THE MAN WITH NO FACE

MARGARET ARMSTRONG

LOST CRIME CLASSICS
www.lostcrimeclassics.com

🪶 PEPIK BOOKS

This edition published 2015 by Pepik Books, Blake House, 18 Blake Street, York, YO1 8QH

Copyright © 2015 Pepik Books

The Man with No Face by Margaret Armstrong (1867-1944) was first published in 1940.

Published by Pepik Books (www.pepikbooks.com) as part of the *Lost Crime Classics* collection.

www.lostcrimeclassics.com

All rights reserved. This book is sold subject to the condition that it shall not, by way of trade or otherwise, be reproduced, lent, re-sold, hired out or otherwise circulated in any form of binding or cover other than that in which it is published and without a similar condition being imposed on the subsequent purchaser.

ISBN: 978-0-9932357-8-8
Printed and bound in the EU

THE MAN WITH NO FACE

MARGARET ARMSTRONG

LOST CRIME CLASSICS
www.lostcrimeclassics.com

PROLOGUE

"Now well a day!" said the heir of Linne.
"Now well-a-day, and woe is me
for when I was the heir of Linne,
I neither wanted gold nor fee."

SCOTTISH BALLAD

The funeral was over at last. As Doctor Ferguson closed his Bible a sigh of thanksgiving rose from the crowd gathered around the open grave. For the service had been long and the day hot, unusually hot even for a December day in Australia. Not a breath of wind was stirring, the leafy fringes of the acacias bordering the road hung limp as rags and the sun beat down out of a dazzling sky. Black coats and stiff collars had become a mortification to the flesh before the service had fairly begun, stout gentlemen longed for home, cold baths and iced drinks like harts for the water brooks, and even the thinnest old ladies took off their gloves.

But now, at last, it was all over and the crowd free to disperse. To disperse, but not to hurry. For this was a decorous crowd, Adelaide's best come in full force to see the last of their old friend Donald Bell and to honour his memory. So the movement across the tombstone dotted grass toward the gates of the cemetery, where a long line of cars stood waiting, contrived to combine determination with dignity, and no comments were allowed – except the usual "excellent discourse," "beautiful flowers," or at most, "A pity Mr Bell was a Presbyterian. The cathedral would have been so much more impressive" – until the grave with its small group of mourners had been left at a safe distance.

Then, of course, voices took a lighter note, heat was forgotten, the crowd broke up into knots, gathered and separated and gathered again like lilies on a cake, as curiosity, held back for the past hour, overflowed the banks of convention. The appearance of the 'heir,' seen just now for the first time by most of those present, was eagerly discussed and questions and answers flew back and forth unhindered. So many more questions than answers, however, that if Sir Wilfred Bennet's chauffeur had been more aggressive – his car stood half way down the line – many would have gone away no wiser than they came.

As it was, Sir Wilfred found himself the centre of such a rapidly growing group that he was obliged to give his wife a share of the interviewing. Fortunately, she too could say that she knew the 'heir,' Percy McGuire, though not so well as Sir Wilfred knew him. It developed that Lady Bennet had met him only once, and that accidentally, at Mr Bell's house years ago while Sir Wilfred and Percy McGuire were boyhood friends. That is, they had gone to the same school in England. Sir Wilfred hinted that 'friend' was not the word one used in speaking of Percy McGuire.

"You don't like him, I gather," General Preston remarked. "Yet the fellow looks harmless enough." And he stared across the greensward at the group still standing watching a mound of earth being patted into shape.

"Harmless!" Sir Wilfred snorted. "Of course he looks harmless. That's McGuire's great card. I assure you he had been at school two full years before any of the masters became aware of his little peculiarities. Even the boys were fooled for a time. It was weeks before they realized Percy's game. Inciting them to mischief and never getting caught himself!"

"More naive than fool, I judge," Dean Marlow put in.

"Oh, McGuire is clever enough," Sir Wilfred conceded. "If his heart were as good as his brain he'd be all right."

"Mr McGuire doesn't look as if he had a bad heart," Mrs Denbeigh whispered to Lady Bennet. "You know, I quite like his face. Not an interesting countenance. Rather dull, in fact. But no evidence of depravity."

"That's what's so disappointing," Miss Coles remarked. "He ought to be tall and dark and romantic looking, and he's short and middle-aged and common place. As for depravity, I simply don't believe it. After all, if Sir Wilfred only knew him as a boy..."

Lady Bennet laughed. "Wilfred," she said, "some of us think you are being rather hard on Percy McGuire."

"I agree," Judge Rivers put in. "Mr McGuire is likely to become a power in the community and although he won't, of course, fill the place of his father..."

"*Adopted* father," Lady Bennet murmured.

Judge Rivers affected not to hear the interruption. "In short," he went on, "a man with such a vast fortune at his disposal deserves, or rather he should receive..."

"You mean," Sir Wilfred broke in, "that as Percy McGuire is rich we should let bygones be bygones?"

"You put it crudely," Judge Rivers said. "But the pranks of a schoolboy can scarcely..."

"Pranks!" Sir Wilfred snorted. "Do you call cruelty a prank? Do you call cheating a prank? Good Lord, if..."

"Hush, Wilfred," Lady Bennet laid a warning hand on his hand. "They are coming."

"And, thank God, here's our car! I shan't have to shake hands with my old friend Percy. Get in, dear! Get in!" Sir Wilfred bundled his wife into the limousine and bounced in himself. "Home," he snapped, and the car moved away from the gate just as the mourners, Donald Bell's 'heir,' his doctor and his solicitor approached.

Sir Wilfred glanced back "Look at them all!" he growled. "All shaking hands and condoling and telling Percy how fond they were of Donald Bell."

"It doesn't mean anything. They're showing respect for McGuire's money, not for McGuire himself."

"I suppose so. But it makes furious all the same. Anyhow, I'm glad I said what I did."

"Weren't you a little indiscreet?"

"What if I was! They had better know just where I stand. Rich or poor, Percy McGuire will never get a leg up from me."

At the moment, however, Percy McGuire was far from depending on anyone for a leg up. For the first time in his life he felt himself firmly in the saddle. The sensation was exhilarating, but he took it quietly enough. His voice was subdued to funeral pitch, his manner, as he shook hands with people he had never seen before except from a respectful distance, couldn't have been better. No one would have guessed that each handshake made a twenty years' dream more real and that he was savouring every polite remark as an epicure nibbles the hors d'oeuvres that prophesy a good dinner. Unfortunately, this interchange of civilities with generals and admirals, deans and judges, and their respective ladies, was cut short by a peremptory 'Mr McGuire's car,' and the 'heir,' accompanied by Mr Lobden, his solicitor, was obliged to depart. But hats were raised as he stepped into the car and all eyes followed it as it rolled away. He leaned back in the softly cushioned seat with a sigh of satisfaction.

Pretty good, he thought, but nothing to the way they'll know me when I start spending my money. I'll give a ball or something as soon as I can get proper clothes... This car is well enough, but I'll need another, a Rolls, and a small car to take girls driving. They say Wilfred Bennet has a pretty daughter... Wilfred. He's always treated me like dirt. I bet he sings a different song now... Oh, well, time enough for all that.

He turned to his companion, who sat looking out of the window. "Very gratifying, Mr Lobden," he said with a sad smile. "A tribute to my dear father that I shall never forget. I was touched, deeply touched."

Mr Lobden nodded and continued to look out of the window. McGuire gave the legal back a meditative glance, seemed about to speak and thought better of it. They drove on for a few minutes more in a somewhat uneasy silence, then McGuire made another attempt:

"I was glad to see that several of my dear father's old servants were present at the funeral. They have been, I trust, remembered in his will."

"Of course. Very liberally."

"That is as it should be. Every smallest detail of my dear father's will must be carried out. You have it with you, I suppose?"

"You asked me to bring it and I have done so. But you won't get me to discuss it now, Percy. I propose to read it in Mr Bell's library and you'll have to wait till we get there."

McGuire nodded, "Of course, of course," and nothing more was said until the car drew up in front of the somber Victorian house which Donald Bell had built, where he had lived for some thirty years and where he had died.

"Here we are," Mr Lobden remarked with a sigh of relief. He got out without waiting for McGuire, mounted a flight of stone steps to a monumental front door, inserted a latchkey and went in, beckoning McGuire to follow. Which, after a moment's pause, McGuire did, though walking stiffly as if in protest.

But as they reached the center of the square, high ceilinged hall, cool and dim after the glare outside, McGuire stopped short and glanced about him with a proprietary and slightly disparaging air. "One moment, Mr Lobden," he said firmly. "I haven't been here for some time, you know, and I confess it's a shock to see the house looking so shabby. I shall have it done over at once. We must get estimates..."

Mr Lobden frowned. "More important business to attend to now," he grunted, and went on across the hall, waving aside a man-servant who came hurrying forward, opened a door, entered and pointed to a chair with an offhand, "Take a chair, Percy," as he sat down. "You've got a shock coming to you, I'm afraid."

McGuire seated himself with extreme deliberation, placed his top hat and gloves on the carpet beside him, leaned back and folded his arms and gazed calmly at Mr Lobden.

The latter coughed, adjusted his pince-nez, extracted a document from an inner pocket and unfolded it. "This," he said, "is the last will and testament of Donald Bell, drawn up six months ago." He glanced at McGuire, but the latter made no comment and he went on: "I will read it: 'I, Donald Bell, being of sound and disposing mind, hereby revoking each and every of the will or wills by me at any time heretofore made.'"

"I suggest we omit the preamble, and the legacies," McGuire interposed. "The bulk of the fortune comes to me, I presume?"

Lobden shook his head. "I'm sorry to say, Percy, that in this new will you are no longer the principal beneficiary. You are remembered, of course. You receive two thousand pounds in cash and an annuity of five hundred a year. Not quite what you expected, perhaps, but a very tidy sum, a very tidy sum."

"You say that this will was drawn up six months ago? Then... But that-that affair was-was adjusted."

"But not forgiven. You went too far, Percy. Mr Bell was a proud man, you know, and forgery – Well, no use going into it all over again now."

"He left everything to a charity, I suppose?"

"No. I only wish he had. It's a peculiar will, most peculiar. I tried to dissuade Mr Bell, but he was firm. Nothing would move him."

"Who gets it then?"

"The Bell family!"

"Impossible. He had no relations."

"True. These heirs are not actually related to Donald Bell. According to the will, the residuary estate is to be divided among 'the descendants of Robert Bell of Irongray, head of the house whose name I bear.'"

There was a moment's dead silence. Then, "As you say, it is a strange will," McGuire remarked dryly. "So strange that I should think it could be broken."

"You might as well try to break Gibraltar. I drew it, and my partner and I are executors. Moreover, the will stipulates that if you make any such attempt you don't get a penny." Mr Lobden rose. "I must be going. But I'll drop in at six this evening. There are several minor matters I want to talk over with you. Here is a copy of the will." He laid a paper on the table. "You can read it at your leisure, but there's nothing much in it except what I've told you."

"One moment, Mr Lobden. About these heirs, the Bell family. Who are they? What do you know about them?"

"Nothing. Nothing whatever except that they're Scottish."

"Will the fortune be divided among a large number of persons?"

"I have no idea. There may be dozens of Bells at the present time, or very few."

"Perhaps the family has died out. In that case, who inherits?"

"Why, you do. But don't let that raise false hopes, Percy. The family can't be extinct, or Mr Bell wouldn't have left them his money. The will was drawn up only six months ago, you know. Mr Bell intended to give me more details, but his illness prevented it. However, it ought to be easy enough to get in communication with them. We shall do so at once."

"I see. Well, they're in luck, whoever they are, and I'm not," McGuire sighed. "I wouldn't mind so much if my father's money had been left to some worthy charity. But these utter strangers. It's something of a shock, Mr Lobden."

"Of course it is. And I don't mind saying that I'm sorry, Percy. To tell the truth, in my opinion you haven't had a fair deal."

"Thank you, Mr Lobden. Then you don't blame me for feeling hurt?"

"I certainly don't. What's more, if you'll permit me to say so, Percy, I think you are behaving remarkably well. Your self control, under the circumstances, is admirable and I congratulate you." They shook hands, and the solicitor departed.

"How did he take it?" Mrs Lobden asked her husband as he came into her bedroom where she was dressing for dinner.

"Like a gentleman!" Mr Lobden sat down, with a sigh. "I was never more surprised in my life. Percy McGuire is a rogue through and through, but I couldn't help feeling sorry for him. He's been badly treated."

"Don't get sentimental, John. Mr Bell knew that Percy couldn't be trusted with any large amount of money and he was right. Think of all poor Percy's ventures, every one a failure!"

"Oh, he's versatile all right and clever! Why, he did so well when he began studying medicine that I agreed with Mr Bell the boy had found his vocation at last – and within the year we were busy keeping him out of jail. All the same it's fantastic to leave a huge fortune to a lot of strangers."

"How do you know there are a lot?"

"I don't. I only wish I did. I told Percy that we would get in communication with them at once. A simple matter if the family is as important as old Donald believed it to be. Not so easy if they've run downhill. We may have to advertise."

"Here?"

"Oh, no, in Scotland. Irongray is a Scottish estate. Donald Bell's grandfather worked on the place, a gardener, I believe. Anyway, Donald started life with nothing but brains to help him along. Brains and luck. He was a lucky man."

"Lucky except in his choice of a son. I never could understand why he adopted Percy McGuire. A foundling, wasn't he?"

"Yes, an orphan Mr Bell came across in the foundling asylum in Sydney. Fancied he saw a resemblance to a dead friend – self-made men are apt to be sentimental. The boy was bright. Mr Bell idolized him; taught him to sing Scotch ballads and dance the Highland fling, and showed him off to everyone who came to the house. Poor old Donald. Before very long Percy had to be sent away – and kept away."

"Does Percy know he is a foundling?"

"Oh, yes. But I've heard him hint at a different version. He likes to imagine that Donald was his father and that he would have been acknowledged except for the old man's pride in the name." He glanced at the clock. "It's late. Time I dressed." He sighed. "It's been a tiring day. I wish I hadn't told Percy I'd be in again this evening."

"Ring him up. Tell him you'll come tomorrow morning instead."

"Well," he hesitated, "I can't see that it would make any real difference. The documents are all at the bank. There are a few papers in the library desk that I haven't examined yet, but it's locked. A good strong lock and I have the key. Yes, I'll wait until tomorrow."

Meantime the subject of Mr and Mrs Lobden's conversation still stood where Mr Lobden had left him after that warm handshake just inside the library door; he stood motionless, head bent, eyes on the carpet. And here he remained for some minutes, immobile as the bronze clock on the mantelpiece. But at length he turned, picked up the copy of the will and read it through once, twice, and sat down in front of an open window, staring with unseeing eyes at the twilight sky showing in pale stripes between the branches of a eucalyptus tree crowded against the wall of the house, and wrapped in what, for some unknown reason, is called a brown study. His fingers absently folded the copy of the will into a smaller and smaller square.

Darkness was falling when, at last, seeming to reach a decision, he dropped the paper – he knew the wording by heart – withdrew his gaze from the window and turned to survey the room. He saw tall arched bookcases, rich with old morocco and vellum, crowned by the marble busts of Scott and Burns, Prince Charlie and the Ettrick Shepherd; revolving globes, celestial and terrestrial; vast tables fit for King Arthur, the centre of a herd of giant armchairs; a carved oak mantelpiece; a mahogany desk...

He rose, switched on a light, approached the desk and lifted the lid, disclosing a row of pigeonholes and a drawer; the pigeonholes were empty and the drawer was locked. He took a small metal instrument from his pocket; in two seconds the drawer was open. A bundle of letters first caught his eye, but the handwriting, he saw with disgust, was his own. Reaching farther back into the drawer, he drew out a long envelope bound around with pink tape, and gave a grunt of satisfaction, for it was labeled, 'Irongray' in Donald Bell's old-fashioned hand. He shook out the contents, and grunted again with annoyance.

Engraving of a gaunt stone house set foursquare against a background of pine and fir; faded woodcut of a garden gate and path; sprig of white heather tied with tartan ribbon; a handful of newspaper clippings recording Scottish events such as a flower show at Dumfries, the Queen's visit to Edinburgh, and the funeral of the Duke of Buccleugh, mixed in with the birth, death and marriage notices of various persons whose names McGuire had never heard. One after the other they were glanced at and pushed contemptuously to one side. A square of cardboard illuminated with a coat of arms – silver bells on a blue ground – held his attention for a moment before it was torn across and across and flung into the wastepaper basket.

He swept together the remaining odds and ends that littered the desk and was about to send them all flying after the coat of arms when he saw that the envelope was not entirely empty. One paper remained; a document yellow with age and crackling so protestingly as it was unfolded that a superstitious person would have fancied the ghost of Donald Bell was attempting to interfere.

But McGuire was not in the least superstitious. He smoothed out the document with an eager hand, bent over it – and relaxed in sudden relief. Here, at last, was what he wanted and what he had hoped to find before Lobden found it: Bell of Irongray's family tree.

More accurately, it was a chart, for the tree grew upside down. The root – Irongray's most remote ancestor – topped the page and the branches descended, spreading wide as the family increased, and coming down almost to the present. Almost, but not quite. The record, to McGuire's disgust, broke off just where, for his purpose, it should have begun. It had not been brought up to date. Four names ended the list: James, Andrew, John and Alexander, sons of a Robert Bell born in 1792 who, as he was the last Robert must be the one mentioned in the will. 1792? A long time ago. Those four sons were all dead by now. Who came after them? Dozens of children, or none? Families were large in old times. If those four all married and all had children and grandchildren there would be dozens of 'heirs' at the present day. On the other hand, very old families were apt to run out. Those four might be the last fruit on the tree and Bell of Irongray safely extinct.

But this was all guesswork, McGuire decided, and he folded the chart and slipped it into his pocket. Facts were what he needed. Vital statistics. Scottish records would tell him what he needed to know. Parish registers, old newspapers...

Old newspapers? He gathered up the clippings, sorted them, and read the notices of births, deaths and marriages a second time... Not a Bell among them. Yet here they were in the Irongray envelope. What link held them together? A common ancestry, perhaps. These people might be descended from Robert Bell through the daughters of the house. The name had died, but the family had gone on in the female line.

So far so good. Was there anything more to be learned from the clippings? Yes, a third reading yielded another fact. Scotland, as well as Bell, had disappeared. These births, deaths and marriages had all taken place, not in Scotland, but in America!

It was a startling idea and opened up a new train of thought. He was still considering it from various angles when the telephone rang in the hall and footsteps came hurrying up the back stairs. Instantly the papers vanished, swept out of sight with a movement as smooth and slick as a cardsharper's, and the drawer was locked. Before the telephone stopped ringing the desk had been closed and wiped clean of fingerprints. The servant had just taken down the receiver when McGuire strolled into the hall.

"For me?" he said.

"Yes, Mr Lobden, sir." The man handed McGuire the receiver, and left him.

"Mr Lobden? Percy McGuire speaking," he said pleasantly. "Of course, of course... A fatiguing day. I shall turn in early myself... Well, no... I hardly think so... A year of travel perhaps, and then... I haven't decided yet. China rather appeals to me. I've never been to China... The sooner the better. I may be oversensitive, but, to tell the truth, I don't feel like meeting any of those kind people I saw at the funeral until... Just so. Awkward for them and awkward for me. So I'd like to get off as soon as possible. Do you think the executors would be willing to advance me a thousand pounds? Thanks very much. See you tomorrow."

"China?" McGuire murmured under his breath, and as he hung up the receiver a smile flickered across his impassive face like a ripple on stagnant water. "No, not China. I rather think my duty lies elsewhere." He walked slowly back to the library and stood for a long moment at the desk, recalling the various places mentioned in the chart, wondering which promised the best hunting...

He had money enough for any of them. What would he need besides money? Letters of introduction. Letters could always be doctored to suit whatever situation might arise. Better not ask Lobden for anything more. Bennet was out of the question. Judge Rivers? The Judge seemed disposed to kowtow a bit after the funeral, and General Preston had been civil enough. They'd both be willing to oblige... Now, where to begin? Big places were safer than little ones. Why not make straight for New York? He liked New York. Yes! New York would be an excellent place to begin.

1

"Lady Isabel put it to her cheek,
Sae did she to her chin;
Sae did she to her rosy lips,
And the rank poison gaed in."

SCOTTISH BALLAD

Mr Minton Marbury finished his second cup of coffee and laid down his napkin with a sense of satisfaction and anticipation. Breakfast could not have been better. An interesting morning lay before him. Sunshine had come at last after a week of rain, bringing a typical New York March day of glittering distances and high white clouds hurrying across a blue sky. Mr Marbury glanced out of the dining-room window, observed that another crocus had come up during the night, and gave himself to blissful contemplation of the back yard.

For the back yard, after months of care and more expense than Mr Marbury wished to remember, was no longer a back yard. It was a garden. Where, for some thirty years – half his life in fact – he would have seen a space of grey flagstones criss crossed by clotheslines, smelling of cats, dusty and yet mysteriously damp, he now saw an agreeable arrangement of grass plots, flower beds, shrubs, sundial and slim dark cedar trees. The grass was already green, the flower beds prickled with green sprouts, the shrubs hinted of pink and white glory to come.

No wonder Mr Marbury smiled! He was about to sally forth to count his crocuses when a maid came in with a message. Mrs Beaumont had phoned to say she'd got the letter from Scotland and she was expecting Mr Marbury to tea.

He nodded and subsided into his chair again. This message from Clare Beaumont meant a change of the day's plans. He had intended to spend the morning in the garden and devote the afternoon to examination of the stamps and coins that were to be sold at the Busby auction tomorrow. However, it would never do to disappoint Clare. The letter from Scotland would revive her interest in genealogy, and she would want her coats of arms at once. Dear Clare was so impatient! There was a morning's work on them. He must start painting as soon as he had read his *Times*. The garden would have to wait.

So eleven o'clock found Mr Marbury in the library. His long thin back and sleek head were bent over his painting table, pince-nez tight clenched to his long thin nose, long thin hand delicately manipulating a watercolour brush as he added dashes of azure, blobs of gules and specks of sable to the various crests, helmets, wreaths and mantles that ornamented the coat of armour of Clare Beaumont's ancestors. Mr Marbury was enjoying himself. He liked illuminating, he liked working for Clare. Clare was a dear. Indeed, more than once since her husband's death five years ago, he had been on the point of proposing but, somehow, he never had.

The morning passed happily away. After an excellent lunch, and a brief siesta, Mr Marbury adjusted his top hat to an exact angle and stepped out into the sun and wind of East Sixty second Street. Clare Beaumont's house was only a few blocks away, farther north and on Fifth Avenue. At five minutes of five he was ringing her doorbell. As the empire clock on the mantelpiece chimed the hour he was seated in her library, waiting – as he had so often waited – for dear Clare. She was far too apt to ignore the passing of time.

Not that Mr Marbury minded waiting. After a busy morning, it was pleasant to relax in a deep armchair and in such agreeable surroundings. Clare's taste was perfect. There wasn't another room in New York, he reflected, that so exquisitely combined elegance and comfort. The somber beauty of books lined three walls, tall windows gave glimpses of the park's treetops, from a panel over the fireplace a magnificent Raeburn – Clare's great-great grandfather, Robert Bell of Irongray, in red coat and riding breeches – beamed down, mellow as his own port. An aromatic whiff of southern fat wood came from the fire sparkling on the hearth and mingled with the scent from vases of roses and mignonette and a row of potted plants on the window sills. A perfect setting for Clare, he thought. Like Clare, beautiful and yet comfortable.

The door opened and Mr Marbury sat erect. But it was only a footman carrying a tea tray. Mr Marbury watched the arrangement of the tea table with interest. As usual, envying Clare that Paul Revere teapot. Did the covered dish contain cinnamon toast or muffins? Those little pink cakes with citron on the top looked delicious. He was glancing hungrily at the clock when the door opened again, and this time it was Clare herself, smiling as only Clare could smile, soft and glowing and full of life.

They had tea. Clare had never looked lovelier, Mr Marbury said to himself, as she handed him his cup. A soft pink rose such a relief in this age of bones and lipstick. He helped himself to a frosted cake, it was as good as it looked and sat sipping and munching.

"What is that? Saccharine?" he asked in surprise, as she uncorked a small bottle and dropped a pellet into her tea. "Aren't you allowed sugar? I was just thinking how well you looked."

"I am well," she laughed. "Fit as a fiddle. But I'm going to a new man, Doctor Costello, and he has cut out sugar. But don't let's waste time on doctors. Have another cup? No? Then ring the bell for William, please." The tea things were taken away, the table cleared, various portfolios fetched from cupboard drawers and Mr Marbury produced a large envelope from his pocket. One by one the illuminations were displayed, admired and exclaimed over.

"Oh, Minton!" she sighed. "They're too too exquisite! You're simply wonderful! I don't know which I like best. The Irving holly sprigs or that enchanting Cawdor deer, or those sweet sweet lambs and cows and leaves of the Durhams and the mottoes – too fascinating! 'Furth Fortune and Fill the Fetters.' Now isn't that quaint! I can hardly wait to paste them in my book."

Her enthusiasm was most gratifying. Mr Marbury slipped the squares of tinted cardboard back into their envelope with a murmur of satisfaction, feeling amply repaid for his hours of labour.

"Now for the documents," she said. "The letter from the Lord Lyon in Edinburgh and the chart!"

She opened a small white velvet bag that lay in her lap and handed him a letter. He read it. "Very satisfactory," he nodded. "The Heralds' office is always most obliging," and bent over another paper she was unfolding before him on the table.

"Look at this!" she cried triumphantly. "My grandmother was right. This chart says that James Bell was one of the Bells of Irongray, and he came to this country in 1812."

"Robert Bell of Irongray," he read aloud, "born 1765. We know all about that Robert, his son Robert married Ellen Dunbar. Nothing new there... Ah, now we come to something the four children of Robert: James, Andrew, John and Alexander."

"And that James was my great-grandfather," Clare broke in triumphantly. "He came to America and his daughter married Alan Carlisle and their son Alan was my father. The Lord Lyon says so I have a right to the Bell of Irongray arms after all!"

"You certainly have. I'll paint it for you at once."

"You're an angel, Minton, is it a pretty one?"

"Three bells argent on a field azure."

"Blue and silver... very pretty. You know, Minton, it's a real satisfaction to find that my grandmother was right. She was a dear old lady. I remember her perfectly though I was only five when she died... She wore a lace cap and a pearl brooch and she used to sing me Scotch songs. The one I liked best began:

> " 'Bessie Bell and Mary Gray,
> They were twa bonnie lasses.

*They built a hut upon the brae
And covered it with rashes.'*

"I named my doll 'Mary Gray' and I used to sit under a lilac bush in the garden and make believe we were the lasses in their hut. Dear me, that was more than thirty years ago!"

"You must have been a very pretty child, Clare."

"And I haven't changed much? Minton, you're a darling!"

He smiled. She rattled on. "Isn't it exciting to think the *Record of my Ancestry* is almost done! As soon as I get the dates Mr Angus Bell of Dumfries is looking up for me, I can have it bound in green morocco, I think, with a little gold tooling. Could you help me get the pages in proper order, Minton? What about tomorrow?"

But before he could answer, there was a knock at the door and William the footman came in.

"Mr Wheeler is on the phone, madam," he said. "He has a lease for you to sign and he hopes tomorrow afternoon about five will be convenient."

"It won't be," Mrs Beaumont frowned. "But I suppose I shall have to see him. Tell him he can come, William."

"Mr Wheeler? Atwood's clerk?" Marbury asked.

"Yes. Mr Atwood told me there would be some papers to sign and I must be sure to read every one of them all through. That means Mr Wheeler will be here for ages, and my book must wait for a day or two. Tomorrow I'm sitting for my portrait. Jim Northcote gave me no peace until I let him paint me. And the next day, oh, well, I'll have to call you up. By the way, there's something I want to consult you about. I am..."

Again the footman appeared. "Mr Northcote," he said, let in a tall good looking young man, and departed. "We were just speaking of you, Jim," Mrs Beaumont exclaimed. "This is Mr Marbury, a very old friend of mine."

"How's the portrait getting on?" Marbury asked as they shook hands.

"We've made a very good beginning, I think," Northcote answered. "Mrs Beaumont seems to like it."

"It's simply wonderful!" she cried. "Not too *modern* and yet not one bit *vieux jeu*. Just the happy medium between Bouguereau and Gauguin. You must come and see it, Minton."

"I'll be delighted." Marbury rose. "Goodbye, Clare. You'll call me up?"

"As soon as I have a free afternoon. Goodbye, and thank you a thousand times for the illuminations."

Handsome fellow, that young Northcote, Marbury said to himself as he left the room. Nice blue eyes. I like him. Hope I'll see him again.

Next morning, true to his word, Mr Marbury finished illuminating the Bell of Irongray arms. But Clare Beaumont did not ring him up that evening. She seemed to have forgotten him. Two days went by. Three. And still she did not telephone. On the fourth day he rang up her house. There was a long wait. Then came a voice – a high, breathless, horrified voice – William's voice?

"Hello! Hello! Yes. Mrs Beaumont's house... No. No. She can't come... Oh, is that you, Mr Marbury? Something awful has happened here, sir! Awful! Awful! The police..."

Sudden silence. Marbury rang again and again. There was no answer. He hung up the receiver with a shaking hand.

"Good God!" he muttered. "William was evidently in a terrible state. Something's wrong. What can it be? The police are there. A burglary, I suppose. I'd better go around."

Ten minutes later he was standing on Mrs Beaumont's steps waiting for an answer to his ring. There was a brief delay and when at length the door opened he was confronted by a policeman.

"Nobody allowed in," the man said.

"But what has happened, officer? I'm an intimate friend of Mrs Beaumont's. I might be of some assistance. Will you just tell her I'm here?"

The man hesitated. Then: "It'll be in the evening papers," he said. "So there's no harm my telling you. Mrs Beaumont is dead, sir."

Marbury turned white, and caught at the railing.

"When?" he gulped.

"Between nine and ten this morning. Committed suicide."

"No! No!" Mr Marbury shuddered. "Impossible. There must be some mistake."

The policeman shook his head. "It's a fact, sir. The doctors are here now, and the lawyer. And no one else is to be let in."

Mr Marbury turned and walked stiffly away. As he crossed the street a taxi driver shouted at him, but Marbury did not see the man's angry face as it whizzed past perilously close. He was back again in Clare Beaumont's library four days ago, he felt her soft hand in his as she bade him goodbye, heard her laughing voice: "Thank you a thousand times, Minton. You're an angel." Clare dead? No! No!

He had almost reached his own house when he remembered that the policeman had said, "It will all be in the evening paper." There was a newsboy at the corner. He retraced his steps and bought a couple of papers. But he did not dare to glance at them. Folding them under his arm, he walked toward home, head bent.

"I beg your pardon!"

He looked up. He had collided with a man. Someone he knew, Northcote, Jim Northcote.

Northcote held an open newspaper in his hand. The two stood staring at each other. Then:

"I see you've heard," Northcote muttered.

Marbury nodded. "Only the – the fact. I haven't looked at the papers. What do they say?"

"That it was suicide!" Northcote exclaimed. "A damn newspaper lie, of course. It's incredible. Why, I saw her yesterday and she was as gay as a lark. I simply don't believe it."

"I agree. There must be some mistake. But I've just been to her house… Couldn't get in… The doctor was there…"

"Damn the doctor! If all the doctors in New York swore it was suicide till they were black in the face, I wouldn't believe it. As for these vile reporters…" Northcote crumpled the newspaper angrily into a ball. "I'd like to thrash every man jack of them."

"This is my house," Marbury said. "Come in, won't you? I'd like to talk it over."

Neither spoke again until they were in the library. Marbury indicated a chair in silence. They sat down. Then he resolutely unfolded his newspaper. Flaring headlines ran across the front page:

"Suicide on Fifth Avenue. Mrs Arthur Beaumont. Prominent in Society. Widow of Wall Street Magnate. Colony Club. Piping Rock." And so on and so on, for a dozen lines. Then, at last, the story, brief enough in all conscience:

"The body was found at half past nine this morning by Miss Jane Grant, Mrs Beaumont's personal maid, when she entered the bedroom in order to remove the breakfast tray she had taken in at nine, Mrs Beaumont having, as usual, breakfasted in bed. Dr Carter of 183 Park Avenue was summoned at once and arrived within a few minutes, but could be of no assistance as Mrs Beaumont was already dead. Poison, probably cyanide of potassium, self administered, is believed to be the cause of death. A note found on the dressing table stated that the unfortunate lady had decided to commit suicide. No arrangements have as yet been made for the funeral."

Mr Marbury read the paragraph thrice over, then looked up to meet Jim Northcote's inquiring gaze.

"Well, what do you think of it?" Northcote asked.

"I don't seem able to think," Mr Marbury quavered. "Here it is in black and white, and yet I can't believe it. I can't take it in. Clare commit suicide? It's incredible!"

"You've said it," Northcote nodded. "It's incredible."

"But it seems she left a letter saying she intended to kill herself."

"So they say. But do you notice how brief the account is? I bet they're hushing things up. There's material for a column and only the bare facts are given."

"That is true."

"They don't tell us whether Mrs Beaumont seemed as usual when the maid brought her breakfast. Or suggest any reason for believing it to be suicide – except the note. They don't give the contents of the note, or say whether it was in her handwriting."

"That is implied."

"Well, do you know of any reason? Was Mrs Beaumont in any financial difficulties? Or mixed up with shady people who might blackmail her? Might she have become involved in an unhappy love affair?"

"Good God, no! Atwood, her lawyer, told me a few days ago that she was the only one of his clients who had not suffered from the depression. As for the other reasons, good God, no!"

"Which brings us back to our original proposition; the suicide theory is untenable. Well, we shall know more after the inquest."

"I suppose there will have to be an inquest?"

"Undoubtedly. And I advise you to attend, Mr Marbury. I most certainly shall. Look here, if the inquest doesn't clear things up – and I have a feeling it won't – may I come and talk it all over with you?"

"Of course, of course."

"Thanks. Goodbye," and Northcote was gone.

Mr Marbury went to the window. Northcote was already in the street, striding along at a great rate. "What energy," Marbury murmured. "Did I ever walk as fast as that, I wonder? Good Lord, how old I feel today," and he returned wearily to his armchair.

"Well, I was right," Jim Northcote said. The inquest was over. He had joined Marbury in the street and they were walking along together. "We don't know any more than we did before. That inquest was a farce. No desire whatever to get at the truth. Looked to me as if the lawyers and doctors just wanted to finish the thing up and get home to lunch. I still feel sure that it was not suicide."

"The letter didn't convince you?"

"No. It may have been forged."

"Mr Atwood and Doctor Costello and Jane Grant all identified the handwriting."

"They aren't experts. Anyway, I still maintain that no woman in perfect health of mind and body, of an unusually sunny disposition and with everything to live for, could by any possibility have killed herself. Another point, how would she have got hold of that poison, cyanide, or whatever it was?"

Marbury sighed. "I can explain that," he admitted. "At one time Clare Beaumont was interested in photography. I used to help her develop the negatives. There might have been some cyanide in her dark room."

Northcote shook his head gloomily. They walked on for another block in silence. Then Marbury said: "It might have been an accident."

"Cyanide of potassium get into food by accident? Out of the question! Now, you see where all this lands us? If it was neither suicide nor an accident, it was murder. Someone killed her."

"It certainly looks that way." Marbury shuddered.

"Well then, who would benefit by her death? Who gets her money? Several millions, wasn't it?"

"I fancy so. Some of it, I know, goes to a cousin, or rather, a cousin of her husband's. A Mrs Chase of Baltimore who is enormously rich already, as it happens. The rest is left to various charities. I don't know the details."

"A cousin of her husband's? Then she had no immediate family?"

"No. She was singularly alone in the world. An only child. Father and mother dead. No near relations. Hosts of friends and acquaintances, of course."

"Who was the most intimate?"

"Well, I suppose I was. I've known Clare Beaumont for years. We had many tastes in common. Gardening, genealogy." Mr Marbury's voice broke. He cleared his throat, went on, "Mrs Harcourt and Miss Alice Hemmingway were old friends of hers, and General Blanchard was there a good deal, and oh, any number of people! Clare was the soul of hospitality and everyone liked her."

"I see. What about the servants? Seven or eight of them, I suppose?"

"About that. I don't know any of them well except Clare's maid, Jane Grant, and William, the second man. All of them had been with her for years, except Green, the butler. He was new. Her old butler died not long ago. William is his son."

"A very respectable lot, I gather?"

"Oh, quite. I have a great regard for Jane, and for William too. They were both devoted to Clare."

"It would be interesting to know what Jane really thinks," Northcote said meditatively. "Didn't you feel that she might be keeping something back at the inquest?"

Mr Marbury did not answer at once, for they had reached his house. When they were seated in the library, he said: "To go back to what we were saying, I did think that Jane's testimony at the inquest was remarkably brief. I'll try to see her later on and..."

"Not later on," Northcote broke in, "but at the first possible moment, as soon as the police will let you into the house. There's no time to lose."

Mr Marbury stared. "Surely you don't think it's up to me to interfere? After all, I'm not a relation."

"You just said she hadn't any relations." There was a tinge of impatience in Northcote's voice. "No relations and very few intimate friends. No one, in short, who cares a damn whether or not the poor darling killed herself, except you – and me."

Mr Marbury only sighed and twiddled his eye glasses.

Northcote went on:

"And we both feel dissatisfied with the coroner's verdict of suicide. Well then, it seems to me a spot of investigating is in order. Suppose you make some inquiries and I quest around a bit, and we pool the results. Don't you feel it's a duty? A duty to the dead?"

"I-I suppose it is."

"That's settled then. Now let's make some notes." Jim Northcote produced a sheet of paper and a pencil from his pocket. "We'll make a list of the persons who ought to be questioned."

"Questioned?"

"We must get a record of the last few days of Mrs Beaumont's life. Find out where she went, whom she saw, what she did, the letters she received. All persons able to throw light on any of these points must be questioned. Now, who shall we put first?"

"The police?"

"Just so. A: the police. And then comes Mrs Beaumont's lawyer, I suppose, Mr Atwood. What is his address?"

"Samuel Atwood, 143 Wall Street."

"B: S. Atwood," Northcote wrote. "Who's next? The doctors? There were two of them; Carter, the man the servants sent for in a hurry, and her own physician, Doctor Costello: they come under C. And D brings us to the servants, more particularly Jane and William. Who else? Some clergyman, perhaps. I have an idea that Mrs Beaumont went to St. Margaret's."

"She did. Dr Brace, the rector, is an old friend of Clare's."

"Good. Then E is Dr Brace. Anybody else?"

"I can't think of anyone."

"That will do to begin with, anyway. Now, let's make a plan of campaign and divide forces. I know a man on the Times who would help me with the police. I'll see him tonight, get in touch with the police and find out what they found out, or think they found out, and, if possible, get a look at that suicide letter. And I have another friend who is an interne at the Medical Center and I'll ask him whether those two doctors have good reputations, and then I'll interview them. Who will you see?"

"Suppose I talk to the rector, Dr Brace, and Mr Atwood? I know them both fairly well."

"All right. Try to persuade Mr Atwood to let us see the servants as soon as possible."

"He won't let anyone into the house until after the funeral in all probability. Atwood is a rigid sort of man, and a stickler for professional etiquette."

"We shall have to wait a day or two then. But when Mr Atwood gives permission and you interview the servants, would you mind if I came too?"

"Not a bit. In fact, my dear fellow, if we are to embark on this investigation you will have to supply the impetus. I feel surprisingly weary – Clare's death has been a terrible shock – and, left to myself, I might succumb to inertia."

"Don't worry. You and I make a swell combination, Mr Marbury. I'll provide the brute strength and leave the brain work to you. Between us we're bound to ferret out something. And if we do –" Northcote's face flushed. "If we find that it was not suicide..." He broke off, and sprang to his feet. "May I drop in again tomorrow afternoon? Would two o'clock suit you?"

Mr Marbury hoisted himself out of his armchair. "I'll be here," he said. "By the way, in my interview with Mr Atwood and Dr Brace I suppose I had better not bring up the question of murder?"

"Let's keep our suspicions to ourselves for the present." Northcote turned to the door, and paused. "I was half in love with her, you know," he went on. "She was ten years older than I, but she seemed so young, and she was lovely to look at. Lovely in every way. I was half in love with her."

"So was I," Mr Marbury sighed. "More than half. A great deal more than half."

"Well, goodbye. See you tomorrow."

As the door closed, Mr Marbury remembered that if Jim Northcote expected to come at two o'clock the next day, he should have been asked to lunch. But not even then, such was the disorder of

Mr Marbury's mind, did it occur to him that two o'clock, his time for napping, was a most inconvenient hour for an appointment. He sat staring into the fire, aware that the happiest chapter in his life had come to an end. Murder or suicide, Clare Beaumont was dead.

2

*"Is there no voice or guiding hand
Arising from the awful void?"*

DINAH MULOCK

Ten o'clock the next morning found Mr Marbury ringing the doorbell of St. Margaret's rectory. But his early start was useless. Dr Brace had already left the house. "To lay the cornerstone of St. Jude's parish house in the Bronx," according to the butler, "and not expected home until twelve." Marbury made an appointment for that hour and took his departure.

This sort of thing isn't in my line at all, he reflected dismally, as he walked across town to the Fifty-first Street subway station, having decided that Wall Street, his next port of call, was too far away for a taxi. I shan't get anything out of Atwood. Might as well try to chat with a gate post.

This sense of futility increased, hung over him like a pall, when, twenty minutes later, he sat facing the lawyer from the far side of a vast expanse of polished mahogany. Mr Atwood was polite, his smile gave an impression of good humor, but there was a watchfulness in the eyes that would have chilled a less sensitive person than Mr Marbury. It was with difficulty that the latter explained his errand.

But Atwood seemed very willing to talk. "Of course, my dear Marbury, I quite understand, he said genially. "As one of my late client's most intimate friends, it is natural you should wish to ascertain the details of her death. Not that I can add very much to what you will have heard at the inquest – I saw you there. But when you speak of not being 'satisfied,' just what do you mean?

Everything was done that could be done. Mrs Beaumont was dead when Doctor Carter arrived."

"I know. That was not what I had in mind. Surely, Atwood, you must realize that Mrs Beaumont was the last person in the world to commit suicide."

Mr Atwood shrugged his shoulders. "Anyone may commit suicide."

"But not without some definite reason. Do you know of any reason? Has anything turned up?"

"Certainly not. But you seem to forget that the coroner's verdict was 'temporarily insane.' Insane persons need no reasons for what they do."

"Clare Beaumont was not insane!"

"If she hadn't been insane she wouldn't have committed suicide."

"Are you sure it was suicide?"

"My dear Marbury, the letter!"

"Yes, the letter," Marbury sighed. "I'd like to see the letter. Would it be possible for me to glance at it? I was so fond of Clare."

"Certainly. I have it right here." Mr Atwood opened a folder that lay at his elbow and turned over the papers it contained one by one. "Sorry," he said at length, leaning back in his chair. "That letter doesn't seem to be here after all. The police wanted it, and I suppose it has not yet been returned. Come in again some time and I shall be glad to show it to you. Anything more?"

"I should like to know exactly what happened the morning of Mrs Beaumont's death. What time did you arrive at the house? Who else was there?"

"I got there about quarter past ten, and went straight upstairs to the bedroom. Doctor Carter was there, and Doctor Costello, Mrs Beaumont's own physician, and Wheeler, my clerk – he's gone to Boston on business, or I'd call him in – and, let me see, who else? Oh, yes, Miss Hemmingway from next door. The servants had sent for everyone they could think of. Jane Grant was in the room and William, one of the men servants, and Doctor Brace, the rector of St. Margaret's, came in just behind me. That was all, I think. I seem to remember a fat woman in a corner, probably the cook. The room was crowded. I may have omitted someone."

"There was a good deal of confusion, I suppose?"

"Oh, yes. Everybody was asking questions in loud whispers. Miss Hemmingway was sobbing, and one of the maids was having hysterics in the hall. It was all very distressing. Very distressing."

"Doctor Carter had finished his examination when you arrived?"

"Oh, yes. Bed covered over with a sheet. Doctor asked me if I wished 'to view the remains,' but I declined... After all, why should I? It wasn't up to me to identify."

Mr Marbury felt a little sick. But he persisted. "When did they realize it was suicide?"

"Almost at once. Jane Grant found the letter, and then there was no doubt about it. None whatever."

"I see. And where is the funeral to be?"

"In California. The remains are now reposing in St. Margaret's mortuary chapel, and will be shipped this afternoon." Mr Marbury winced, "As you know, Mr Beaumont died while they were living in San Rafael. We felt that she would wish to rest beside her husband, regardless of expense. Money, in this case, being of no consequence. A noble fortune, Marbury – well over five million. A noble fortune!"

"And most of it goes to Mrs Chase, I suppose?"

There was a moment's pause. Marbury fancied he caught a gleam of satisfaction in the legal eye, as if Atwood were saying to himself: "Aha, now we're getting somewhere! Marbury wants to find out whether she left him anything." But there was no hint of this in the legal voice. "I'm afraid it's rather soon to discuss the will, Marbury," he said, regretfully. "It is to be read this afternoon. Until then it wouldn't be proper for me to talk about it even with you."

"Of course not." Marbury rose. "Well, thank you very much, Atwood." They shook hands and he got himself out of the room.

"Callous, close-mouthed, avaricious brute!" he muttered indignantly as he stepped into the elevator. "Thinks of nothing but money. I wouldn't trust him around the corner."

A revolving door shot him out into the windy street. He hurried along to the subway, holding on to his hat and still muttering:

"Cold-hearted money grabber. No touch of compassion. Might have been speaking of an utter stranger, yet he's known Clare for years. And what did I learn? Nothing. I hope the rector will be easier to talk to. If he isn't, I shan't have much to tell young Northcote this afternoon."

Fortunately, however, the Reverend Septimus Brace was very easy to talk to. The clerical handshake was soothing. There was sympathy in the rector's mellow voice, sorrow in every line of his handsome face. Mr Marbury's sense of futility vanished, lost in mournful satisfaction as the two sat ensconced in deep leather armchairs beside the study fire, recounting the many charming qualities of their departed friend and lamenting her demise.

The conversation had gone on for some time when the chimes ringing the quarter hour from the nearby church tower reminded Mr Marbury that the object of his visit was still to be attained, and he asked the rector to describe the scene in Mrs Beaumont's bedroom on the fatal morning. But Doctor Brace could add little to what Marbury already knew. He had been sent for at a little before ten – William, the second man, having telephoned – and had reached the house within fifteen minutes. Several persons were already in the bedroom when he entered and others might have arrived shortly after, but he had been too overcome to be sure just who they all were. "I'm sorry to be so indefinite," he went on. "I remember seeing the two doctors, and the two lawyers, Atwood and his clerk, and Alice Hemmingway, besides Jane, Mrs Beaumont's maid. But people kept coming in and going out. Atwood was discussing something with Doctor Costello in a louder voice than I thought suitable – I don't like the man, he showed no reverence for the dead. Alice Hemmingway was crying and I tried to soothe her, but she couldn't stop, and Jane brought her a glass of water. Then Mrs Beaumont's little dog ran in and began to bark. It was all very painful."

"Who found the letter?"

"I don't know. I was too occupied with the dreadful fact that Mrs Beaumont was dead to think of anything else. Somebody handed it to Mr Atwood and he read it aloud. We were all horrified."

"You are quite sure it was suicide, I suppose?"

"But surely the letter made that plain? In a moment of insanity, of course. A tragic end. I can't tell you what a shock it has been to me."

Marbury sighed. There seemed nothing more to ask or say. He went sadly away again.

Quarter before two. Mr Marbury looked at the clock on the dining room mantelpiece, rose from the lunch table, and left the room without so much as a glance at his garden although another crocus had ventured to appear.

As likely as not that young man will be late, he grumbled to himself as he mounted the stairs to the library. I daresay he won't come at all. Probably forgotten all about Clare by now. Young people are like that.

But he was wrong. As the clock struck, Jim Northcote came into the room.

"Any news?" he asked eagerly.

Marbury shook his head.

"And you?"

"Mighty little. I saw both the doctors. They repeated what they said at the inquest. It was cyanide. Everything on the breakfast tray had been analyzed and it was found in the coffee cup. The autopsy left no doubt whatever. Doctor Costello admitted that he had never observed any symptoms of insanity in Mrs Beaumont but said he didn't know her well, as he had first seen her only a month ago. She wanted to reduce, and he told her to take saccharine instead of sugar, and she might try the banana and milk diet if she wanted to, but he didn't advise it. In his opinion she was in perfect health of mind as well as body. But you never knew. Might have been something wrong he hadn't noticed. He didn't profess to be a nerve specialist. Doctor Carter couldn't tell me anything new either."

"And the police?"

"They were polite enough. I asked them to let me see the suicide letter, as they call it. But they didn't have it, said it had been returned to Mr Atwood's office."

"And Atwood told me the police had it."

"Really? I don't know that it matters much though. We know what the letter said. I asked them whether the bottle containing the poison had been found and they said it hadn't been, but didn't seem to think that was important."

"Did they show any uncertainty as to its being suicide?"

"Not an atom. Just said the case was finished as far as they were concerned. And that was that. Tell me how you got on?"

Mr Marbury described his two interviews, so unlike yet equally unprofitable.

"We are just where we started," he ended, rather hoping that this energetic young man would now have his fill of investigation. "I don't think there is anything more we can do."

"You forget the servants. They're our best bet by a long shot. We'll go right around there now – the house must be open again – and have a heart to heart talk with Jane. Come along. Where's your hat? In the hall? Then come on down."

And Mr Marbury found his hat on his head, his stick in his hand, and himself in a taxi, before he had time to protest.

A housemaid opened the door of Mrs Beaumont's house, a

stranger to Mr Marbury. But she seemed to know him; said she would call Jane and apologized for leaving them in the hall. "The drawing room is all upset, sir. The furniture is being packed."

"Already?" Marbury exclaimed.

"Yes, Sir. Mrs Chase arrived late last evening and she wants to get everything cleared out and the house closed as soon as possible. It's an awful change for us, sir. That dear lady..." She sniffed, and hurried away.

In a few minutes Jane Grant – a gaunt, middle-aged woman, repressed in manner – came downstairs and greeted them in a subdued voice.

"I don't know where to take you," she went on, uneasily. "The appraiser is going round upstairs and the packers are in the drawing room."

"We can sit here." Northcote indicated some chairs by the window. The three sat down, and Jane gazed at them expectantly.

"I needn't say, Jane, what a shock this has been to me," Marbury began, "and how deeply I sympathize with you..."

"If you please, sir!" She held up her hand. "Let's take all that for granted. You know and I know, and we don't have to talk about it. To tell the truth, I've had about all I can stand and... Was there anything else, sir?"

"Well, I don't quite know how to express it." Marbury hesitated. "But Mr Northcote and I don't feel satisfied and..."

"You don't, sir!" Her voice was eager. "Just what do you mean?"

Again Marbury hesitated, and Northcote broke in.

"Let's leave that for the moment, Jane. If you can bear to do it, we would like you to tell us everything that happened on the morning of Mrs Beaumont's death. I assure you it is not idle curiosity on our part."

"I realize that, sir," she nodded. "Well, I went in to shut the bedroom windows as usual at quarter before nine. Mrs Beaumont was fast asleep, but she woke up and said: 'Good morning, Jane. I'm glad it's a nice day. How's your sciatica?' I said it was better, and I went and got the breakfast tray. There was the usual breakfast; orange juice and bacon and toast and coffee. No butter or cream or sugar. She thought she was getting fat. But she wasn't. She was just right. Well, she picked up the letters – the mail was on the tray – and she said: 'Oh, dear, I wish they wouldn't send me so many appeals. It just breaks my heart. Give me the *New Yorker*, Jane. It's on the dressing table.' So I gave it to her, and then I went into the bathroom and found the bath salts bottle was empty, so I went to get some. And she was laughing, and she said, 'That's really funny!' And that was the very last thing I ever heard her say. I was gone about ten minutes – I had to go down to the basement – and when I got back… Oh, Mr Marbury, Mr Marbury! There was the tray and everything on the floor and coffee all over the bedspread and my dear, dear lady…" Jane fumbled for her handkerchief and burst into tears.

But in a moment she went on: "I'm sorry, sir. I won't do that again. Well, I saw at once that she was dead. I ran out into the hall and called down for William, and he came and he and Green telephoned for everybody. And that's all, Sir…"

"I believe it was you who found the letter?" Northcote asked.

"Yes, Sir. Somebody said something about suicide… I don't remember who it was – and that she might have left a message and we'd ought to look for it. So we began looking and there it was under the scent bottle, just a corner showing. And I gave it to Mr Atwood. That was right, wasn't it, Mr Marbury?"

"Quite right. Thank you, Jane. Is there anything else, Northcote?"

"About that letter," Northcote said. "You say you gave Mrs Beaumont the New Yorker, having found it on the dressing table. Was the letter there then?"

"If it was, I didn't see it."

"But wouldn't you have seen it?"

Jane passed her hand across her eyes and sighed, "I've asked myself that a thousand times and I can't be sure. I was in a hurry.

It might have been there and I missed it. Or she might have put it there while I was out of the room."

"Did you read it before you handed it to Mr Atwood?"

"Yes, I did. Maybe I oughtn't to of. But I couldn't help it, somehow. And I can see it just as plain as if I had it in my hand now."

"Can you indeed! What did it look like?"

"It was a half sheet of paper. Mrs Beaumont's best Tiffany note paper. Smooth grey, a rather small sheet."

"A half sheet, you say? With the address stamped at the top, I suppose?"

"No." Jane paused. There was surprise in her voice as she went on: "Why, no! Now I come to think of it, there wasn't any address at the top."

"Then it was the last half of a double sheet, torn off?"

Again Jane reflected. "Yes," she said at length. "The left edge was a little rough. The sheet must have been torn in two."

"Could you get us a sheet of that paper, Jane?"

"Of course." She hurried away.

In a moment she was back again, and handed Northcote several sheets of note paper. He tore one sheet in two. Then produced a letter from his pocket. "This is a letter from Mrs Beaumont that I got from her last week. It's the same kind of paper and gives us her handwriting. Now, Jane, I am going to write the words of the note they call the 'suicide letter' on this half sheet. I made a memorandum of it when it was read at the inquest. I know it by heart. I'll copy her handwriting as well as I can."

" 'This is no sudden determination,' " he read aloud, as he wrote. " 'I have had it in my mind for some time. I have no family, and only a few intimate friends will miss me. I am tired of life.' " Northcote looked up. "Is that right, Jane? Is that how you remember it?" He handed her the sheet of paper.

"Yes, sir. That's what the letter said. And it looks just like her handwriting too. Beautiful writing, but peculiar, not like anybody else's."

"I have made five lines of writing. Would you say there were five in the original?"

"I'm sure there were. And it began with a capital like you have it, Sir. But somehow the last word looks different. In her letter the word life was sort of squeezed up at the end. I mean there wasn't any space after it, with a dot, as you've put it."

"You mean there wasn't any period, Jane?" Northcote demanded, with such eagerness that Mr Marbury stared at him in surprise. Northcote turned to him: "You see what this implies, Marbury?"

Before Marbury could answer, Jane broke in, "I think I see, sir! You mean she hadn't finished the sentence? She was going to say something more on another sheet of paper?"

"Then why didn't she write on the back?"

"She never did. She always took another sheet. Oh, sir, I feel as if you've got hold of something important, though I don't know just why, or where it leads us."

"It leads to something pretty awful, Jane."

"Oh, sir! Then ought we to tell the police?"

"Not yet. They said at headquarters that they considered the case closed. And what have we to go on? The omission of a period in a letter that, according to their theory, would have been hastily written! Don't you agree, Marbury?"

"I agree with everything you have said, Northcote, and I am much impressed by your powers of deduction. If we knew how Mrs Beaumont intended to finish that sentence the 'suicide letter' might turn out to be nothing of the sort... Also our theory, based on the psychological impossibility of suicide, has been immensely strengthened by Jane's account of Mrs Beaumont's last moments. But I doubt if the police would take much interest in theories based on psychology."

"Just so. And you remember that this aspect of the case was

ignored at the inquest... Why were you so reticent, Jane?"

"Mr Atwood told me not to volunteer anything, sir. Just to answer yes and no. So when they asked if Mrs Beaumont appeared to be in her usual health and spirits that morning I said yes. And they went right on to how long I had been out of the room, and pretty soon they told me I could step down."

"I remember. Now, Jane, let's go back a little. Did anything out of the way happen during the few days before her death? Did she get any disturbing letters, or seem in any way unlike herself?"

"No, Sir, she was in fine spirits. She liked having her portrait painted, and she walked every day in the park with Cocoa, and she dined out several times. She had meant to dine with Mrs Cathcart the evening before she died, but they put her off at the last minute because Mr Cathcart had influenza, and she said she was glad to have a quiet evening because she wanted to get on with her book, you know, Mr Marbury, the book about her ancestors. She showed me the little pictures you made for it. The papers are all strewn about the library table just as she left them. Oh, dear! Oh, dear! But I mustn't let myself go. I've got a lot to do for Mrs Chase and..."

There were footsteps on the stairs, and a maid appeared.

"If you please, Mr Marbury," she said, "Mrs Chase would like to see you in the library, and the other gentleman too, if you can spare the time."

Jane said, "Then I'll be going, sir. You'll let me know if anything turns up?" and slipped away.

The afternoon sun was streaming in through the windows of the library and a fire crackled on the hearth, but to Marbury and Northcote memory gave the room a strange dreariness. Stiff, dumpy, hard featured Mrs Chase, with her perfunctory, "How do you do? How do you do? Isn't it terrible about poor Clare!" was a painful contrast to Mrs Beaumont, lovely and serene, as they had last seen her here.

They all sat down. Mr Marbury glanced at the table and saw, with a constriction of the heart, that the genealogical papers were still there as Jane said Clare had left them. Mrs Chase's glance followed his. "All that genealogical stuff," she said fretfully. "I don't know what in the world to do with it. Poor Clare was crazy about that sort of thing. But old grandfathers and grandmothers don't interest me one bit. I suppose I'd better throw them away..."

"Please don't do that, Mrs Chase," Mr Marbury broke in. "If no one else wants those papers I should like very much to have them. I might be able to finish Clare's book."

"Very well. Is everything there that you want?"

Marbury walked over to the table and examined the various folders and documents that lay upon it. "All the material for Clare's book seems to be here," he said at length, "except a certain chart and a letter. Jane may know where they are. Tell her they were the papers that came from Edinburgh last week."

"She will find them for you. Well, that's one thing off my mind. I'll have Jane put all the genealogy papers together and send them to you as soon as I can. Mr Atwood says nothing is to be taken out of the house until the appraiser gets through – inheritance tax, you know. Perfectly outrageous. I'm worn out. You can't imagine the amount of junk poor Clare had accumulated. However, I've made a beginning. The kitchen furniture and everything out of the servants' rooms labeled for the Salvation Army, and Clare's clothes for those protégées of hers in the South, and all the really good furniture I'm sending to my daughter in Chicago. She's getting married and won't mind having old things to start off with."

"And the Raeburn?" Northcote asked, gazing at the rubicund countenance smiling down from over the mantelpiece.

"Clare left that to the Metropolitan. It's rather effective. I'll take it myself, if the Museum doesn't want it. But Mr Atwood seems to think they will. But what I really wanted to consult you about is Clare's dog. The Peke. I don't keep dogs. So smelly. Yet it seems a pity to have him chloroformed for that sort of dog is so expensive. I know Clare paid a perfectly absurd price for him. Jane would like to have him. But it seems too valuable a present to give a servant.

Particularly when she gets such a handsome annuity. What do you think, Mr Marbury?"

"Give him to Jane by all means. Cocoa would be homesick with strangers and you might have him back on your hands."

They talked a few minutes more on indifferent subjects and then, with a last glance at the room they would never see again, the two men took their departure.

"Lord, what a woman!" Northcote groaned as they went downstairs. "Oh, there's William! William, can you spare us a moment?"

William expressed his willingness to be interviewed. But little came of it. Though he said again and again: "It wasn't suicide, sir! Believe me, it wasn't suicide!" he could give no reason for his conviction except the one they shared with him: "She would never have done it! Never!" When Green, the butler, was asked for, it appeared that the man had already taken another place.

"We haven't seen Miss Hemmingway yet," Marbury remarked, as they went down the front steps. "That is her house next door. But I hardly think it's worth while to talk to her. She's a good soul and Clare was fond of her because they went to school together. But she is near-sighted and a little deaf. I can't imagine her seeing anything the others missed."

"We mustn't leave any stone unturned. I'll wait for you in the park, one of the benches behind the museum."

Northcote did not wait long.

"She was out," Marbury said, as he sat down on Northcote's bench. "They didn't know when she'd be in."

The day had grown warmer. Marbury would have liked to relax for a while, think about nothing, watch the pigeons tiptoeing back and forth and the children playing ball and chalking games on the pavement. But Northcote opened a notebook and began at once.

"I have made a lot of notes," he said briskly, "and I'll amplify them when I get home. I propose to put down everything we know. First, a list of the persons who were in Mrs Beaumont's bedroom that morning. Then what each person observed, as far as possible in their own words. The accounts vary. Atwood saw the cook and heard a maid having hysterics in the hall. Doctor Brace mentioned Cocoa, the dog, and said Miss Hemmingway was crying. I've noted everything that Jane told us, of course. I shall add what I can recall of the last time Mrs Beaumont came to my studio. We didn't talk much that morning. She asked me if I had ever been to California, and I said I hadn't. And we talked a little about Scotland. That was it, I think. I was too busy for conversation." He sighed. "God, how hard I would have worked if I'd known it was the last sitting!"

"Is the portrait nearly finished?"

"Two more mornings would have been enough. As it is, I'm going to make a try at it."

"Good. I hope you'll succeed."

"I hope so too. Now, what about the last time you saw Mrs Beaumont? Think back and try to recall every detail."

"Let me see. We sat in the library. I showed her the coat of arms I had painted for her genealogical record, and I read a letter she had received from the Lord Lyon King at Arms..."

"Who's he?"

"The head of the Heralds' office in Scotland. Clare had written to him asking for some information about the Bells of Irongray. He wrote a nice letter and sent a chart."

"A chart?"

"A sort of family tree; the descendants of some particular branch set down so that one can see the various relationships at a glance. We talked about that for a while, and then you came in and I went away. I forgot, before that we had had tea. William brought it. She gave me mine, and I ate a pink cake..." Marbury's voice quavered but he went on: "Then she poured out a cup for herself and I asked her what she was putting in and she said saccharine because she was getting too fat and her doctor, a new man, Doctor Costello, said she must cut out sugar and –"

"Saccharine? What sort of container was it in? What does saccharine look like?"

"It comes in small white tablets. Clare took hers out of a little glass bottle with a screw top. It was about a quarter full."

Northcote drew a long excited breath. "Now we're getting somewhere!" he exclaimed. "Don't you see, Marbury? That was how it was done!"

"Done?"

"Yes. Yes. That was how they poisoned her!"

"They?"

"He-she-it – poisoned Mrs Beaumont by putting one poisoned tablet in the saccharine bottle! Just one. When she had taken it, there was nothing left to tell the tale."

Marbury stared in silent horror.

"You're right," he muttered at length. "That was how it was done."

3

"The land of tears gave forth a blast of wind,
and fulminated a vermilion light,
which overmastered me in every sense,
and as a man whom sleep hath seized I, fell."

DANTE

March in Vermont. A grey sky hung low over blue-grey hills and grey-brown fields; a fretful wind nibbled at the drift of last year's leaves lurking in the hedges and picket fences of Durham's single street and gathered them up, only to find them valueless and toss them away again. Left to themselves, the leaves circled aimlessly for a moment around the tall red chimneys of Durham's twenty seven houses and the tall white spires of the two churches – Congregational and Episcopal; if a stranger wanted Mass, he had to go to Dresser's Fall – they stared at each other amicably enough from opposite ends of the common, before drifting back to their birthplace in the branches of the over arching elms, or, realizing the end had come, went spiralling down and were swept into a bonfire by some tidy householder spring-cleaning his back yard. It was very cold. A lacy line of ice bordered the brook that slanted across the street under a narrow white bridge, patches of snow still streaked the hollows of the hills.

"Seem's if spring wouldn't ever come," Miss Whittaker complained, as she met Mrs Parsley coming out of the butcher's shop. "Ain't so much's a skunk cabbage up. Don't you think it's an awful late spring?"

"Don't know's I ever remember a spring that wasn't late, 'cept the year of the Centennial. I recollect the arbutus was out by May Day that year, and I put on my cotton drawers earlier than I have ever since. And, my, wasn't it hot in June! Hotter than hinges, as the old saying is."

"I could do with a little heat." Miss Whittaker shivered. They both sighed. "This everlasting frost and snow, frost and snow," she went on, prodding at the ice in the gutter with her umbrella. "I get so fed up with it I could scream. Why, there's a ridge of snow under my rose of Sharon won't thaw no matter what! I poured a kettle of hot water over it yesterday and it froze solid again in the night. Thaw and freeze, thaw and freeze. I'm sick of it!"

"March is the meanest month of the year, I guess. How was it in church, Sunday? I didn't get to go, Martha's folks run over from Dresser's Falls."

"Cold. I got so stiff I couldn't hardly yank myself up off the hassock and I had to quit kneeling. What you going to make for the church supper?"

"Veal loaf. I took spice cake last year."

"And pound the year before, I remember. Rector's Hannah, she asked me would I help her with the chickens. Seems Lucy won't be back from New Haven in time so I don't guess I'll take anything much but a few doughnuts. Hope the weather'll moderate some before Wednesday. The parish house ain't any too warm with just that base burner."

"It's a sight warmer than the church. Seem's if the Ladies' Aid might stir their stumps and do something about that old hot air. The men'll never get round to putting in steam heat like they'd ought to. What you going to bring for Evie's kitchen shower?"

"A sink strainer."

"That'll be nice...There comes Doctor!"

They watched a tall man alight from a Ford and hurry into a nearby house.

"Won't anybody in this town be gladder to see spring come along than what Doctor will be," Mrs Parsley remarked. "My, how bone weary he must get traipsing ten fifteen miles most every day helping folks in and out the world. Looks half froze, don't he?"

"Nose's as red's a beet."

"If he's as cold's he looks, he's real glad to get indoors." Mrs Parsley agreed, and the two parted, as is the custom of New England, with no word of farewell.

Doctor Peters was just as cold as he looked. He dropped his bag on the hall table, flung down coat and hat, hurried into the dining room and drew an armchair close to the fire.

"God, I'm thankful to get in," he muttered, as he pulled off his arctics, propped his feet on the brass fender and leaned back in his chair, relaxing for the first time that day.

"What you giving us for supper, Matty?" he asked, as a stout young woman entered the room. "You know Mr Robinson is coming."

Matty grinned, slapping plates and knives and forks down on the dining table. "Pot roast and lemon pie," she grunted. Matty was no conversationalist. "Not quite all there," the village said, "but awful willing, and a fair to middling cook."

Doctor Peters glanced at the clock. "I hope he's on time," he remarked. "I could eat a house." A grinding of brakes sounded outside. "There he comes now."

Peters did not rise as the door opened and a young man came in. But his "Hullo, John, my boy!" was warm with affection. "Pull up to the fire. Matty will have supper ready in two shakes of a lamb's tail and I bet you need it."

"I should say I did. Never was so hungry in my life." The Reverend John Robinson sank thankfully into a chair. "Half frozen too."

"Where you been?"

"Dresser's Falls."

"Twenty miles and a mean road. What you go for?"

"To christen the Butler baby. I couldn't let them bring the little thing to church in this weather. It's a delicate child."

"I know. How did Mrs Butler look?"

"Rather pale. And the baby is tiny, felt no bigger than a mouse when I took it in my arms."

"They'll both be all right when warm weather comes. How did the ceremony go off?"

"It was all very nice. I like the Butlers. Jacob Sprigs, the fellow that won the ploughing contest was godfather. We had coffee and sponge cake afterwards. I needed that coffee, I can tell you, before starting home. The wind in the Notch was bad enough but coming through Avery's Gore it cut like a knife."

"The cold certainly does hang on. But the winter has been healthy on the whole. Not much measles and only two deaths. For that matter, you can't hardly count Deacon Grimes – he was over ninety. I felt bad about Sam Tryon's girl though. But she was born peaked. I did my best."

"How is Mrs Brundage?"

"Going strong. Just likes to scare her daughter once in so often. I bet the old girl outlives the two of us. What do you hear from your sister? In New Haven, isn't she?"

"Yes. I got a letter from Lucy this morning. She's having a lovely time seeing all her old friends."

"Good. But I guess you'll be glad to have her back."

"Indeed I shall. The house seems terribly empty without Lucy."

"But not quiet!"

"No." Robinson laughed. "Poor Hannah never stops talking when Lucy is away. But she's a good soul – I oughtn't to mind."

"Supper," Matty remarked.

Both men were too hungry for conversation. Nothing more was said until John Robinson had finished a huge triangle of pie and Matty slapped another on his plate.

"There's not a girl between here and the Boundary Line," he said, looking up at her with a smile, "can't beat you, Matty, when it comes to lemon pie. I wish my Hannah could learn the trick."

Matty grinned, slapped a pitcher of cider on the table and vanished.

For some two hours the friends sat smoking, sometimes talking, sometimes silent, but always entirely contented with their surroundings and with each other. Yet they were oddly unlike. The doctor, tall, gaunt and weatherbeaten, pessimist and agnostic, was ten years older than the parson, a short thickset red-haired young man with bright brown eyes, and an air of good humoured laziness that was deceptive. John Robinson was the best man on the best hockey team the village had ever seen, and ran three parishes a dozen miles apart.

When they talked, the range was wide. Village affairs, the cure of bodies and the cure of souls. New books, the new deal, crops, fishing.

"Joe Blackett told me he saw two trout in their brook yesterday, where it leaves the meadow," Peters remarked. "Said they were fairly good size. They'd be bigger further up, of course. Could you go some day next week, John?"

"Not till Thursday. There's the church supper on Wednesday, and Tuesday I have to go to an archdeaconry meeting, worse luck."

"Thursday then. In the meantime I may try the brook with that fellow who is boarding at Mrs Parsley's. Man by the name of Parker. Asked me to go fishing with him some day. Have you met him?"

"Yes. He came into the church the other day when I was there. He said he was interested in colonial architecture and wanted to look around. He seemed intelligent, admired the steeple, and thought it was a pity the chancel had been done over. I agreed, of course. He said the church must have been built about 1830 and the gothic stuff put in somewhere around 1875. So I took him into the vestry room and we looked it up in the records, and he had got the dates right within a year or so. I remember now that he spoke of hoping to get some trout fishing."

"It seems he motored through Durham last summer on his way to Quebec and thought then that Blackett's brook looked promising. So he came again this spring. Did you like him?"

"Like him? Why, he isn't the sort of man you either like or dislike. One of those colourless people that you forget as soon as you stop talking to them. I wouldn't know him again if I met him a month from now. But I must be off. I have some things to attend to at the church. Tomorrow is Sunday, you know. Goodbye, old man. I'll keep Thursday free if it's humanly possible, and we'll come romping home with our creels brimming over."

For some two hours more Doctor Peters sat nodding by the fire, too sleepy to go to bed. One after the other the neighbours' lights went out. The street was dark and silent when, at a few minutes after twelve, he sat bolt upright, roused by a knock on his front door. He hurried to open it. A boy stood on the threshold.

"Hello, Joe!" the doctor exclaimed. "What brings you here at this hour?"

"Is Mr Robinson here, Doctor?"

"No. He left here hours ago. He must be at home."

"Well, he ain't, And Mrs Brundage's daughter wants him. Old lady's had a bad spell. She woke me up..." He yawned. "And sent me to fetch him. So I went round to his house and the lights was lit downstairs, but nobody come when I knocked. Then I threw a pebble up at Hannah's window and she stuck her head out awful scared and I asked her was Mr Robinson home and she went and looked and he wasn't."

"When he left here he spoke of going to the church, but he wouldn't stay there as late as this, unless... Look here, we'd better go round there. I'll get my coat."

At first sight the church appeared to be in darkness. But as they turned a corner, light shone out from the vestry room window.

"So he's here after all," Peters said with some relief, pausing at the window. "Hi there, John! Come out! You're wanted!"

But there was no response. Man and boy looked at each other, then they hurried back to the door of the church. It was open, but the interior was in darkness. They snapped on the lights and hurried up the aisle to the door of the vestry room. The door was locked. They knocked. There was no answer.

"He ain't here," Joe said.

But the doctor turned and ran out of doors again back to the lighted window, Joe at his heels.

"We've got to get a look inside," he said. "I'll brace myself against the wall and you climb up on my shoulders. Take hold of the vine and you can pull yourself up to the window sill."

After several false starts Joe drew himself to the desired position, but only to exclaim:

"I can't see in after all! This church glass is too thick."

"Of course it is. I ought to have thought of that. Break out a pane with your elbow, Joe. Press on the lead and it will give way."

Joe obeyed. The panel tinkling inside the room. Joe applied one eye to the opening.

"Oh, Lord!" he cried, choked, clutched at the vine, and came down head over heels.

Peters caught him and set him on his feet.

"Is he there?" the doctor cried. "Damn you, Joe! What's the matter? Can't you speak?"

For a moment Joe stood gasping. Then:

"Something smelly blew out at me!" he whispered hoarsely. "Sort of caught my wind... Oh, Doctor, Doctor, he's there! I saw him. Mr Robinson is in there laying face down on the floor, and all curled up like he was sick!"

"We must get in somehow! Come along!"

Back in the church again, Peters tore the brass eagle lectern from its base; together they dashed the bird's head against the vestry door. At the second blow the panels splintered.

"Keep back, Joe," Peters said. "I'll get him out."

Holding his breath, the doctor pushed through the opening, gathered a limp figure up into his arms, staggered down the aisle, out into the open air, laid his burden down on the grass and dropped to his knees.

"Too late," he said, after a minute. "He's dead. Suffocated. Run for my bag, Joe. In the hall. On the table. But it's too late. Oh, my dear John! My dear John!"

Joe ran for the bag. Neighbours arrived. They worked over the body until daylight. But it was too late.

"Dead as a doornail," Grigg, the butcher, said at last. "What do you guess it was, Doctor? A stroke?"

"No!" Peters said angrily. "Some poison gas or other got him. Came from that God damned furnace, of course. Just like you damned penny wise Christians. Too stingy to buy a decent furnace. So you go and kill the finest man ever set foot in Vermont!"

"The furnace? But furnace gas don't kill as I ever heard tell."

"Then you haven't heard much. What about those Dartmouth students last winter? Six of them. Killed in their beds. Didn't the coroner say it was gas from a defective flue?"

"Guess you're right. Guess it must of been gas. But would it knock him out so quick he couldn't open the door?"

"The door was locked. I can't imagine why. And he was lying face down over the open register. The registers in the church must be closed, for Joe and I didn't notice anything peculiar in the air when we went in. I wonder why he locked the door."

"It won't stay shut," Joe put in, " 'thout you locking it."

"That accounts for it then. Well, get a pew cushion and we'll carry him home."

Early next morning Joe was back at the church again with half a dozen friends. They stood staring at the shattered door and into the vestry room in awestruck silence. They gazed at the empty flower vases, the piles of prayer books and hymnals, Mr Robinson's cassock hanging from a hook, the broken window pane. They picked up bits of wood from the door to take home as souvenirs. Joe, feeling himself a star actor in the tragedy and worthy of a more important memento, looked about for the key. There was no key on the inside – he did not, of course, expect to find one in the outside lock – no key anywhere on the floor. He was obliged to content himself with a scrap of paper inscribed with the numbers of next Sunday's hymns in Mr Robinson's handwriting.

The inquest was over. The funeral was over. Miss Whittaker and Mrs Parsley stood talking on the church steps.

"To think," Mrs Parsley said, wiping her eyes, "to think that Lucy should have been taken too. I tell you Durham won't seem the same place without Mr Robinson and Lucy."

Miss Whittaker nodded mournfully. "I don't know's I ever liked anybody much better'n I did those two. And it certainly is what you might call a coincidence. Reverend Robinson poisoned by gas on Saturday and his sister killed in a motor accident the very next day. She was a real good driver too, Lucy was."

"Something wrong with the steering gear, they said. It was one of those monstrous big cars, not Lucy's, but one her friends had hired. They're kind of risky, I guess."

"Too big to be safe, I guess. Somehow or other I always feel safer in a Ford. Well," Miss Whittaker blew her nose, " 'God moves in a mysterious way his wonders to perform,' and we didn't ought to question it, I presume."

"One thing, the men folks will have to hump themselves now," Mrs Parsley said comfortably. "They won't have the face to say it's up to the Ladies' Aid to get a new furnace now. Not after what's happened, they won't!"

4

"While poring antiquarians search the ground."

WORDSWORTH

When Marbury and Northcote left Central Park after coming to their horrifying conclusion as to the cause of Mrs Beaumont's death, they had, of course, intended to meet again very soon and continue their investigations.

But fate was against them. Mr Marbury awoke next morning with a sore throat. Tonsillitis developed. He was in bed for several days, too ill to talk or receive visitors – at least, too ill for a visitor so exuberant as Jim Northcote – and, when at length he was up again, seemed so debilitated that his doctor insisted on a change of air.

"Two or three weeks at Jekyl Island," he said, "and you'll come back as good as new; warmth and sunshine are what you need."

Mr Marbury was too languid to offer any resistance. He told Sarah to pack his bags.

He was consuming, without appetite, a last meal before leaving home when it occurred to him that Clare Beaumont's genealogical papers promised him by Mrs Chase might be arriving any day now. He told Sarah that if a package came from Mrs Chase it was not to be forwarded, and went slowly upstairs to the library. His legs felt like tissue paper; as for his head, if it didn't clear up at Jekyl he wouldn't be able to work on Clare's papers when he got back. Had Jane found the missing chart, he wondered, and glanced at the clock. He wasn't leaving the house for another hour yet. There was plenty of time to write to the Heralds' office in Edinburgh to send him a copy of the chart, in case Jane didn't find it. And it would be as well to get the address of the Mr Bell of Dumfries Clare had spoken of that day; it might be useful. He dragged himself unwillingly to his writing desk.

The change of air prescription was a good one. Marbury's strength returned. He began to take a more cheerful view of life. He thought less about Clare Beaumont. Not that he had forgotten her, of course; but the strange circumstances surrounding her death ceased to obsess him. By the time he was ready to return to New York, he could tell himself that it might, after all, be best to let sleeping dogs lie. Why stir things up? Nothing would bring Clare back and that was all that really mattered. But this mood was short lived. The sight of a large package marked 'from Mrs Chase,' which he found waiting for him on his library table brought the whole affair back with a rush.

Clare's papers, he said to himself, as he cut the string. Yes, here they all are. The pedigrees, and the photographs she took in Scotland, and all the rest of the material for her book. He sighed, opening one folder after another. And here are the coats of arms I painted and we looked at together the last time I saw her. It's all here, a little mixed up – dear Clare was so unsystematic – the Dalzell book plate has got into the Conway folder. And these baptisms – surely they must belong with the Rutherfurds.

But the small carelessnesses that had occasionally fretted him in the past, seemed now endearing. He was obliged to blow his nose more than once as he examined and sorted out the papers.

So Jane didn't find the Bell chart after all, he reflected, as he closed the last folder. It is not here. What under the sun can Clare have done with it? It wasn't with the papers that William brought in that last afternoon. She took it out of a little white velvet bag she had in her lap.

He went to the telephone. Clare's house might not have been closed yet; if Jane were there he would inquire about the velvet bag.

Jane answered his ring. Yes, she knew the bag Mr Marbury had in mind. White velvet. Yes, she had looked in that bag hoping to find the chart, but there were only some business papers and she had given them to Mr Atwood. Nothing that looked as if it had anything to do with genealogy. She had searched high and low for that chart. It just wasn't in the house. She was very sorry. And she was keeping her eyes open like Mr Marbury said, but nothing had happened. She supposed Mr Marbury hadn't any news either? Oh, dear, oh, dear! Yes, she was staying on in the house for the present, with Annie the cook, to oblige Mrs Chase. The other servants had gone. The house was awful sad. She didn't know how long she and Annie would be able to stand the lonesomeness. She was sorry to disappoint Mr Marbury about the chart.

Marbury thanked her. As he hung up the receiver, the door opened and Jim Northcote came in.

"I thought you might be back by now," he said. "How are you, old man? Why, you look fine! Fresh as the first rose of summer. What have you got there? Coats of arms? The ones you painted for Mrs Beaumont?"

"Yes. Mrs Chase has sent me all the material that Clare had collected for her ancestral record. I found the package here when I got home today. There are some nice old book plates and old prints to use as illustrations, besides the various family trees. But the chart I spoke of to Mrs Chase – Bell of Irongray – is still missing."

"I suppose you could get a copy from Edinburgh?"

"I wrote to the Heralds' office before I went south. There may be an answer here." Mr Marbury picked up a handful of letters. "I haven't looked through my mail yet. It's about time I had a British stamp. This must be from the Lord Lyon."

It was. The Lord Lyon regretted to hear of Mrs Beaumont's death. The address Mr Marbury wished, that of Mr Angus Bell, was 34 Burns Crescent, Dumfries. It gave him pleasure to enclose a copy of the chart, Bell of Irongray, and he had the honour to remain, etc., etc.

"Polite old chap," Northcote remarked. "And what a dressy

envelope he uses! 'On His Majesty's Service. Court of the Lord Lyon. Edinburgh.' Doesn't that reek of tournaments and chivalry!"

"The Heralds' office is useful as well as ornamental, however. See what a neat document this is." Marbury spread out a large sheet of paper on the table. "Does this mean anything to you?"

"Not a thing. It looks to me like a peculiarly awful variety of crossword puzzle. Tear yourself away from the past for a moment. I want you to go over my notes with me. My notes about our 'case.' I amplified them while you were away, and then made a digest. I'll read you the important points and you tell me how the affair strikes you now.

" '*Persons present* in Mrs Beaumont's bedroom the morning of her death,' " he read. " 'In probable order of appearance: Jane, Doctor Carter, Miss Hemmingway, Doctor Costello, Mr Wheeler, Mr Atwood, the Rector, the cook and William – I don't know when they came in – and Cocoa, the dog.

" '*What and whom they saw.*' I won't read the accounts in full, only essential items. Mr Atwood saw all the persons mentioned above. So did both the doctors. The Rector noticed all except the cook and William. He spoke of Miss Hemmingway's crying and Jane bringing a glass of water, and he was the only one who remembered seeing the dog. We have not interviewed Wheeler or the cook or Miss Hemmingway. They may have something to add, though I rather doubt it. Anyway, we ought to get in touch with them some time or other. *Method* comes next; poisoned saccharine tablet. That's easy. But *Motive* remains obscure. For *Clues* we have nothing but the omission of a period after the word 'life' in the 'suicide letter,' and its having been written on a half sheet of paper. Next I have put down what Mrs Beaumont spoke of the last day in my studio; a word or two about Scotland, something about California. Then comes your last visit: tea, the saccharine tablets, your coats of arms, the chart. Have you anything to add?"

"Nothing of any consequence," Marbury said. "But I have been thinking back, and I remember now that when we had finished looking at the coats of arms Clare said there was something she wanted to consult me about. Then William came in with a message from Mr Atwood's office, and she forgot to finish what she had tended to say."

"You have no idea what it was?"

"Not the slightest."

"I'll make a note of it, anyway. It might have some bearing on the case that will show up later on."

"Do you know," Mr Marbury remarked, "calling it a 'case' and talking it over in this business-like way robs the affair of its horror. We might be fitting a puzzle together."

"It's a puzzle all right. I wish we could ferret out something queer. Something apart, I mean, from the improbability of suicide. Something that did not fit. All we have so far that is queer is the appearance of the suicide letter. I wanted to have a look at the original, but when I called up Atwood's office they said the police still had it, and I let it go. We don't want to attract the attention of the police unless we have something pretty definite to suggest. Can you think of anything else that seems in any way peculiar?"

"Well, I find the disappearance of the Scottish chart extremely puzzling. What can have become of it?"

"Mrs Beaumont may have thrown it away by accident."

"I don't think so. Clare was careless only with things that didn't matter. Just as small annoyances vexed her unreasonably. She would get pink with anger if a mosquito bit her, but when she broke her arm she never whimpered. No, Clare valued that chart and she would not have thrown it away."

"Mightn't it have blown into the fire without her noticing?"

"That's the same thing – carelessness. The letter from the Lord Lyon accompanying the chart is also missing. Surely she would have observed two papers burning up."

"So you think Mrs Beaumont put the chart in some fairly safe place?"

"I do. But then why didn't Jane find it? She says she searched high and low."

"And I bet Jane is thorough. I'm going to add 'Chart missing' under *Clues*, and under that: Mislaid? No. Accidentally destroyed? No. What else? I have it! Stolen! I tell you that chart was stolen!"

"But why? Who would want it?"

"You spoke of it as a valuable paper."

"Valuable at the moment, and to Mrs Beaumont. But anyone could procure a copy from the Heralds' office in a few weeks just as I did."

Northcote sighed with exasperation. "No more motive for stealing the chart than there was for murder. But I have a hunch we'll find a link between the two. Let's have a look at the damn thing. Do any of the names strike you as peculiar? Or the dates?"

"They seem all right to me. I have not had time to verify them of course."

"Here's another idea. The last row of names are of fairly recent date. Uncles and aunts and cousins of Mrs Beaumont's, I suppose. What would you think of tracking them all down?"

"With what object?"

"We are trying to find a motive, aren't we? These people are Mrs Beaumont's nearest relations, and relations are potential heirs. One of them may have expected to inherit, found he was cut out and harboured a grudge – five million is not to be sneezed at! Or he may have believed she was intending to change her will and wanted to prevent her doing so."

"You think money is at the bottom of it, then?"

"I do. Those heirs certainly ought to be interviewed. Another thing – relations might know of something queer in the family background."

"It all sounds pretty far-fetched."

"Poor clues are better than none."

"I agree. Let us consider the possibilities." Marbury bent over the chart. "All the male Bells of recent times seem to have died unmarried or left no issue. The women were more fortunate. Five of them married and their children – Clare among them – are second cousins."

"And their married names?"

"Carlisle – Clare was a Carlisle; Van Horne, Pride, Robinson, Starkweather and Carroll. I know about the two Van Hornes; one of them was killed in the War, and the other died of typhoid two years ago. Neither left issue. It was the same with the Carroll family, a girl, never married. The other names mean nothing to me. They could be traced. Robinson would be the most difficult as it's so common."

"Wouldn't there be some allusion to them in Mrs Beaumont's papers?"

"I doubt it. She did not intend to bring her record down to the present time. It was the past that interested her. The Conway folder might mention the Robinsons. Ella Conway married a Robinson... No, it's a different branch and this one contains only book plates, and such little odds and ends."

"There is something written on that folder: 'Ask Polly.' Who is Polly?"

"Polly? I don't recall any Polly in Clare's family."

"Might be a friend?"

"I don't recall a friend of that name either."

"Who could tell us?"

"Alice Hemmingway might know."

"We ought to see her, anyway. Let's trot around there now."

Miss Hemmingway was out. But as they were walking down Fifth Avenue a figure approached, and Mr Marbury exclaimed: "There comes Alice Hemmingway now!"

The lady's advance was both rapid and reluctant. She came on at a canter, drawn by a small dog tugging persistently at his leash, and sloping backward as if she leaned against the wind.

"Why, Minton!" she panted, jerking to a standstill. "I haven't seen you for ages... Be still, Bunny! I do wish he didn't think it was fun to trip me up... How do you do, Mr Northcote." Mr Marbury had contrived to fling an introduction into the flow of talk. "You were painting poor Clare's portrait when – oh, dear, wasn't it just too too tragic about darling Clare!" Emotion flushed Miss Hemmingway's kind and foolish face. "I can't get the poor lovely darling out of my mind... Bunny, will you be quiet. Mother wants to talk... What was I saying? Oh, yes, poor dear Clare. She spoke of you the last time I took tea with her. She said she was going to consult you about nice places in California and..."

"So that was it!" Marbury exclaimed.

"What was what?"

"The last time I saw Clare she spoke of wanting to consult me about something and we were interrupted. I'm glad to know what it was. Do you mean she was thinking of returning to California? Buying a place there? Leaving New York for good?"

"Yes. She hadn't said much about it, but I fancy she had had it in mind for some time. You see there was nothing much to keep her here since Arthur's death. She said she was tired of life in New York and... Why, what have I said?"

For Northcote had exclaimed: "The suicide letter! Tired of life. Oh, my God! Don't you see, Marbury? The sentence would have read, tired of life in New York, if she had finished it!"

"You're right," Marbury groaned. "You're right."

Miss Hemmingway stared. "I don't understand."

"Didn't you read the account of the inquest in the newspaper?" Marbury asked.

"I couldn't," she shuddered. "It was all so horrible. Why, at one time I was afraid I might have to go to the inquest. You know I was in the room that morning, the servants sent for me. But a man called and asked me some questions and said I wouldn't be needed. Such a relief!"

"I see. If it is not too painful, Alice, could you tell us one thing more? Did you see anyone in Clare's room that morning besides the two doctors, the two lawyers, the Rector, Jane, William and the cook?"

"Let me think. I don't remember seeing the cook. I remember the others you mention. I think that was all. Except Cocoa. He ran in barking. I was glad I hadn't taken Bunny; Cocoa is jealous of Bunny. That was all, I'm sure. Oh, there was a boy with a box."

"A boy? That's the first we have heard of any boy."

"He was just a boy from Thorley's. He came in, out of curiosity, I suppose, and somebody shooed him right out again... I wish you wouldn't talk about it, dwell on it like this. Clare is my best friend! – I mean *was*. Oh, isn't it tragic when our loved ones go into the past tense!"

"It is indeed," Mr Marbury sighed. "Well, I'm very glad we met you, Alice. You have cleared up several obscure points and..."

"Not that it makes much difference now whether Mrs Beaumont was thinking of going to California," Northcote put in.

Marbury took the hint, and went on: "Do you happen to remember any of Clare's friends or relations, Alice, by the name of Polly?"

"Polly? Could it be Polly Harkness? No, she's a Hartford girl I used to see at Bessie's. Clare didn't know her... I remember! Clare had a friend in St. Louis named Polly Conover. A very old friend, a girl she'd been to school with. You could find the address in the St. Louis Social Register. Why do you want to know about her?"

"I thought she might be able to supply some genealogical data for Clare's book, the record she was working on. I hope to finish it."

"As a sort of memorial? How sweet of you, Minton. Poor dear Clare was so interested in that sort of thing. Rather mouldy, if you ask me. Grubbing in the dead past. We should all look to the future, heads up, hearts... Oh, *Bunny*! Goodbye! Goodbye!"

As they watched Miss Hemmingway's plump figure being whirled away from them, Northcote said "I'm glad you took my hint. It would never do to let this murder theory of ours get about too soon. I hope Miss Hemmingway won't think over what we have said and begin to conjecture."

"Alice Hemmingway never thinks," Marbury smiled, "chattering keeps her too busy for reflection."

"We learned something from her chatter just now, however. The 'suicide letter' seems to have been merely a note telling some friend or other that Mrs Beaumont was going to California to live."

"Which disposes of it as a clue, I suppose?"

"Quite the contrary! If that sentence had been finished, the letter could not have been accepted as proof of suicide. Murder would have been as plain to the police as it is to you and me!"

Marbury shuddered. "You may be right," he sighed. "It's all very distressing and very fatiguing. Let's go and sit down on one of those benches along the park."

They crossed the avenue and found a vacant bench. Northcote whipped out his notebook.

"There's a lot to add!" he exclaimed. "Part of our first 'something queer' is disposed of. No period comes after the word life because she went on writing on another page. But there is still the torn off page to account for, and when you remember that the letter reconstructed points to murder, every smallest detail becomes vitally important – even a half sheet of paper! Why did she tear off the first half?"

"Perhaps what she had written was badly expressed, or she had blotted it."

"Somehow that doesn't quite satisfy me," Northcote frowned. "The letter, proving suicide, was found so opportunely. Let's think back... If the letter was put there on the dressing table..."

"You mean put there by the murderer!" Marbury breathed.

"By the murderer, or someone he had bribed to do so. Either way, it suggests that the murderer must have had access to Mrs Beaumont's house. He may have found that letter in the wastepaper basket, and realized the use that could be made of it..."

"You mean," Marbury groaned, "that the murderer tore off

the first page, destroyed what went before and what came after, because the sentence that was left implied suicide, and that was the impression he wished to give!"

Northcote nodded.

5

*"Treason has done his worst, nor steel, nor poison
Malice domestic, foreign levy, nothing
Can touch him further."*

SHAKESPEARE

"What do you think, Julia? Shall we put a row of salvia in front of the golden-glow and verbena along the edges, same as last year? Or would you care for a change?"

Julia let the branch of crimson rambler she was clipping snap away from her gloved hand, and came across the grass to the flower border where her husband stood, leaning on a hoe. Fred wore baggy overalls and a straw hat pushed to the back of his head. He always dressed the part in these first warm days of spring when farming seemed the right occupation for a manly man. So did Julia, in her own feminine way; she wore a purple smock.

They stood gazing intently at the strip of pale baked clay that ran below the piazza railing.

"It looked nice and bright that way last season," Fred went on. "That is, it would have if the drought hadn't been worse than usual."

"We can't have less rain than we had last summer, that's one comfort." Julia brushed an early mosquito from her plump red cheek. "And it was a pretty arrangement. But I sort of thought I'd like a canna somewhere, and perhaps a castor-oil plant."

"A very good idea." Fred gave his wife an approving glance. Julia certainly had an original mind! "Suppose we put a castor oil plant in the middle of the bed among the salvias and a canna in front? Just the same but a little different, if you know what I mean."

"That's a good idea. And when the hydrangeas grow taller and it's warm enough to get out the beach umbrella and the new blue seats and the rabbits, the garden will look simply swell."

"I only hope the hydrangeas will pull through. They looked pretty sick when I brought them up out of the cellar."

"They'll be all right. The one at the left has a sprout already. Miss White told me what to do for them. She says they need vitamins, and a teaspoonful of castor oil every morning will work wonders. Do you suppose our castor oil plant will grow fast enough for us to get any from the seeds or whatever it is they get it out of? Or shall I buy some?"

"I wouldn't depend on our plant. Probably you have to have a grove to get anything much in the way of oil. If it's a success I'll tell Banks – he's the man I talk to on the train about gardening. Banks told me the other day that what hydrangeas needed was pig manure. He says it's terrible nobody keeping anything but Fords these days. I don't believe there's a stable or a pigsty within twenty miles." Fred stared disconsolately across the dry swamp that lay beyond the vacant lots of the development to the patch of scrub oak melting almost imperceptibly into the level line of the horizon. Not a barnyard anywhere in sight! Even a very distant barnyard would, he felt, have enabled him to speak with more assurance of "my place way out in the country," when Banks began bragging about newlaid eggs. "I don't know where I'd find any kind of manure, let alone pig," he ended with a sigh.

"Well, I wouldn't want anything of that sort in my flower pots," Julia said firmly. "I'd rather – oh, dear, here comes Father! I told him it was too hot for a long walk this afternoon. And he won't even take an umbrella."

A very tall, very thin old gentleman dressed in tweeds of an old-fashioned sporting type was descending the piazza steps. Field glasses in a case hung from a strap over one shoulder; he carried a plump red cushion under his arm.

"Oh, Father!" Julia said fretfully. "You promised you wouldn't go out until it got cooler. The sun is too hot for you. Look, Fred will bring out a chair and you can sit over there beside the conifer."

"The what?" Mr Starkweather turned stiffly, and gazed at the indicated corner of the lawn.

"The spruce," she snapped. "Conifer is its real name, you know. Spruce is only a nickname. But that's neither here nor there. I'm sure you'll see just as many birds right here in the garden as you will in the woods. There's a robin now!"

Mr Starkweather allowed himself a condescending smile, then pulled his panama hat well down over his nose and turned resolutely to the front gate.

"Won't you let Fred get you an umbrella, Father?"

"You talk as if this was July instead of March, Julia," he flung back over his shoulder as he stalked down the gravel path. "It's bad enough to have to carry this confounded cushion just because you think the woods are damp. I refuse to burden myself with an umbrella."

He was fumbling impatiently now with the latch of the gate, and Julia started forward.

Fred held her back. "Leave him alone," he said. "He likes to do things for himself."

They stood watching the tall figure marching along the straight asphalt road that ran in one direction to the town between two rows of houses – varying outwardly from moorish to modern, but conveniently alike inside – and in the other made for the open country.

Mr Starkweather despised towns. His objective was the patch of scrub oak that Julia called the woods. Spurred by opposition, he walked faster than usual – surprisingly fast for a man of seventy-eight – and was soon lost to sight behind a clump of maples.

It was pleasant there in the shade. Mr Starkweather drew a deep contented breath. Even these puny trees gave out a good smell, he thought, as he selected a hump of moss. He placed his cushion with care so that he could lean against a tree trunk, lowered himself stifly to this comfortable seat, and waited for a moment to get his breath before he took the field glasses from their case and directed them toward the tree tops.

But the view was disappointing. Not much bird life anywhere about today. The fox sparrow had gone. A distant tap tap was to be heard, probably a downy getting grubs. On the other hand, it might be a sap sucker. Mr Starkweather half rose, then sank back again, too lazy to follow the alluring sound. He laid down the field glasses, closed his eyes and let himself slip away from the present – far, far away from this New Jersey suburban town where fate had landed him.

The woodpecker's tap sounded nearer, but he did not open his eyes. Mr Starkweather was getting what he had come for – escape. Escape from home life. Birds were only an excuse.

There under the trees – so still except for the flutter of birds, a distant pattering of squirrel or field mouse, the hum of insects, with the feel of moss under your head – you could dream yourself across the continent. You were back in California again, in a real forest – not a measly dried up little thicket – a primeval forest. Above you the massive red column of a sequoia topped with feathery bronze rose a hundred feet into the blue blue sky. All about you, dozens of massive red columns ranged themselves like the pillars of a cathedral aisle. Douglas firs, too – poor little Julia and her spruce! Flowers sprinkled the forest floor. No daisies or buttercups. Huge white trillium, blood red snowplant, the little creeping vine that smelt of tar. And birds! There were birds worth seeing in the sequoia groves. They didn't sing much though, not in midsummer, anyway, when the High Sierras were at their best. If you wanted to find singers you had to go to the coast. Why, the golf links below Monterey were so thick with larks on a sunny morning, popping up out of the grass at your feet and tearing up into the sky and singing fit to burst, that you forgot to play when your turn came. No Eastern lark could sing like that.

The tap-tap came very near. Mr Starkweather sighed, opened his eyes, picked up the field glasses and watched the woodpecker scraping furiously at the bark of a wild apple tree. The bird flew away. An empty snail shell lying on the moss caught Mr Starkweather's attention. He closed his eyes again.

Shells made you think of sea beaches. The beach at Carmel. The pool hollowed out of the rocks, pink with sea anemones. Close your eyes tighter still. Now you could look down down through the green water, clear down to the golden floor. The anemones opened and shut their tentacles; little crabs scuttled; in one corner under the weeds you saw a pale pointing finger. Then a wave coming in from the sea lifted the weed and you saw the whole starfish, a great orange coloured creature, its back patterned with white like the bead work of an Indian moccasin...

A beetle crawling over his hand brought Mr Starkweather back to the present. He looked at his watch. Almost time for supper. Julia would be worried if he were late.

Worried. As if a man couldn't take care of himself after nearly eighty years. Julia meant well and so did Fred. They were kind. It was natural they should be proud of their stuffy little house for they had never known anything better. They couldn't realize that 'Father' felt suffocated by the warm smallness, puzzled by the new fangled devices that were supposed to make life easy. But Julia and Fred had been very kind after the crash. Written sympathetically when Ellen died and he was, as Julia said, 'alone in the world' offered him a home. Alone. Yes, it was bad to be alone. Worse to be old. A lot worse. But you could get along if you weren't poor as well. There wasn't a day that you didn't miss Ellen, of course, but if you had money you could fill up your time so you wouldn't have to think about her so much. You could travel. Julia and Fred had been talking that morning about what they would do if they had money. Fred would like to buy the vacant lot; Julia spoke of fur coats and another bathroom, but she wasn't quite sure.

God! Mr Starkweather muttered, scrambling to his feet. It wouldn't take long for him to make up his mind. Tell him he had inherited fifty thousand or so – fifty thousand didn't look like much before the crash – and ten minutes would see him at the station buying a ticket for California!

"Good afternoon. Can you tell me if Mr Starkweather lives here? Mr Dayton Starkweather?"

Julia, on her knees beside the hydrangeas, looked up, slid a bottle and teaspoon behind a flower pot, and rose, with some difficulty. "Yes, he does," she said, smiling. "But he isn't in just now. He's gone for a walk. Can I take a message?"

"No, thank you. I'll try to stop in again. But I may be leaving any day now. Depends on business."

"Was it anything important you wanted to see him about?"

"Oh, no. I was passing and thought I'd look Mr Starkweather up. An unusual name you know. Last night at the hotel they were talking about the prominent citizens of Mountain View and someone mentioned Mr Starkweather."

Julia looked gratified. "Father used to be a very important man," she said. "But that was a good while ago and in California. I didn't know they knew about him here. He's only been with me since last summer."

"Mr Starkweather is your father?"

"My stepfather. My mother married twice. She died two years ago."

"Sad. Very sad. Well, I must be going." He raised his hat.

"Who shall I say called?"

"My name is Wilson. E. G. Wilson. Your father will remember me, I'm sure, though I haven't been in San Francisco for over ten years. Tell him Ed Wilson, the bookkeeper at Watson & Watts, corner of Center and Pine. He'll remember me. A fine man, Mr Starkweather."

"Father will be back any minute now. I do wish you'd wait... Here's my husband."

Fred came around the corner of the house, followed by a stout child of three or four.

"Fred, this is Mr Wilson, an old friend of Father's. Sistie, take your thumb out of your mouth!"

"Glad to see you, Mr Wilson," Fred said heartily, mopping his face with a bandana handkerchief. "Hot, isn't it! A farmer's life is no cinch, let me tell you!"

"Is this your little girl?" Mt. Wilson smiled down at the child.

"Shake hands nicely, Sistie. No, the other hand. Her name is Barbara. We just call her Sistie because it's sort of cute."

"A pretty child. Do you know, I think I will come in for a minute after all. I'm very fond of children."

Mr Wilson came through the gate. They all moved to a circle of chairs ranged on the grass under a striped umbrella guarded by two wooden rabbits.

"These modern style chairs look as if they'd buckle under you," Fred remarked as they sat down. "But they said at Macy's they'd hold up as well as our old wicker ones did, and maybe longer."

Mr Wilson lifted the little girl on to his knee.

"Have you got anything in your pocket?" she demanded.

Everyone laughed.

"Let me see." Mr Wilson took out his watch. "Blow hard," he said, "and see what happens."

"I know about that," she said coldly, looking off into space.

Mr Wilson fumbled in his pockets and brought out a piece of candy wrapped in coloured paper.

"Only butterscotch." He looked pleadingly at Julia. She nodded. "Look, Sistie, isn't this pretty paper? Tartan, you know. Like what they wear in Scotland."

"Why do they wear paper?"

Everyone laughed.

"You can't get ahead of that girl," Fred remarked.

They all sat watching while Sistie absorbed the sweet. "Where's Scotland?" she said at length.

"Dear me! I'm surprised a big girl like you doesn't know where Scotland is. That's the country where they hunt deer in the heather and sing Scotch songs."

"Sing me a Scotch song."

Mr Wilson shook his head. "I don't know how to sing," he said. "But I'll say one for you, Sistie:

> " *'Bessie Bell and Mary Gray,*
> > *They were twa bonnie lasses.*
> *They built a hut upon the brae*
> > *And covered it with rashes.*
>
> *Bessie kept the garden gate*
> > *And Mary kept the pantry.*
> *Bessie always had to wait,*
> > *While Mary lived in plenty.'* "

Sistie reflected for a moment. Then, "I think Mary had the most fun," she remarked. Everyone laughed.

"She's taken a great fancy to you," Julia said. "Usually she's rather shy."

"Children and dogs always like me." Mr Wilson smiled, set the child down from his knee, and rose. "I really must be going."

"Father ought to have been back before now," Julia said frowning. "He has a bad heart, and I feel worried whenever he stays out late. But he gets so absorbed watching birds that he doesn't keep track of the time."

"Birds?" Mr Wilson asked.

"Mr Starkweather is a bird lover," Fred explained. "It's wonderful how much he knows. Why, he can tell just by the colour whether or not it's a bird he's seen before. You should hear him describing the blue-bellied gnat-catchers and what not, that he finds in those woods over there."

"It's too long a walk for him," Julia sighed. "I do wish Father wasn't so self-willed. He knows he oughtn't to smoke, but he won't listen to a word I say. Well, goodbye, Mr Wilson, if you must go."

Fred and Julia stood watching Mr Wilson walk away up the street.

"I hope Father will remember him," Julia said. "But Father's memory isn't what it was by any means. And Wilson is a rather usual name. I kept wondering if I had ever seen him before, but I guess it's just that he looks like lots of other men."

"That's it," Fred agreed. "Every second fellow you meet in the business section of any town looks just like him. Clothes too. His suit isn't new, but it's not shabby. And you can tell his hat didn't come from a Fifth Avenue store, but it's pretty good all the same. Sort of protective coloration, I guess. Like the birds your father talks about."

The next morning brought grey skies, and by afternoon it was raining so hard that Mr Starkweather was obliged to admit that it was no day for a walk. Julia placed a chair for him in the living room window and pointed out some feathered objects on the lawn.

But Mr Starkweather refused to be interested and the afternoon went by so slowly that when, next day, the sun came out while they were at breakfast Julia greeted it with relief. Yes, he might go birding as soon as the ground was dry.

By four o'clock Mr Starkweather was on his way, having refused, however, to put on rubbers – Julia would be pretty mad, he said to himself, if she knew I'd buried my overshoes in the woods long ago – and by half past he had settled himself comfortably on his favorite tuffet of moss.

The woods were even more delightful and sweet smelling than ever today. A gentle breeze stirred among the young leaves, so fresh and green after the rain. More birds too. For a long time, Mr Starkweather sat watching a pair of cedar waxwings fluttering in and out of a nearby tree. He was so absorbed that he did not hear approaching footsteps and turned with a start as a voice at his elbow said:

"Good afternoon. I see that we have tastes in common. I too am a bird lover."

"You don't say so." Mr Starkweather smiled up at the newcomer. "Then you'll enjoy seeing these two little chaps over there in the cedar. Will you have my binoculars?"

"Thank you. I brought my own." The stranger sat down on a fallen log, drew a pair of field glasses from his pocket and pointed them at the cedar tree.

"You have a Lemaire," Mr Starkweather said enviously. "Makes my old glasses look pretty clumsy."

"It's the knowledge that counts." The stranger smiled. "Not the glasses. I see you don't remember me, Mr Starkweather. My name is Wilson. Ed Wilson. I used to be head book-keeper at Watson & Watts."

"Why, of course, of course. Let me see; you aren't the red-headed boy. No, his name was Thomas."

"It's a long time ago," Mr Wilson said soothingly, "and it doesn't really matter anyway. This is a pretty spot. Nothing pleasanter to my mind, than the woods in early spring." He took a cigar case from his pocket, and drew out a Corona. "Have a cigar?"

Mr Starkweather gazed at it longingly.

"Julia says I oughtn't to smoke," he said at length. "But I don't believe just one cigar could hurt anybody." He took the cigar, bit off the end.

Mr Wilson struck a match, gave Mr Starkweather a light, lighted up himself.

The two puffed for a moment in silence. Then Mr Starkweather removed the cigar from his mouth, looked at it meditatively, and replaced it. A slightly bewildered expression stole over his face. Bewilderment gave way to drowsy satisfaction. Another puff and his eyes closed.

That starfish again, he thought… No, not a starfish. It's a real star. Dropped down out of the sky. Crawling about there in the water. Now you see it and now you don't… Warm water… Great big soft warm waves. Rising higher and higher and full of stars…

The pool is filling up with waves and stars... Now the waves are half way up the trunk of the sequoia. If they rise much higher the stars will stick. Stick in the branches... One more heave and the water will splash right over the topmost bough... and wash all Calfornia out to sea...

Mr Starkweather's hand dropped limply on the moss; the cigar rolled away; his head drooped to one side.

Mr Wilson watched him in silence. He seemed to think it would be as well not to disturb the old gentleman. Sleep was good for the aged.

The cedar waxwings flew off. A squirrel came running along the log, paused with a jerk, chattered angrily away again. Mr Starkweather did not stir.

Mr Wilson glanced at his watch and rose. He stood looking down at Mr Starkweather for a moment, then picked up the half smoked cigar and slid it carefully into his pocket. He looked about him; at the ground, the log where he had been sitting; smoothed a roughened place in the moss, brushed off the log. Then he moved rapidly away among the trees.

6

*"Wisdom is oft times nearer when we stoop
Than when we soar."*

WORDSWORTH

Mr Marbury sat in his dining room window reading the *Times*; not, however, with his customary thoroughness that omitted only baseball and advertisements, for he had missed seeing a New York paper on several occasions during his recent convalescence in the South and was now trying to catch up. After the weather report and the more startling headlines on the front page, he turned to the death notices. He had an insatiable appetite for vital statistics and often regretted that marriage notices had recently gone out of fashion and that the English custom of recording births – 'Mrs Snooks, of a son' – was seldom followed in America. However, this left all the more time for the deaths. As a rule, he pondered each name. Matthews? There was a boy at Groton named Matthews. No, he spelled it with only one t... Griffin? That must be a sister-in-law of the Mrs Griffin I met on the steamer last summer.

Sometimes this intensive study brought a real harvest. "Bogardus!" he would exclaim. "Now that's interesting. I never knew before that one of those Bogardus brothers had married a Stevens." And he would cut out the notice for his genealogical records.

Today, however, he ran hastily through the names of the departed, with only a brief pause here and there, until he came to a sudden stop.

"Starkweather?" he murmured. "Starkweather. Why, that is one of the names of Clare Beaumont's cousins that Northcote said we ought to track down. Poor fellow, death tracked him down before we got a chance." He read the notice through:

"Starkweather. On the 15th instant at Mountain View, N. J., Mr Dayton B. Starkweather in the 79th year of his age. Funeral services two o'clock Saturday at the residence of his daughter Mrs Frederick Cotton. No flowers. San Francisco papers please copy."

"Dayton," Mr Marbury nodded. "Yes, one of the Virginia Daytons married a Starkweather in 1850 or there abouts, and the Daytons were connections of Clare's. This old gentleman must be the one we were after. Too bad we didn't find him sooner. Now it's too late. However, I'd better call up Northcote and see if he thinks it's worth looking into."

Northcote did think so. He would be around in a few minutes.

"I hope you were not busy," Mr Marbury said, as Northcote came in. "The light is so good today I should think you would be working."

"I was working." Northcote dropped discontentedly into a chair. "Or trying to. The light is fine and I had a good model; but I haven't been able to get really interested in anything since I finished Mrs Beaumont's portrait. I'm stale. Stale as the 'remainder biscuit.'" He ruffled his hair with a gesture of annoyance. "But don't let's talk about my work. Tell me about this Starkweather who's just died."

Marbury handed him the *Times*.

Northcote read the notice, and reflected. Then:

"If we follow up every lead," he said, "and interview every potential heir as we planned to do, we ought to have a word with this Mrs Cotton. She is Starkweather's daughter, so his death makes her an heir, and she may have known Mrs Beaumont."

"That is true. And Mountain View isn't far."

"I don't mind going. Have you decided how the other families are to be reached? The Prides, for instance. That is a Massachusetts name, I suppose. Isn't there a place called Pride's Crossing?"

"Not the same family; I know that much. The Prides we want came from New Orleans. Also, I got thinking about Clare's relations last night, and I remember now that she spoke of playing with some little cousins named Pride one summer in Newport."

"We ought to find them easily enough. By the way, I too had an inspiration last evening. Some of these relations we are tracking down may be mentioned in Mrs Beaumont's will. Do you suppose it has been probated yet?"

"Probably. Atwood is fairly brisk – for a lawyer."

"You wouldn't care to ask him, I suppose?"

"Nothing would induce me to. When I alluded to the will, during my interview with him after Clare's death, he hinted that I was hoping for a legacy!"

"I remember. Well, he can't think that I have any expectations. I'll call him up. May I use your telephone? Thanks."

Northcote twirled the dial. "Mr Atwood's office? Mr James Northcote speaking. Is Mr Atwood in? Oh, yes, Mr Wheeler will do just as well... How do you do, Mr Wheeler? It's about that portrait of Mrs Beaumont that I have been working on. I just wanted to let Mr Atwood know that it is finished. I thought he might like to see it... Of course, delighted to have you come too. I was just going to suggest... Yes, indeed. I'd be glad to know what you think of the likeness. I am going to call up Doctor Brace of St. Margaret's. In fact, if he's pleased with it I may present it to the church; for the choir room, perhaps... The A.I.C.P. might like it? Good. What other charities were mentioned in Mrs Beaumont's will?... Yes... Any intimate friends? I know about Mrs Chase, of course, and the Raeburn being left to the Metropolitan, and Jane Grant's annuity. Any other names mentioned?... Mrs Blueberry?... I hardly think an old nurse – don't know though. She might like to see the portrait. What's her address?... 114 West 127th Street? Thanks so much. I'll let you know when I'm ready. The portrait isn't framed yet."

"Are you giving the portrait away?" Marbury asked in surprise as Northcote hung up the receiver.

"No, indeed. And I'm not showing it yet. I invented that as an excuse to get Wheeler talking about the will."

"Has it been admitted to probate?"

"No. But Wheeler didn't seem to mind talking about it. I'm glad I got him on the wire instead of Atwood, whom you found so reticent. You gathered what Wheeler told me, I suppose? Not a name mentioned in the will that we didn't know already except a Mrs Blueberry, an old nurse."

"I seem to remember the name. She might be the best person to ask about the Prides."

"Then we have two leads now. Which will you take? Starkweather or Blueberry? It's all the same to me."

Mr Marbury twiddled his pince-nez and considered the question from all sides.

"I can't make up my mind," he said at length. "You, my dear fellow, would undoubtedly handle any investigation more skilfully than I. On the other hand, if the conversation happened to require a knowledge of genealogy, I should probably prove more expert."

"We'll toss up then. Heads, you go to Jersey. Tails, I go." He spun a coin, caught it. "Heads it is. Off you go to the untrodden ways of the Hoboken Hinterland! I'll take the high road to Harlem and make friends with dear old Blueberry. Call me up when you get back. And, for God's sake, ask Mrs Cotton plenty of questions! It's the little things that count. Remember what vast continents and seas 'little drops of water and little grains of sand' have manufactured for our benefit! Think of the coral insects! And make notes of everything."

A dreary prospect, Mr Marbury reflected, staring out of the window of the parlour car. It is difficult to realize that these wastes of ashes and garbage were once a grassy meadow bright with marigolds, butterflies hovering, birds building nests. Not so very long ago, either. My father used to go snipe shooting on the Jersey flats. If New York and its environs were to be wiped out by some cataclysm, how many years would nature require to bring meadow and marsh back to their primeval state? A hundred years? Perhaps less. I daresay ten years would be enough to tinge these smoking grey hillocks of tin cans and cinders with living green and...

"Mountain View, Sir!" It was the porter. "Next station, Sir."

The train stopped. Mr Marbury alighted and looked up and down the platform. It was empty, most of the citizens of Mountain View having gone to town at an early hour, except for a man piling crates of chickens on a baggage truck. Mr Marbury approached him.

"Can you direct me," Mr Marbury said, "to the residence of Mrs Frederick Cotton?"

The man scratched his head. "Cotton? Cotton? There's a man works at the meat market by the name of Cotten. Wouldn't be him, I suppose? I tell you what you better do. You go right over there across the street to the telephone office. Miss Beasley she'll fix you up all right. She's acquainted with every Tom, Dick and Harry in this God damn town."

"Cotton? Frederick Cotton? Woodland Avenue, 304, I think." Miss Beasley reached for a telephone book, ran an expert finger down the page. Yes, 304 Woodland Avenue. It's quite a ways out. You better taxi. I guess you'll find one in front of the Eagle House. Turn to your right, and it's one block up Grand Street. No trouble, I'm sure."

"By the way," Mr Marbury said as he was leaving the telephone once; "Why is this place called Mountain View?"

"I guess because Snake Hill is only fifteen miles away. You can see it real well on a clear day."

The Eagle House was easily reached, but Miss Beasley had been over sanguine. No taxi was waiting there. It was some time before it was located in a side street and its owner routed out of a grocery store by an obliging boy. When at length Mr Marbury was deposited at the gate of 304 Woodland Avenue he thought it wiser to keep the taxi in order to make sure of being able to return to the station.

No one answered Mr Marbury's ring. He experimented with

the knocker. Rap-rap-rap the head of a brass Pinocchio battered itself against the door, and now footsteps could be heard inside the house. The door was opened half way; then flung wide open. A plump young woman, out of breath, panted on the threshold.

"I'm so sorry," she said. "Have you been ringing long? It's the maid's day out, and the bell doesn't sound upstairs. Yes, I am Mrs Cotton. Won't you come in?"

Julia, adjusting her bobby-pins with one hand and her belt with the other, led the way into the living room. They sat down and she gazed at him expectantly. He can't be selling anything, she thought, not even the Encyclopedia Britannica; he's too well dressed.

Mr Marbury cleared his throat. "I trust you will pardon this intrusion, Mrs Cotton," he said. "You may think it an impertinence for a stranger – my name is Marbury, by the way – to call upon you so soon after your bereavement."

Julia glanced down at her black frock, and groped for a handkerchief.

"It was so sudden," she murmured.

"Really? I hope the end was peaceful?"

Julia blew her nose. "I don't know that you'd say it was peaceful. Father died of a heart attack in the woods while he was watching birds. Father was a bird lover. We didn't find him for quite some time. It's a real forest over there. Just as wild as can be. It was simply terrible for me."

"Very sad. Very sad," Mr Marbury murmured soothingly. "Was your father subject to these attacks?"

"No, but the doctor knew he had a bad heart and told him not to smoke. But Father couldn't resist a cigar now and then, and he would walk in the sun. Well, anyway, they didn't have to have an autopsy. Thank goodness!" She shuddered. "That would have been too much. We gave him a beautiful funeral, though the hardware business isn't what it was before the depression. Mr Cotton is in hardware, wholesale, of course. And Mr Starling, our minister – we're Presbyterians, though I'm afraid we don't attend as regularly as we should, Mr Starling spoke so nicely about Father. How he had been such an important man in the old days in California. Why, at one time, they thought of making him mayor of San Francisco!"

"You don't say so!"

"They would have but then he got unpopular because he didn't approve of bringing water from a beauty spot he thought oughtn't to be spoiled, maybe there were birds there. But how I am running on," Julia dried her eyes. "What were you saying, Mr Marbury, when I got talking about Father?"

"I was about to explain my errand. I am interested in genealogy, Mrs Cotton, finding out about one's ancestors, you know."

"I know," Julia nodded brightly. "The Mayflower and all that. My mother was a D.A.R."

"Then you will sympathize with me in my quest. I am preparing a book which is to include the family trees of several American families which have not as yet appeared in genelogical publications. The Starkweather pedigree is among them. Can you tell me anything of the late Mr Starkweather's ancestry?"

"Why, no. Not very much, I am afraid. You see, he was only my stepfather, my mother married twice. She was an Updyke, one of the Newark Updykes, and my father's name was Marvin."

"I see. Excellent names, Updyke and Marvin. But the Starkweather family is what interests me most at present. Do you know anything about Mr Dayton Starkweather's forebears?"

Julia meditated. "I'm almost sure that his mother's first name was Eliza. And the last name was either Hall or Call. It was written on the back of an old photograph I threw away yesterday – a girl in a hoopskirt and bonnet – while I was clearing out Father's room. He had collected a lot of old rubbish, of course... Oh, I know! I found a little Bible in his trunk with some names written in it, and I didn't quite like to put a Bible in the ash barrel. I'll get it for you."

She was back again in a moment. Mr Marbury's eye gleamed

with anticipation as he took the small thick volume from her hand, and examined it carefully, stroking the cover of worn red morocco and fingering the brass clasp, before he opened it.

"Ah, 1704!" he said with satisfaction. "Printed in Edinburgh, for McTavish & McTavish, 92 Prince's Street. A nice old book." He fluttered the yellowing pages.

"The writing came about the middle," Julia put in.

"Of course. Between the Old and New Testaments." He found the desired place. "This is just what I want!" he exclaimed. "Father and mother. Grandparents. Why, it goes back four or five generations! May I copy these names and dates, Mrs Cotton?"

"Why, certainly. But there's a lot to write. Suppose you take the book along, Mr Marbury. As for that, I'd be glad to give it to you, if you would like to have it. The Starkweathers are no kin of mine, you see, and books do accumulate so – my husband is quite a reader and we subscribe to the 'Own a book Club'."

"Thank you, thank you," Mr Marbury positively crowed with delight. "You are too kind. I..."

He broke off, disconcerted by the gaze of a stout child who had entered the room.

"Shake hands nicely, Sistie. No, the other hand. She's rather shy, Mr Marbury."

"What have you got in your pocket?" the child demanded, leaning heavily against Mr Marbury's knee.

"Why – why – nothing very interesting, I'm afraid."

Julia came to the rescue. "Now, Sistie, if you ask silly questions I shall have to send you upstairs."

Sistie continued to lean heavily. "Tell me the song about that Bessie Bell and Mary Gray who built a house," she said.

Julia laughed. "I know what she has in her mind," she said. "A strange man called here asking for Father just a day or two before he died, and Sistie took a great fancy to him. He gave her candy and repeated an old song about some children named Bessie and Mary. She thinks you're the same man, I suppose, though you don't look one bit like Mr Wilson."

"Not so thin as I am, perhaps?" Mr Marbury said. "Nor so tall?"

"He was just medium. Medium in every way. Sort of inconspicuous, you know."

"I see. Well, Mrs Cotton, I must be going." Mr Marbury removed the leaning child and rose.

"You have been most kind. Thank you a thousand times."

"Must you go? I'd like to show you the garden and..."

"Another time, perhaps. I fear I must hurry away now. I have a taxi waiting in the road and it will have cost me a king's ransom already. Thank you again and again."

I must remember to send that very unattractive child a box of candy, Mr Marbury said to himself as he walked down the garden path. I was lucky to get this Bible. On the other hand, did I or did I not glean any of the useful trifles that Northcote wants? I must make some notes anyway.

He stepped into the taxi, got out a notebook and scribbled busily as he was rattled back to the station. "Mr S. died suddenly of heart attack while alone in woods. Had been forbidden to smoke. No autopsy. He was a bird lover. Woods very wild so body not discovered for some time." He paused and reflected. "Oh, yes," he murmured and wrote: "Mr S. would have been mayor of San Francisco if he had not been so fond of birds. He was a Presbyterian. A strange Mr Wilson came to call a few days before Mr S. died and gave that child candy and told her a rhyme about Bessie and Mary Gray..." He paused again. Why does that remind me of something? he asked himself, shook his head and went on writing: "Mountain View is as flat as a pancake."

Again he paused; but he could think of nothing more to add, and turned with glad anticipation to the Starkweather Bible.

The Starkweather statistics occupied him so agreeably that the return journey seemed short. He compared the record of births, deaths, marriages and christenings with similar records in other family trees so far as he could recall them, and never once thought of his recent interview until he was at home again.

Then he took out his notes and re read them, with some dissatisfaction. Trivial indeed! And all that about Mr Starkweather not being made mayor of San Francisco because he liked birds didn't make sense. Jim Northcote would laugh his head off. The nursery rhyme too – Bessie and Mary. Such rubbish. Better tear it up. Oh, well, Northcote might as well have it. Remember the coral insect... Bessie and Mary, Bessie and Mary... Now what under heaven did that remind him of?

7

*"He took his vorpal sword in hand.
Long time the manxome foe he sought –
So rested he by the Tumtum tree,
And stood awhile in thought."*

LEWIS CARROLL

"You seem to have had a fairly interesting day," Northcote remarked. He had dropped in on the afternoon of Mr Marbury's return from Mountain View and as the weather had turned remarkably mild for the season they were sitting in the garden. "The trip was less common place than mine, anyway. Let's have a look at your notes."

Marbury handed over his notebook, with some reluctance. It was as he had feared. Before Northcote had half finished reading, he broke into uncontrollable laughter.

"This is priceless!" he cried. "Simply priceless!"

Mr Marbury flushed. "Well, you said to remember the coral insects and put down everything."

"No insect could have been more industrious," Northcote declared. "And your description of Mr Starkweather – an ancient bird lover from California who *would* smoke – is so vivid that I feel as if I had known him all my life. I get a pretty good idea of the stranger too, the man who came to call on the old gentleman a few days before he died and entertained the child with candy and song. Mr Wilson seems to be a harmless soul. You don't suspect him of any foul deed, I suppose?"

Mr Marbury laughed, a little ruefully. "Of course not! Those notes are perfectly useless and I realize that as well as you do, Jim, except in one particular. Mr Wilson's rhyme about Bessie and Mary awakes some recollection that persists in eluding me. I have heard those two names recently, but, for the life of me, I can't think where. Anyway, my subconscious tells me that I must try to recall the circumstances, for the song is more important than it seems."

"Really? Well, let us hope it comes back, bringing a clue in its mouth. Now for my story. I found Mrs Blueberry, first name Ella, easily enough. Second floor front in a Harlem walk up. A nice old lady, bulging figure controlled by tight black satin. Very respectable and respected. Room crowded with Victorian furniture – evidently all Mrs Beaumont's flotsam went to dear old nurse; terrible 'photo enlargement' of Mrs Beaumont over the mantelpiece. As was to be expected, Ella's tears were near the surface and I had to let her mourn Miss Clare for a while. But at length I maneuvered her into the past. She remembered the Pride children, Frances and Charlotte, perfectly well. Nice little things, but awful plain compared to Miss Clare. My, how it all came back! That summer of 1900 was real warm for Newport, and the children could dig in the sand, and go swimming most every day, and so on and so on. I had a hard time getting her away from Bailey's Beach, and when at last she began searching her memory for more recent news of the Prides, she could tell me nothing important except that Mr Pride – first name Albert – had gone to live in Chicago soon after that Newport summer. This wasn't much, and I was saying goodbye when she remarked casually:

" 'Miss Frances and Miss Charlotte will be sitting pretty now they got all Miss Clare's money.'

"And Ella knew what she was talking about, Marbury. It seems she witnessed a will some years ago and Mrs Beaumont spoke of the Prides and said they would inherit her fortune after Mr Beaumont's death. Now what do you think of that!"

"I think it's worth following up. Did you get their address in Chicago?"

"No, Blueberry couldn't tell me, and they don't appear in the

Chicago Social Register, or directory or telephone book. But, as it happens, I have to go to Chicago myself before long to see Mr Bainbridge, Edith Lansing's father. She wants a portrait of him, and I'm inclined to undertake it, for he is to be with Edith at Bar Harbour all summer and I like Bar Harbour. But I didn't commit myself. I must have a look at the old gentleman first – I will not paint a dull, heavy, business face!"

"Chicago is a large town, Jim. How would you go about finding these Prides?"

"Well, there's a Miss Jerningham I used to see at my mother's – an authority on old Chicago society – who would be sure to remember them."

"If they are not in the Social Register, they must have left Chicago."

"I shall unearth them. People who have been done out of a cool five million are worth finding. Anyway, I feel restless. The Prides are exerting a strange influence upon me, Marbury. I swear that no matter how long the trail may be, nor how wild and woolly the landscape may become, 'my purpose holds to sail beyond the sunset!' "

"Good!" Marbury smiled. He liked to hear the younger generation quote Tennyson. "Don't get so enamored of the 'baths of all the western stars' that you forget to come home."

"No chance of that. I was just thinking that I'd like to paint your garden, Marbury. The tulip border would make a swell background. If my search is successful and I come galloping home with one of the Pride sisters, Frances or Charlotte – whichever has most improved in looks – across my saddlebow, I shall paint her lolling in your garden plot."

The journey to Chicago was uneventful and uninteresting. Northcote engaged a room at the Blackstone, went out again into Michigan Avenue, and stood gazing about. A mighty fine sheet of water, he said to himself, and a mighty handsome town. Appearances are deceitful, of course. No doubt if you were to tip over one of those magnificent skyscrapers, swarms of gangsters would come crawling out like beetles from under a stone. Yet I hear no sound that remotely resembles the rattle of a machine gun, there is no taint of mustard gas in the air. In fact, the air blowing in from over that rough blue water makes me feel like a million dollars! But idle admiration must wait for a more convenient season. He hailed a taxi. In another half hour his interview with Mr Bainbridge had been brought to a satisfactory conclusion – the old gentleman turned out to be extremely paintable – and he was free for the more romantic half of his expedition: tracing the Prides, via Miss Jerningham.

Another taxi took him to her boarding house – Miss Jerningham had come down in the world –16 Salmon Place, a quiet neighbourhood once fashionable, now sunk to mere respectability. He mounted the front steps and rang the bell, but with a shudder. The house, like Childe Roland's tower, was "built of brown stone without a counterpart in the whole world," and also heavily encrusted with lions, cupids and cornucopias in terracotta, sadly defaced by wind and weather.

The parlour proved equally distressing to the spirit. Very large, very dark, enormous pieces of furniture lurking in the corners as ominously as the boulders and precipices of Wagnerian scenery, and smelling of moth balls. Jim Northcote fidgeted, wishing he didn't mind bad smells so much more than other people seemed to. Might be a good idea to get one of those isinglass masks that nose and throat specialists wore suspended from their spectacles.. At length a boy appeared and he was ushered into another large parlour on the next floor.

"How do you do, How do you do!" came chirping from an armchair in the window. "Can't get up, you know. I'm a shut-in."

Northcote approached, and shook a soft pale hand. Miss Jerningham's figure was muffled in white wool, her large pale flat face emerged from bunches of blue white hair topped by a lilac boudoir cap. What strange flesh tints! he said to himself as he sat down.

The half-tones are sea-green. She looks like something bleached and bloated that has floated up to the surface of the water.

Miss Jerningham was most affable. She was delighted to meet Mr Northcote again and to assist in his search. Old Chicago? Well, there wasn't much she didn't know about old Chicago. Long before the fire, her father had... she prattled on. Northcote tried to wean her from Chicago in general to the Pride family in particular. She wouldn't wean...

It was a good ten minutes before she finished her lamentations over the decadence of Chicago society in general and the contrast between her present quarters and the luxury she had been accustomed to in the old days, and was brought reluctantly to the Prides.

"Of course I remember the Prides!" she chirped. "A New Orleans family – the Alfred Prides... Oh, you say the name was Albert? You may be right – I never knew them intimately – merely a bowing acquaintance. Anyway, they lived near us on Carroway Street. I remember when Carroway Street was a cow pasture – that was before the fire, of course... Oh, you want to know where the Prides live *now*. Why, Miss Pride used to live right here in this boarding house!"

"You don't say so. But I thought there were two Miss Prides, sisters."

"Not that I recall. She didn't have any sister, just a friend, Miss Prime. We used to make jokes about 'Prime and Pride wait for no man' – they were so energetic, you know, always in a hurry..."

"Was this Miss Pride's name Frances or Charlotte?" Northcote broke in.

"Frances? Fanny? Oh, yes, Miss Prime used to call her Fanny. Nice girls. We were sorry when they left us. You see Miss Prime wrote poetry and Miss Pride painted pictures, and after a while they decided Chicago wasn't stimulating enough, and off they went to Arizona."

"Arizona!"

"Yes, Tucson. It's not a large place, I believe. You would find them quite easily, I'm sure. Such nice girls. Especially Miss Pride. No nonsense about her. A fine upstanding girl with honest blue eyes."

Northcote sighed. He thanked Miss Jerningham warmly, and tried to escape. It took some time for she was enjoying herself, but at length he was allowed to depart, and returned to his hotel in two minds what to do next. Arizona was a pretty far cry. On the other hand, a third of the trip was behind him. He decided to long distance Marbury.

"An hour of Victorian Chicago has left me rather disintegrated," he told Marbury. "But I found the Prides – that is, I found one of them. Miss Charlotte still eludes me – she may be out of reach in another world, for all I know. But Miss Frances is alive and kicking."

"Did you see her?" Marbury asked.

"I did not. She has withdrawn herself rather deeper into the baths of the western stars than I bargained for. She lives in Tucson."

"Tucson? What a strange coincidence!"

"Coincidence?"

"I tried to call up Mrs Conover a few minutes ago, to find out what that 'ask Polly' meant and it seems she has gone to Tucson for the winter."

"That settles it. Two clues are five times better than one. I start for Arizona tonight."

"But that's absurd, Jim. Travel a thousand miles on a wild goose chase!"

"Don't forget we have two geese in the offing now! If I miss one I may wing the other. As a matter of fact, I hate to give up any sort of chase. Now don't discourage me. I'm stale, I tell you! I need inspiration. If Miss Frances Pride can find it why should not I?"

Marbury laughed and made no further objection. After all, Jim Northcote was well off, he could afford to waste as much time as he chose on the pleasures of the chase, and there was always a possibility that Mrs Conover or the Pride girl might have useful information to impart.

It so happened that as Jim Northcote's train slid smoothly out of the Chicago railway station a few hours later, Julia Cotton in far off Mountain View was stepping down her garden path to take a package from the postman.

"Look what's come, Fred!" she cried, as her husband joined her. "Candy!" She tore off the wrapping paper. "It's from that nice old gentleman, Mr Marbury – here's his card – for Sistie. Look, it's addressed to Miss Cotton. Isn't that cute!"

She was about to open the box when Fred took it from her.

"One moment, Julia," he said solemnly. "We ought to think this over. Candy sent by a perfect stranger seems sort of risky to me. How do you know they aren't poisoned?"

"Fred! If you had seen him, you wouldn't be so absurd. Of course Mr Marbury is all right. He's a gentleman, the kind that puts on a Tuxedo for dinner, whether there's company or not. And he had a perfectly lovely Harvard accent and a carnation in his buttonhole."

"But why should he send candy to Sistie?"

"Just to be nice. She didn't like him much and I'm afraid he realized it. I guess he wanted her to feel differently about him."

"Well, I don't approve of allowing our child to eat candy sent by mysterious strangers."

"You didn't mind her eating the butterscotch that Mr Wilson gave her."

"There wasn't anything mysterious about him. He was just an ordinary man. This la-di-da fellow that wears a Tuxedo when he doesn't have to, and comes borrowing Bibles sounds fishy to me."

"Nonsense!" Julia snatched the box. "It's Sherry's. One of those lovely lilac tin boxes. We can keep flower seeds in it." She opened it. "Have one?"

Fred looked uncertainly at the rows of glossy sweets smiling from their paper frills, and yielded.

But he munched warily, and Julia's face also took on a watchful expression, as if she too were following the chocolate's downward course with some anxiety. They looked at each other. Fred laughed.

"Mine is resting easy," he said, and took another. "This kind in silver paper is fine. Better try one. I guess your old gentleman is all right."

"Of course he is. I must write and thank him. No, I'll have Sistie write. Children's letters are so cute. I hope she hasn't used up all the lovely bunny paper she got last Christmas."

Meanwhile Northcote's train was taking him southward with dignified determination. Mile after mile slid into the distance, but the landscape remained singularly commonplace. He was bored. It was not until the second day, Chicago far behind, that a glance out of the window brought his startled attention. The landscape was changing at last! With growing excitement he watched green plains fade to silvery desert spotted with cactus, and the flat country begin to heave into ridges as if thrust up by a subterranean giant stirring in his sleep. Toward sunset a succession of huge red castle-like mesas appeared against a turquoise sky. One after the other they ranged themselves along the track, whirled past, dwindled, were lost in an opalescent haze... Gosh! Northcote sighed with delight and refused to leave the observation platform until the castles had retreated into a blue night peppered over with stars.

But Mr Marbury, although left behind in prosaic New York, was also enjoying the beauties of nature, for Jim Northcote's departure had left him free to resume his gardening. Several days went by pleasantly and profitably. He had finished a long job of weeding and was bending over the iris bed uncertain as to the ancestry of a half open bud, when Sarah appeared bringing him the second mail.

He sat down on a bench and ripped open one envelope after the other. Appeals and advertisements. Advertisements and appeals.

One by one he dropped them into an empty flower pot... A letter – a note from Alice Hemmingway. He read it and laid it aside... Another letter; he frowned at the envelope. It was small and pink and ornamented with a picture of rabbits drinking tea. Someone selling rabbits? Mr Marbury asked himself, as he glanced at the contents. No, it's from a child. That Mountain View child. He was about to send the pink letter to join the appeals and advertisements in the flower pot when a word caught his eye. He read:

> "Dear Mr Marbury,
>> "Thank you ever so much for the candy. I get a piece after dinner and another piece in the afternoon when I go to play Bessie Bell and Mary Gray in the bushes. Mother is writing for me and I tell her what to say.
>>> Your loving little friend,
>>> Sistie."

"Bessie Bell and Mary Gray!" Mr Marbury muttered. "Bessie *Bell*!"

He let the pink paper fall from his hand and sat staring down at the iris bed with unseeing eyes.

Jim Northcote arrived at Tucson late in the evening so the search for Miss Pride could not begin until the following day. But he breakfasted early and then went to the desk for advice from the clerk.

"Miss Pride?" the clerk said. "I don't recall the name, but I'm new here. Buffalo is my home town. I'll ask Mr Jose, he's sure to know." He retreated into an inner office, and returned. "Mr Jose says Miss Pride and Miss Prime live a little ways out on the road to the Mission. He says to tell the taxi driver it's the pink adobe just before you come to Mr Plunkett's residence – that's the big blue mansion with the palms. Funny names, Prime and Pride, makes you think of the old saying..."

"Thank you very much."

As Northcote turned away, the clerk called after him: "Be sure you tell the driver to run you out on the desert a ways and show you where June Robles was imprisoned in a living tomb."

Northcote laughed and stepped into a taxi.

Ten minutes later he alighted at a low rose-coloured adobe, bearing a sign, "Pride Studio," and rang the bell. The door was opened by a green smocked woman of thirty-five or forty. She acknowledged herself to be Miss Pride, and he was ushered into a large low-ceilinged living room. A blue-smocked woman rose from a settle.

"This is my friend, Miss Prime," the green one went on.

Northcote bowed, they all sat down. He explained his errand.

"I'm so sorry," Miss Pride said. "You have had a long journey for nothing. My Christian name is Florence, not Frances, and my people didn't come from New Orleans. We're a Massachusetts family. You may have heard of Pride's Crossing."

"But Miss Jerningham said your friend called you Fanny," Northcote insisted.

"Florry, not Fanny. Miss Jerningham's memory isn't very good except for the remote past. She can tell you all about the Chicago fire and..."

"A wonderful old lady," Northcote put in. "Well, thank you very much, Miss Pride." He rose.

"I hope you are not going back to the East at once, Mr Northcote," the blue smocked friend remarked. "Have you been to the Mission? You haven't! Then come out into the patio for a moment. We are very proud of our glimpse of the Mission."

They went out. The patio was gay with marigolds and poppies, bounded by a low adobe wall. Beyond it lay a stretch of desert centered by a group of snow white buildings – the Mission of San Xavier del Bac – whose glistening towers cut sharply into a sky of hot cloudless blue.

"It's magnificent!" Northcote exclaimed. "As fine as Spain!" "Splendid. I'll have to paint that Mission some time or other. If I don't stay on now, I shall return," and he took his departure.

Why hurry back to New York? he asked himself as he was driven back to the town. There's lots to paint here besides the Mission; that great plain shimmering in sunshine; the circle of blue and violet mountains... And I still have Mrs Conover – 'ask Polly' – to interview. I'll stay a couple of days anyhow.

But back in the hotel as he was about to tell the clerk he had decided to stay on for a while, a boy came in with a telegram. It was for him, from Marbury. He read it and stood hesitating.

The message wasn't insistent. Marbury only wanted to let him know that a clue had turned up, faint, but leading in an entirely new direction, that might perhaps be worth following. Marbury didn't ask him to return at once, and he wanted to stay on in Tucson... On the other hand – a new clue.

He turned to the clerk. "Get me a compartment on the first train east," he said. "Leaves at five? All right," and he went upstairs.

He had begun packing when he suddenly remembered his 'second goose,' Mrs Conover, and turned to the telephone. Mrs Conover was as easily found as Miss Pride – and equally unsatisfactory! The explanation of the 'ask Polly' marginal note was simple enough. Poor dear Clare had written just before she died, but it was only about binding that book... Oh, Mr Northcote knew about the *Records*? Well, dear Clare wanted the address of a girl they both knew who had gone in for book binding. Clare's cousins? She couldn't remember any cousins – except the Prides of course. They were living in Paris at one time – or was it Florence? She really couldn't be sure... Sorry not to be more helpful... Any friend of poor dear Clare's...

He was about to break in with an apology – he had a train to catch – when she added a remark that held him for a moment:

"It's strange you should be asking about the Prides," she said. "Just before I left home last week somebody called me up to get their address."

"Really? Did he give his name?"

"I suppose he must have – it was some commonplace name – I've forgotten what it was. He had an old family portrait to sell and thought the Prides might be interested."

Northcote remarked that it was an odd coincidence, thanked her, and rang off.

"Well, here I am!" Northcote blew into Mr Marbury's library. "What's the news? Arizona is swell. I didn't want to leave one bit. But my trip was a washout as far as the 'case' is concerned. You seem to have done better staying at home. Tell me what you have discovered. Something big, I hope?"

"Big? Oh, no. It's just one or rather, two of those trifles you think so important."

"Get along, my dear man! Little or big, what is it?"

"You will remember that when I went to Mountain View to inquire about Mr Starkweather, Mrs Cotton's child came into the room. Well, here is a letter from her."

Jim Northcote took the pink paper, read, looked up inquiringly.

"Why do you attach any importance to this?" he asked. "I gather that you sent the Sistie child some candy, but I can't see why you think it strange that she – or rather, her mother – should write and thank you for it."

"It's not the letter itself," Marbury explained, "but something it recalled. I told you, Jim, that ever since I heard that rhyme about Bessie and Mary – the rhyme the stranger told the child – I have been haunted by it. I knew I had heard it recently, but I couldn't remember where or when."

"The stranger? You mean the Mr Wilson who called just before Mr Starkweather died?"

"Of course I do."

"Well, what of it?"

"The name Bell in this letter has revived my memory. The song has come back to me. Listen, this is how it goes:

> *" 'Bessie Bell and Mary Gray,*
> *They were twa bonnie lasses.*
> *They built a hut upon the brae*
> *And covered it with rashes.'*

"Now, where do you suppose I heard that song? In Clare Beaumont's library, the last time I saw her! She sang it to me. It was a song of her grandmother's."

"I still don't see. Oh, you mean that Mr Wilson's knowing the song indicates an interest in the Bell family and therefore he may be in some way connected with Mrs Beaumont and her death?"

"It was just an idea. When you put it so concisely it does seem rather far-fetched."

"Worth thinking over, anway," Northcote said encouragingly. "Anything else?"

"Only that I have heard from Alice Hemmingway. She is staying in Boston. I had written to her asking if she could tell me where any of Clare Beaumont's cousins were to be found. It seems the people Alice is staying with know the Robinsons. They live in Portland."

"Maine or Oregon?"

"Maine."

"Thank the Lord!"

"That is, they were living there two or three years ago. There was a boy named John. Alice's friends think he went into the Church and a girl named Lucy. I suppose we ought to look them up. I understand Portland is an attractive town."

"Are you implying that you wish me to dash up there?" Northcote laughed. "Do you expect me to leave no stone unturned between Mexico and Canada?"

"Not at all. In fact, I was about to say that it was my turn. A trip to Maine would be rather pleasant."

"I was only teasing you. There's nothing to keep me here. The Pride family – not gone before, but lost – still pull at my heartstrings, and even if these Robinsons prove a washout in themselves, they may point the way to Frances and Charlotte, those two fine upstanding girls with honest blue eyes – I'm getting mixed. It's Florry not Fanny who is upstanding. Anyway, I don't mind running up to Portland. You went to Mountain View."

"That was nothing."

"Don't be too sure. You dug up a mysterious stranger. My thousand miles gave me only a tantalizing glimpse of San Xavier del Bac. You look obstinate. We'll consult the oracle." He flipped a coin. "Heads, you go to Portland. Tails, I go. Heads it is."

Pretty chilly for the time of year, Mr Marbury reflected as he emerged from his hotel the morning after arriving in Portland. I wish I had brought my winter overcoat. Foggy, too. It is to be hoped that my lumbago won't return.

But these reflections were not allowed to interfere with the plan of campaign he had mapped out on the previous evening with the assistance of the desk clerk. Blake's real estate office came first; then the cashier of the First National Bank, Dr Combes and Judge Travers, ending with the Reverend Andrew Ogilvie.

Mr Marbury took them in order. Real estate, bank, doctor and lawyer all knew any number of Robinsons, but in every family they offered there proved to be a flaw. If there happened to be a John, there was no Lucy. If a Robinson had gone into the Church, it was of the Baptist or Unitarian, not the Episcopal, persuasion.

Mr Marbury returned to the hotel at lunch time depressed by his lack of success. There was still the clergyman, the Reverend Andrew Ogilvie, to visit. If he wasn't of any use, he, Mr Marbury, had a great mind to give the whole thing up.

But the clergyman turned out to be extremely useful.

"John Robinson? In orders?" Mr Ogilvie said briskly. "Let me get my clergy list. There you are! 'The Reverend John Robinson; Trinity College, Hartford; General Theological Seminary, New York; Rector of St. Stephen's Church, Durham, Vermont.' Does that fit? It does? Good! So glad I could be of assistance. I hope you are staying over Sunday, Mr Marbury? The Bishop is coming for confirmation. You can't? Too bad. Goodbye. Goodbye. Always glad to welcome you at any time."

Mr Marbury and Dr Peters sat side by side on the porch of the doctor's house in Durham. Lilacs were out in Vermont's door-yards, arbutus in the woods. The breezes, prettily termed by seamen 'light and variable airs,' mingled these scents with the aroma of balsam and pine brought from distant mountains. The sun shone, the birds twittered.

But neither of the two men was conscious of their agreeable surroundings.

"John was my best friend," the doctor ended – he had been talking for some time. "I can't tell you how lonely the place seems without him."

"It must indeed," Mr Marbury said feelingly. "I am sorry that I never had the pleasure of meeting Mr Robinson. Does his sister live here? Or do you know her address?"

"Hadn't you heard? Lucy was killed in an automobile accident the day after John died!"

"You don't say so!" Mr Marbury had risen to go, and now sat down again. "What a strange coincidence! There was nothing, nothing peculiar about her accident? From what you tell me, the brother's death was accounted for by a defect in the furnace."

"Yes, John's death was an accident, and so was Lucy's. I believe they found something wrong with the steering gear of the car she was driving. It must have been something of the sort, for Lucy was no tyro."

"I see. Well, thank you very much, Dr Peters. It is very sad about the Robinsons. You said they had no immediate relations, I believe, so I shall have to get the genealogical data I want from some other branch of the family."

Mr Marbury walked back to the railway station in a very

thoughtful frame of mind. As he strolled up and down the platform – the New York train was not due for more than an hour – he continued to meditate. Finally he decided that the knowledge he had acquired ought to be followed up, but that the affair was too complicated for him to handle alone. He went into the station and wrote a telegram:

"Robinsons both died suddenly two weeks ago. John killed here by furnace gas, Lucy in New Haven motor accident. If this seems as strange to you as it does to me please come. I shall wait here. Remember Starkweather."

He was about to add Northcote's name and address, when he hesitated, and re-read what he had written. Then:

This won't do he said to himself, and tore it up; realizing that a more discreet message must be given to the station agent to dispatch or the man would become suspicious and the whole village begin to wonder and speculate.

This time he wrote:

"Unexpectedly good fishing here in Durham. Hope you can join me at once. Am staying on for the present." He handed this message to the agent, and as he paid for it, remarked:

"I had intended to return to New York this evening but Durham seems such an attractive place that I have decided to postpone my departure. Could you direct me to a good inn or boarding house?"

"There ain't any. But Mrs Parsley she don't object to putting up a transient now and again. She'd have to look you over though. She's awful choosy. No harm trying. Four houses up street, on this side. The one with the larch in the yard."

8

I cannot tell what you say, brown streams,
I cannot tell what you say;
But I know that there is a spirit in you,
And a word in you this day."

CHARLES KINGSLEY

"Hello Marbury! Isn't this early morning air glorious? How I love the smell of Vermont! Balsam and pine and maple sugar! A pretty village too." Northcote glanced approvingly at Durham's elm shaded common with its guardian churches, and picked up the luggage that the porter had deposited on the station platform. "Nice of you to meet me. Is there a bus to the hotel?"

"No, not even a hotel. I'm stopping at Mrs Parsley's, a good lady who occasionally takes pity on transients. It's only a step. Let me carry your rods and the creel."

"Your telegram mentioned fishing, so I thought it would be a good idea to dress the part and brought along some fishing tackle for both of us. Lord, how hungry I am! I hope Mrs Parsley's breakfasts are adequate?"

"Her breakfasts are excellent and the dinner quite good enough. But I regret to say that supper leaves much to be desired."

"I know – apple sauce and tea and soda biscuits. I suppose New England begins thinking higher and higher as the day goes on, and by suppertime living is at its lowest. The diet doesn't seem to have quenched your activity, however. Your telegram was terribly exciting. Tell me what you've discovered."

"Here we are." Marbury pushed open a white gate. "Let us postpone our conversation until we have had something to eat."

Breakfast was satisfactorily over. Marbury and Northcote sat on Mrs Parsley's front porch, smoking. Marbury had finished describing his adventures: the many futile inquiries in Portland and final success; his arrival in Durham, ending with the tragic story of the sudden taking off of the Reverend John Robinson and his sister Lucy.

For a moment Northcote sat smoking in thoughtful silence. Then he said:

"I'm mighty glad you sent for me. We seem to have struck oil at last!"

"You really think so?"

"I do. Mr Starkweather and the two Robinsons are cousins of Mrs Beaumont's, and the four cousins pop off at about the same time!"

"And all suddenly."

"And all suddenly. It can't be coincidence. No coincidence would be so long armed as to grab four cousins at one fell swoop."

"We must look into the Robinsons' accidents and get the details."

"We certainly must. Our landlady will know something. Here she comes now."

Mrs Parsley's ample figure appeared in the doorway. "Would meat balls and custard be all right for dinner?" she demanded. "Or would you relish a mince pie? I'm partial to mince myself, but some folks finds it lays heavy."

"Of all pies mince is my favourite," Northcote declared. "But it's cruel of you, Mrs Parsley, to discuss dinner when we have just put away such an enormous breakfast."

Mrs Parsley smiled and smoothed her apron.

"Perhaps we can bring you some trout for supper," Northcote went on. "We're going fishing. Do you know which are supposed to be the best brooks around here?"

"Most folks seem to think Blackett's is the best. You go right up the road apiece, past the Episcopal Church, and you'll see it. But you better ask Doctor. Doctor, he'd rather fish than eat any day. But I don't know's he'd want to go with you. No, I don't guess Doctor will feel to go fishing yet awhile!" She paused expectantly.

"You mean the doctor is ill?"

"Oh, no. But when Doctor went fishing, Rector he most always went along."

"You are alluding to Mr Robinson's death?" Marbury remarked. "I was just telling Mr Northcote about that sad affair. He died from the effects of furnace gas, I believe."

"That's what the coroner said."

"The furnace must have been in bad shape. Very old, I suppose?"

"Yes, it was old, and nothing but a hot air, at that. A hot air don't make much impression when it's twenty below. The Ladies' Aid been talking quite some time about putting in steam heat, but you know how 'tis. Folks kind of hang on to their dollars when it ain't their own house that's cold. As for that, I got a hot air myself; feels awful good when you stand right over the register."

"I gather it was the cold more than the gas that worried the congregation?"

"That's so. I don't know's anybody complained of the gas till after the accident. They said then something must of broke. Worst of it was, the pipe, or whatever 'twas, must of give way only a few hours previous. They'd had choir practice that afternoon, and Miss Whittaker, she sings soprano and her throat's delicate – didn't notice any gas. Everybody felt awful bad, of course, most especially Doctor. So you see, he won't be going fishing yet awhile."

"Of course not. I suppose you get a good many fishermen here in the spring, Mrs Parsley?"

"Not so many. Durham is a good ways off the main line, you know. I haven't had but one transient this season till you two, and Mr Parker he didn't stay but a few days. He wouldn't have went quite so soon – Doctor and him was going fishing – but this awful thing happened to Mr Robinson and Mr Parker he thought he might's well leave."

"He had been here before, I suppose?"

"No. He was a stranger."

Mr Marbury let out a curious crowing sound that he tried to turn into a cough. Northcote frowned at him, and went on "Parker? There was a William Parker in my class at college. I wonder if it's the same man. Bill Parker loved fishing. A tall red haired fellow about my age, with a long hooked nose."

"No. This one's hair was sort of brown and he was only middling tall. Far's I can recollect he looked older than what you do, Mr Northcote. But I wouldn't swear to it. Anyway, his given name was Henry."

"Henry? Why, I bet that's William Parker's older brother. Had a heavy moustache. You remember him, Marbury?"

Mr Marbury nodded and blew his nose violently. "A moustache?" Mrs Parsley remarked. "I don't think this Mr Parker had any hair on his face."

"My friend may have shaved. I certainly would like to see dear old Hank again! And Bill too. We used to have the best times. Your Mr Parker didn't leave his address by any chance, I suppose?"

"No, he didn't... There's my kettle boiling over! I got to run!" and Mrs Parsley hurried away.

"The plot thickens," Mr Marbury said.

"I should think it did! It's as thick as pea soup now. I believe your hunch about the fellow who called on Mr Starkweather was a good one after all, Marbury!"

"Two strangers lurking in the background most certainly add to the mystery."

"Two strangers are sufficiently peculiar. What do you say to three?"

"You don't mean you have heard of still another?" Marbury asked.

"That's how it seems to me. Now listen. After you left for Portland, I got brooding about those Prides. It piqued me to think they were still in the offing somewhere and I determined to make another try. Well, as I was wondering how to go on, I thought of the Public Library – you had spoken of looking up data in the genealogical room, and so…"

"I went there the other day, and they haven't a thing about the Prides."

"You went too soon. Now, let me tell my story. After miles of granite steps and acres of marble corridors and an enormous catalogue room and a huge reading room, with a blackboard flashing red numbers and dozens of people watching for their numbers to come…"

"My dear Jim," Mr Marbury said impatiently, "I am quite familiar with the Public Library. What did you discover?"

"Don't interrupt! I was about to say, when you broke in, that I am afraid I have claustrophobia!"

"Claustrophobia is a morbid fear of small places."

"So it is. I mean agoraphobia. I always get them mixed – like concave and convex. Well, anyway, when I got into that last enormous room full of readers with long hair and spectacles and piles of books and green lamps, looking studious and Germanic, I felt so depressed that I could have cried. My sense of humility was such that by the time I had reached a door that should have said 328 Genealogy, not 300 History, and knew I'd taken a wrong turn, like the children of Nineveh not knowing right from left, and gone back and found 328 and asked at the desk if they knew a family called Pride and been told to sign a register with a pencil chained up like a dangerous dog and make out a slip and didn't know how, I felt like a child again just for that night! While I pondered over those damn slips I could feel the years dropping from me, and I toddled to the desk and I'm sure I talked baby talk when I begged for help, for the man spoke to me exactly as if he were my nurse."

"Nonsense, Jim," Marbury protested, but with a laugh. "He is a very business-like person."

"Well, anyway, he was kind. 'The Prides?' he said. 'The Pride's Crossing Prides?' 'Emphatically not,' I said. 'Oh, the New Orleans Prides?' he said. 'Why, it so happens I do know something about that family. It's extinct. I only found that out the other day. You see a man – man named Williams – came in asking for those New Orleans Prides, and I told him to drop in again next day and I might have the information for him, for my sister was in town, and she used to live in New Orleans. My sister said that Miss Frances and Miss Charlotte Pride were the last of the family and they both died some years ago, just after the War.'

"So that was that. I thanked my kind nurse and toddled away, hoping I'd feel older and stronger when I got out into the air. And I did. But I also felt very sad to think that I never would get even one glimpse of the sisters' dear plain faces this side of Paradise! Oh, I forgot one important detail. I asked Nursie what this Williams looked like, but he couldn't remember. He said Williams looked like every other man you met in the street. Then he found the fellow's name and address for me in the register: 'S. Williams, 115 East 72nd Street.'"

"Did you go there?"

"I did. It's a vacant lot. Now what do you make of it all?"

Mr Marbury evidently made a good deal of it. He sat smoking and frowning in silence for a moment. Then:

"I realize the implication," he nodded. "You think, Jim, that these three strangers, Starkweather's Wilson, Robinson's Parker, and the Public Library's Williams are one and the same individual, the same man under different aliases?"

"It would seem so. If only we could get a good description of any one of the three! But neither Mrs Cotton of Mountain View, nor our landlady here, nor my Public Library nurse can remember what he looks like."

"Isn't that, in itself, a resemblance?"

"I was hoping you would say that. This complete absence of any salient feature suggests camouflage. All three strangers are so commonplace in dress, speech and appearance that they might as well be invisible."

"Commonplace even in name," Marbury remarked.

"You're right – which suggests another possibility. That man who called up Mrs Conover to inquire about the Prides, she couldn't recall his name because it was such a common one!"

"If we add him to our list we get four persons searching for Clare Beaumont's cousins!"

"We do. Four – who may in the end boil down to one. But whether or not we add Mrs Conover's man to Wilson, Parker and Williams, we shall have to abandon our first theory, Marbury. We thought Mrs Beaumont had been murdered by an heir – that the motive was either revenge for a disappointment, or to make sure of her money by killing her before she left it to somebody else. That theory won't wash now. Tracking down, and eliminating these cousins – persons that Mrs Beaumont's friends have never heard of, and are, therefore, out of the picture – doesn't fit into that theory. We must work out another motive."

"That's true. On the other hand, one man ought to be easier to find than four."

"But how? We were proposing to interview these various cousins of Mrs Beaumont's, her heirs in the hope they might tell us something useful. And they are all dead!"

"We shall have to make a fresh start," Marbury sighed. "Have you anything to suggest, Jim?"

"Well, until now we have been exploring fairly remote horizons. Suppose we drop a fly into the nearest pool, and see if we get a bite. Don't you feel there is something unconvincing in that furnace gas story?"

"I do indeed."

"Let's trot over to the church and see if we can pick up any suspicious crumbs. Shall we take our rods?"

"The afternoon is a better time for fishing."

"So it is. We'll have a spot of sleuthing first, anyway. I see two churches. Which is Mr Robinson's, do you suppose?"

"The one with a cross on top of the spire, of course."

"Of course," Northcote agreed. They walked up the road.

"Lovely!" Northcote exclaimed, as they reached the church. "How prettily that white spire rises into the sky! Nice fanlights too and swell cornices. Those New England builders knew what they were about. If it's open, let's go in – though I have a premonition that it's been 'done over' inside."

"Just as I feared," he sighed, as they entered – the door was not locked – and walked up the dim aisle. "It's gone Gothic. Cheap Gothic too. Why was it that a mixture of black walnut, brass, and red and green glass seemed 'churchly' to the Victorians? Just look at that chancel window! German, of course. Makes you sick. Come on! That must be the door to the vestry room over there in the corner..." He stopped short. "What's that noise?"

"It comes from the cellar. Workmen, no doubt."

"Of course. They're putting in a new furnace. We'll go down there as soon as we have viewed the scene of the crime."

"You can see where it has been repaired," Mr Marbury remarked, as they stood looking at the closed door of the vestry room. "Two of the panels are new."

"Yes. But the lock..." Northcote bent to examine it. "The lock is an old one fitted with a brand new key." He opened the door. They looked into a small neat room. Flower vases, hymnals, prayer books, black cassocks hanging from a hook, broom in one corner, empty water pitcher.

"Not a clue to be seen," Northcote said. "It's all been swept and garnished, of course, and..."

Both men started. Tremendous crashing noises came from below, iron falling upon iron.

"Come along," Northcote exclaimed. "Let's see what those experts in the cellar have to say about furnace gas."

The cellar door was at the back of the church. A deafening clamour rose to meet them as they came to the opening and stared down. Two men in overalls were at work, surrounded by a ring of boys – it was Saturday – squatting on kegs and various metal objects that strewed the cellar floor.

"May we come down?" Northcote asked, and without waiting for permission he and Marbury descended. The workmen stopped hammering, the boys grinned inquiringly.

"We are strangers here," Northcote explained. "Come for the fishing. I believe this is the church where that terrible accident occurred. Mr Robinson was poisoned by furnace gas, I understand?"

"That's what they claim," one workman grunted. The other said nothing.

"I'm a builder," Northcote went on, "so I'm interested in furnaces. What is your theory as to the trouble? What was the break?"

"Waren't nothing broke 's far as we could see when we took her down."

"Really? I thought that gas from a defective flue was supposed to be responsible."

"Doctor, he said it was gas," one of the boys put in eagerly. "Mr Robinson was laying with his face right over the register and that register was open and all the others shut. Me and Doctor. It was me and Doctor found him. We knew it was gas the minute I saw him like that all curled up. Doctor, he said it was likely the same kind of gas that killed those Dartmouth students."

"Your head's swelling so fast, Joe," the more talkative workman grunted, "you'll have to buy a new hat. Them students was different. From what I heard tell, the old stinkpot they had at Dartmouth was rotten as hell, would have laid down and died if you'd of give it one kick."

"But if the furnace here was all right," Northcote asked, "why put in a new one?"

"I didn't say it was all right. I said we didn't find no break nowhere. It's nothing but a hot air and old at that, so it didn't give any heat 'cept in warm weather."

"The congregation ain't going to complain of cold when we get through," the other man remarked.

"They will not. They'll sweat in January 'most as good as they will in July, when we're done." He picked up his hammer. "We'd ought to be getting on with it. Hand me that bolt, Elmer."

Northcote and Marbury took the hint and departed. As they reached the upper level, they found the boy Joe at their heels.

"Say, Mister!" he said. "Have you been inside? Come on and I'll show you round. Show you just where me and Doctor found him and all."

"Very well," Mr Marbury said. "We have already been inside the church, but it will be more interesting to have a competent guide."

Once more Marbury and Northcote stood looking into the vestry room. Joe told his story, pointing out important details: the register, Mr Robinson's cassock, the broken pane in the window.

"And he'd locked the door on the inside," he ended, "so we had to break it down, me and Doctor."

"Is this the key?" Northcote asked. "It looks like a new one."

"It is new. Funny thing. I came round first thing next morning and I looked high and low for that key. I thought 'twould make me a dandy souvenir and I couldn't find it, nor any of the other boys couldn't."

"Perhaps some boy picked it up when you weren't looking."

"Maybe. But he'd of got bragging about it, by now, and I'd of heard of it."

"I daresay. Well, thank you very much, Joe. By the way, which is the best trout stream hereabouts?"

"There's stacks of trout in our brook where it comes out the woods. But they're small. If you went up a ways you'd do better, I guess. That's the brook yonder."

"Thanks. We'll have a try this afternoon." It was pleasant by the brook. Sunlight shimmered through overhanging branches, lay on the pools in ovals of gold, sparkled on the swift current, mingled and was lost where the water broke to foam over the stones.

A path near the edge made casting easy for the first half mile, then the ground rose abruptly and a small waterfall came tumbling down out of a rocky gorge.

"I've had about enough," Marbury remarked, as he paused and dropped several good sized trout into the creel Northcote carried slung from one shoulder. "These aren't very big, but I don't think I shall go any further. It will be rough walking up there and I mustn't get wet. I've managed to keep fairly dry so far. The finest trout in the world wouldn't repay me for an attack of lumbago."

"All right. Wait for me here. I'll go on a bit further. But I shan't stay long."

"Don't hurry. I brought a book with me."

Marbury settled himself comfortably on a log, his back against a tree trunk. Northcote went up the waterfall. An hour went by. Marbury had almost reached the last page of his book, when Northcote reappeared.

"I got some beauties," he said, and opened the creel. "Look at that one! Isn't he gorgeous? It was lots of fun up there, but you were wise not to attempt it. I'm soaked through up to my waist."

"Hadn't you better go home and change?"

"No hurry. I never take cold," Northcote dropped on the moss. "Did you enjoy your book? What is it?"

"It is called *Letters from Scotland*," Marbury said, "*by an English lady*. I found it in our landlady's parlour. The authoress's adventures were tame enough, and her style lacks everything that a style should have. Nevertheless my time has not been wasted. Read this paragraph."

Northcote leaned over the book open on Marbury's knee, and read:

"Methinks, my dear Sister, I have yet to describe to you the entertainment I enjoyed some two weeks since at Irongray. The Laird was civility itself and his good Lady most attentive to my comfort. The tea equipage was near as elegant as that of dear Lady Bobbit. We supped off venison and roast fowl, the latter, however, lacked the embellishment of bread sauce. You will recall the witty remark of our friend Doctor Johnson, that roast fowl without bread sauce is like a judge without a wig. Heaven has blessed the Laird with five stalwart sons, but one of whom, James, has as yet flown the paternal nest. Being the proud wearer of His Majesty's uniform James is at present with our forces in Canada, ready to repel dastardly invasions from our rebellious colony. The youngest son, Charles – a handsome child, but sadly spoiled – expressed to me his intention of emigrating to the States or some other Barbarous land. I told him 'twere better to starve by his 'ain fireside' than grow rich among the enemies of Our King, but I doubt he heeds my warning. From Irongray I proceeded to –"

"You may stop there," Marbury said. "This paragraph is all that's important to us in the book, but it tells me something I didn't know – or the Lord Lyon either, for that matter. Bell of Irongray had *five* sons. The Lord Lyon's chart showed only four, and not one of them is named Charles."

"How do you account for it?"

"If Charles carried out his boyish plan of emigrating to America, he might easily have been lost sight of – it often happened. To be sure, the oldest son, James, mentioned by our authoress as wearing His Majesty's uniform, settled in America some time after the War of '18. But James prospered; his family would have kept in touch with him."

"This Charles may have been a black sheep."

"Just so. Moreover, the Bells of Irongray ceased to be important in that generation. James sold the old place, the other brothers died, and the family records were scattered no one knows where."

"A black sheep is apt to be forgotten."

"Oh, yes. Probably, after a year or so, Charles left off writing home, and his family were rather glad to take for granted that poor Charles was dead."

"Does a fifth son make any difference to us, to our investigation?"

"It does. You see, we thought we had accounted for all the descendants of Bell of Irongray – you remember the chart showed that only James had issue – and as Mrs Beaumont, the Robinsons, the Prides and Mr Starkweather are dead, we believed the line was extinct. Now this Charles crops up. If he had children there may be any number of Bell descendants we know nothing about."

"Here in America?"

"Or some other colony. If Charles had stayed by his 'ain fireside' his family would not have forgotten him."

"Pretty discouraging, isn't it!"

"I don't think so. We hoped to get information about Mrs Beaumont's murder through some of her cousins and were balked by their sudden taking off. Now, if we can track down this Charles's descendants they may tell us something."

"I'd rather track down the mysterious stranger."

"That goes without saying."

"Well, we've got a lot to think over." Northcote got to his feet. "But let's call it a day. If Mrs Parsley is going to cook these trout for supper we ought to be on our way."

Marbury nodded. As he rose, he dropped the book. Northcote picked it up.

"Do you observe that it opens of itself at the page you showed me?" he remarked. "And – yes – as I live, the corner of the page has been turned down!"

"Not by me. I never dog ear a book."

Northcote held the book at a slant, and squinted across the paper.

"There are marks here," he said. "Not pencil marks, but indentations, as if someone had been writing with a hard pencil on a piece of paper laid on the page."

"Making a note of something in the book, perhaps."

"He may have been copying this very paragraph. Now, the question is who was it? Who turned down the page? If that particular paragraph was copied, it would indicate some person interested in the Bell family. But Bell is not an uncommon name and..."

"Why couldnt it have been Parker, Mrs Parsley's mysterious stranger? He found the book in her parlor just as you did, and copied that paragraph about Bell of Irongray's family, because it told him what it told you – that there was a fifth son named Charles."

"I'm afraid you are right," Mr Marbury sighed. "If you are right, – if this Parker has discovered the possibility of there being some Bell descendants still in existence – what will happen?"

"If he is the murderer we think him, he will start out to make another killing! Good God, Marbury, do you see where this leads us? If we can't find the descendants of the fifth son, Charles Bell, before the stranger finds them, they will meet with mysterious accidents as sure as God made little apples!"

"It's a terrible responsibility for us."

"I don't mind responsibility. Gosh! I'm glad you found that book, Marbury. But we've got to hump ourselves, work like the devil."

"I suppose so," Mr Marbury sighed. "A life may be hanging by a thread at this moment! An appalling thought."

"That's not the way to look at it. To my mind, the affair is a lot more exciting than it was. It has a human element now that it lacked while it was merely a problem to be worked out. I was anxious to solve it because of my friendship for Mrs Beaumont, and I was fretted by the indifference of the authorities. But now... Gosh, Marbury! We're more than sleuths, we're lifesavers! Not the peppermint variety, but the genuine article, ready to climb ladders and fling ropes."

"That's all very well," Mr Marbury said dryly, "but our job would be easier if we knew just where to plant a ladder, or could get the remotest glimpse of a ship in distress anywhere on the horizon."

"You'll feel more sanguine after supper," Northcote laughed.

9

"Little Miss Muffet sat on a tuffet,
Eating her curds and whey;
There came a black spider and sat down beside her."

MOTHER GOOSE

"Hurry up, Aunt Henrietta! The popcorn man has come and they're lighting the bandstand."

"One minute, dear. I am just finishing a letter."

Laura sighed. No use trying to hurry Aunt Henrietta. If you told her there was a mad bull coming up the front steps and she was finishing something, she'd finish it before she looked out of the window.

From the piazza rail where Laura sat perched, restless as a hungry bird, she could watch every change of light and color in the park on the far side of the road as if it had been a scene on the stage. Night would soon be here and already the foreground of lawn and hedge was dark. But the road beyond, where cars were slipping in and out maneuvering for good places, caught illumination from the street lamp at the corner, and the park itself – a level grassy space – showed arsenic green in the lights that encircled the eaves of the white bandstand like a crown of stars. Before long the real stars would show themselves in the indigo sky, the moon would come up, and at nine o'clock the band would begin to play...

Here came the band now – Mr Spring first, then Mr Lambkin, Mr Spaulding, Sam Dickie and the others. The brass gleamed like gold serpents. The drum was a pale disk that seemed too heavy for Mr Spring's slight figure. He walked slanting backward. One by one the musicians climbed the little ladder, stepped on to the high platform of the bandstand, ranged themselves in their places. Squawks and screams came from protesting instruments, they were tuning up. The road was lined with cars now on both sides, leaving only a narrow lane. New arrivals had to take the far end; cars indifferent to music and bound for points beyond could barely squeeze through, heralded by a tremendous blowing of horns. Already the popcorn man was doing a good business; you could smell the crisp toasty buttery salty flavour as he jiggled his popcorner over the stove and stuffed paper bags until they bulged and oozed and overflowed with hot foam...

More people were coming every minute, all talking and laughing. The park benches were filling up. From the lake came the puff puff of motor boats, and you could see canoes sliding by, their paddles splintering the lake's dark glass with silver...

A final squeal from the clarinet. Laura sprang to her feet.

"I'm going, Aunt Henrietta!" she called, and away she went, across the dark lawn, through the gate in the hedge, dodging between the cars, past the bandstand, down to the shore. As she reached it, with a blare and boom and thump, thump, thump the band began to play. Peter and his canoe were waiting for her. She stepped in, light as a feather. The canoe moved out on the water. Over her shoulder she could see the bandstand reflected in the water, a white birthday cake stuck full of candles. The music dwindled to fairy music, thin and sweet. You could imagine yourself in Venice, Laura thought, in a gondola...

"I don't like Laura staying out there on the water so late," Miss Henrietta Sands said to Judge Evans sitting beside her on a bench near the bandstand. "She will catch cold, with thin slippers and nothing on her head."

"Seventeen, my dear lady," the Judge remarked, "can afford to disregard dampness as you and I cannot. Laura is as sound in mind and limb as any girl I know and by far the prettiest girl in the county. I doubt if you'll find a prettier girl anywhere in Massachusetts... Good evening, Mr Price!" The Judge rose.

"Miss Sands, may I present Mr Price? Mr Price is stopping at the inn for a few days on his way to Bar Harbour."

Miss Sands smiled and bowed. Mr Price murmured politely and sat down on the bench beside her. The judge moved away.

"A pretty scene," Mr Price remarked, "and very nice music. Do you have these concerts often?"

"Every Saturday during the summer. Are you stopping here long, Mr Price?"

"Oh, no. In fact, I hadn't intended to spend more than one night, but the village is so attractive that I shall probably stay over the weekend. Do you live here all the year round, Miss Sands?"

"Yes. That is our house on the terrace, the white one with pillars on the other side of the road."

"A fine old colonial mansion. Your old homestead, I presume?"

"No. I bought it about ten years ago. I had a little niece to bring up. Her parents died and this seemed a pleasant place for a child."

"It certainly is, and so much healthier than a city. You are a Bostonian, I suppose?"

"No, we came here from Cleveland."

"Indeed! I wonder if you know my old friends the Herbert Barlows, and the Wighams?"

"Of course I do. I knew the Wighams intimately, and the Barlows are cousins of mine. Have you seen them lately, Mr Price?"

"No. I haven't been in Cleveland for years..."

"Ah, the band is playing 'Home, Sweet Home,' the concert must be over."

They both rose. "Do stop in some afternoon, Mr Price," Miss Sands smiled. "We can have a nice chat about our mutual friends in Cleveland." Mr Price expressed gratitude. "I should like you to meet my niece. Oh, here she is now. Where have you been all this time, Laura?"

"Out on the lake. The moonlight was too lovely for words. We went almost as far as the island."

"Mr Price," Miss Sands turned. "Oh, he's gone."

"Who has gone?" Laura asked.

"A friend of Judge Evans I was talking to just now. He knows the Wighams... Come along, dear. It's late and you ought to be in bed."

"A heavenly day," Laura remarked. "Too nice a day to sit around doing nothing in particular." She rose from the piazza step and stretched her bare arms over her head with a sigh. "How I wish we had a car, Aunt Henrietta. I'd like to get into a car and drive all day all by myself, without the slightest idea where I was going, and stop when it got pitch dark at some little inn and go on again the next day and the next and the next, perhaps forever!"

She stood staring out over the water, her hand plucked absently at the vine climbing to the piazza roof, stripped off a leaf and sent it fluttering.

Miss Sands looked up from her needlepoint.

"You're so restless, Laura!" she remarked. "Aren't you happy? I've done the best I could and..."

"Oh, you have, you have, darling!" Laura flung herself on the floor at her aunt's feet. "And I'm a wretch to grumble. But this is such a tiny village, and I've hardly ever been out of it. Only three times to Boston, and never once to New York. I want to travel. I want to go to Venice and London and the Vale of Kashmir!"

"My income seems to get smaller every minute," Miss Sands sighed. "I couldn't risk selling any stock. I might sell some furniture, perhaps. There's that sideboard in the attic with a broken leg that Judge Evans admires so much. But I don't know anyone who would buy it."

Laura jumped to her feet. "A car has stopped at the gate, Aunt Henrietta!" she exclaimed, "and a man is coming across the lawn. A strange man."

"Who can it be?" Miss Sands' gaze followed Laura's. "Why, it's that Mr Price I met last evening in the Park, Judge Evans' friend. Tell Emma to bring tea."

"Let me fill your cup, Mr Price. Laura, give Mr Price another gingersnap. You say you are leaving for Bar Harbour this afternoon, Mr Price? Motoring, I suppose?"

"Yes, I prefer that way of traveling. It leaves you free to go or stay just as you please."

"A Buick, isn't it?" Laura remarked, glancing at the car in the road.

"Yes. I'm all for a Buick. To my mind, it's a happy medium between a Ford and a Cadillac."

"We haven't even a Ford," Laura said. "If I had any sort of car, I'd explore the world."

"My niece longs to travel," Miss Sands said. "I suppose it's natural at her age."

"I wish I wasn't leaving Derby Centre so soon," Mr Price said. "I might have persuaded you to take a drive with me. As it is, I shall have to say goodbye. That is a very handsome desk, Miss Sands. I envy you your fine colonial furniture."

"We have some very nice pieces. Goodbye, Mr Price. If you come through on your way back from Bar Harbour I hope you will drop in to see us."

"A pleasant man," Miss Sands remarked, as she and Laura watched Mr Price cross the lawn and step into his car. "I rather hope he will come in again some time."

"I didn't think he was so hot. His voice is flat, and he has such an expressionless expression. Would you say he was from the West?"

"I don't think he can be. He hasn't any Western but he doesn't speak like a Southerner either, or a New Englander."

"He has probably traveled so much – lucky man! – that he has lost whatever accent he was born with. He liked our furniture, didn't he?" Laura glanced meditatively at the desk.

"I couldn't part with that desk!" Miss Sands exclaimed. "It's a Duncan Phyfe and belonged to my great grandfather."

"The sideboard then. The one in the attic."

"Well, if Mr Price does stop in on his way home, we might show it to him. But it is worth a good deal, Laura, and I didn't think he looked like a very rich man, did you?"

"No, I don't believe he's rich," Laura considered. "Not really rich. That Buick is last year's model."

"He was not particularly well dressed. However, he might know of some friend who would buy the sideboard. It's worth at least five hundred dollars. That would give us a month in Florida next winter."

"And then what? We'd be back here again with nothing to look forward to! Oh, Aunt Henrietta, I don't want to nibble at life. I want a great big fruity slice and I want it now, while I'm young and able to enjoy every morsel, every currant and bit of citron and last crumb of icing!"

Aunt Henrietta sighed, prodding her needlepoint with a worried needle. "There's your great-aunt's silver. It's to be sold at auction this fall."

"We can't count on that. They told you silver wasn't bringing much nowadays."

"Well, stocks may go up again. Until then, l don't quite know how."

"You do know, Aunt Henrietta. You know perfectly well that I ought to get a job. I keep on saying it and saying it and you keep on making believe it's a new idea to sell the sideboard and let me have the money to get started, and I promise you I'll make good. I will, I will!"

"Well, if this Mr Price does come back, I promise to let him see the sideboard, my dear. But he probably won't come."

"No," Laura agreed forlornly. "He probably won't."

But they were wrong. Three weeks later the Buick stood again at Miss Sands' gate.

Laura had gone on a picnic up the lake, but Miss Sands was at home and very pleased to see Mr Price. He seemed quite an old friend now. They had tea on the piazza. Before long the conversation slid easily toward the collection of antiques. When tea was over he was taken into the house to admire the Lowestoft china and Stiegel glass, the highboys and lowboys, samplers and fire screens that adorned the parlour and dining room.

"I am not a collector myself," he said. "Can't afford it. But I have a friend who is always on the lookout for really choice pieces. I wish he could see your treasures, Miss Sands. You have never considered parting with any of them, I suppose?"

"Why, no. That is, I couldn't let any of these things go. But I have a sideboard we never use. It's in the attic. If you don't mind going upstairs…"

When, half an hour later, Mr Price had said goodbye, Miss Sands stood watching the Buick move away from her front gate with a frown. She was troubled by a mingling of regret, satisfaction and indecision so foreign to her placid nature, and so uncomfortable, that a superstitious person would have taken it as prophetic of disaster.

But Miss Sands was not superstitious, and her uneasiness was momentary. For as she turned from the window, Laura came tearing across the lawn and up the path.

"Aunt Henrietta!" she cried, as she dropped a wet bathing suit on the piazza steps, let the screen door slam behind her and burst into the parlor. "Aunt Henrietta, was that Mr Price's car? Has he been here? Did you show him the sideboard?"

Miss Sands hesitated. "Yes – I did. And he has a friend who might like it. But it's an heirloom, Laura… I hardly think… However, he's coming again."

Laura flung both arms around her aunt's waist, and jumped her up and down. "He's coming again? Then it's all right! The friend will buy the sideboard. You'll give me the money and I…"

"Let me go, Laura." Miss Sands panted. "Stop bouncing me about. It makes me dizzy. And don't imagine that anything is settled. It's all quite in the air still."

"When will we know?"

"Fairly soon. That is, Mr Price said he would communicate with his friend at once. But of course he may not hear for some time."

"And if he doesn't hear, Mr Price may get tired of this poky little place and go away!"

"I don't think," Miss Sands smiled demurely, "that Mr Price has any intention of leaving at present. He spoke of staying over the Fourth anyway."

"Good! Hadn't we better ask him to dinner?"

"He has asked us. It seems there's a nice little inn near Salter's Beach, and he has invited you and me and Judge Evans to drive over and have a shore dinner. It would be pleasant, don't you think? That is, if Judge Evans can accept. I should not care to go without him. Mr Price is such a recent acquaintance. Though his knowing the Wighams and Barlows makes a difference, of course."

"There's the club dance that night," Laura hesitated.

"Mr Price spoke of letting you drive the car."

"Then I'll go! I shall tell Peter it's a matter of business and he will understand. We mustn't let Price slip through our fingers."

Mr Price showed no intention of slipping. The Fourth came in due time. The party started off, Laura at the wheel. Miss Sands and Judge Evans sat in the back, chatting amicably. The front seat was less talkative. Laura was too absorbed in learning and Mr Price in teaching to have time for conversation, but she was enjoying herself. They all seemed to be enjoying themselves. They all agreed that the roadbed was smooth, that the afternoon had proved cooler than might have been expected, and that the sea breeze blowing in their faces as they neared the coast was simply delicious.

"You drove very nicely, Laura," Miss Sands remarked, as she

and her niece went upstairs to the ladies' dressing room at the inn. "I didn't feel at all nervous." She bent in front of the mirror, powdering her nose.

"It was fun driving. But, oh, dear, I do think Mr Price is the dullest human being I ever struck!"

Laura took her aunt's place at the mirror, ran a comb through the fluffy curls over her ears, smoothed the satiny top of her head and regarded the reflection in the glass with approval. "I'm glad you didn't let me have my eyebrows plucked, Aunt Henrietta," she went on, adjusting her hat to an exact angle. "It gives you such a bulgy picked chicken look. I wonder if Mr Price will let me drive going home."

"Probably not. It will be dark and I daresay he will prefer to drive himself."

"If he does, please sit in front, Aunt Henrietta. The Judge isn't any too scintillating, but he's a ball of fire compared to Price."

"I don't find Mr Price so very dull," Miss Sands smiled, "but he and I are about the same age which makes a difference, of course. Let's go down. It's almost time for supper."

"How good the lobsters smell!" Laura cried, skipping down the stairs.

The shore dinner, an excellent meal of various succulent sea foods, was over. After coffee on the verandah, Mr Price escorted his party down to the beach and found seats on the platform running in front of the bathing houses where the ladies would be sheltered from the wind and yet have a good view of the fireworks to be set off by the inn management in honour of the Fourth.

"Nothing very elaborate," he explained. "Only a few rockets and Roman candles."

The beach was not particularly attractive, Laura thought. Just a crescent of pebbly sand backed by low rocks and huckleberry bushes that rose at each end to thickets of scrub pine and cat-briar. But a good many people had come to see the fireworks. They sat in groups dotted about on the sand, waiting.

"I wish they'd begin," Laura remarked, suppressing a yawn. "But I suppose they can't until it's really dark. There comes the man with the fireworks at last!"

Everybody peered through the dusk as a man with a hamper approached, and watched him with intense concentration as he took out rockets, Roman candles and Catherine wheels and laid them in rows on the sand.

"The effect might be prettier from a distance," Mr Price remarked. "Shall we leave Miss Sands and Judge Evans to entertain each other, Miss Laura, and stroll up the beach a little way?"

Laura rose obediently – Pricie must be humoured – and with a word of explanation to her aunt followed him down a rough path to the shore and along the beach.

"The fireworks will show much better here," Laura remarked. "It's pitch dark now that we are away from the lights of the inn – and so nice and quiet."

"I thought you would like it. Shall we sit down? This smooth stone ought to be comfortable for you – it's just the right height. Ah, the fireworks are about to begin."

The fireworks were a great success. One Roman candle blew out unexpectedly and most of the Catherine wheels either refused to spin or spurted sideways. But the rockets, everyone agreed, could not have been better. Children screamed in ecstasy, little boys ran about waving lighted sticks of punk, ohs and ahs of admiration came from every group of spectators as, one by one, sometimes two by two, the rockets rose with a long hissing sigh, built a bridge of fire over the waves as if they meant to span the Atlantic, spat out a mouthful of splendid red and blue balls and dropped, plop, plop, into the dark sea.

"They're marvellous!" Laura cried. "Simply marvellous! I'm glad it's such a dark night. Pitch dark. You can't see a single star and the waves are jet black. Do you think a storm is coming up, Mr Price?"

"I daresay. It's getting colder. Are you warm enough?"

"Yes, indeed."

"Shan't I fetch you a wrap?"

"No, indeed."

"Well, I feel chilly myself." Mr Price rose. "I think I'd better get my coat. I'll be back in a minute. Stay right where you are, Miss Laura. It's so dark that if you move I shan't be able to find you again."

He turned away. At once his figure was swallowed up in the darkness. Laura relaxed, glad that Mr Price had gone. Such a dull dull dull man!... That rocket was the best yet. How dark it all was! Sand like grey asphalt, water ink, sky closed down over everything like a big black umbrella... Three rockets going up at once now, their fiery paths criss-crossing... They would seem brighter still if you looked at them upside down, everything looked brighter that way, you used a fresh part of your eye.

She rose, bent low, gazed at the sea from under her arm...

A hiss – a roar – a ghastly oncoming rush! She screamed, lost her balance, toppled over. A hot blinding flash whipped past her. Deafening, scorching, flattening her on the sand. She screamed again. The world went black...

Voices shouting... People running... Spurt of a match... Faces bending close – strange faces... Somebody crying... A woman's voice, saying over and over: "Is she dead? Is she dead?..."

The light of a torch blazed in her face. Laura opened her eyes. Aunt Henrietta's arms were around her. Aunt Henrietta was crying:

"Oh, my dear, my dear! Are you sure you aren't hurt? Do you feel pain anywhere?"

Other worried voices: Judge Evans, Mr Price, asking questions:

"Are you sure you aren't hurt? Are you sure?"

Laura sat up.

"I'm all right," she said impatiently, brushed back a lock of hair, stared about her. "What happened?"

A confused clamour answered her. "A rocket!... You had a mighty close shave... Rocket missed you by a couple inches... A wonder you weren't killed... Came from behind those bushes... Boys... Boys... were running up the beach a minute ago... They ought to be thrashed... You might have been killed..."

I feel queer, Laura thought. I hope I'm not going to be sick. She tried to get up. A dozen hands were outstretched to help her. She struggled to her feet.

Leaning on Aunt Henrietta's arm, she walked waveringly toward the lights of the inn. Judge Evans and Mr Price followed. The crowd fell back.

They reached the car. "I'm quite all right," Laura said. "A little dizzy, that's all." Her foot fumbled for the step. She got in. Aunt Henrietta was beside her. She dropped her head on Aunt Henrietta's shoulder. The car started.

"This is the lousiest evening I ever spent," Laura remarked. "I don't want to see so much as a rocket again as long as I live."

10

"Books are not seldom talismans and spells."

COWPER

It was full summer now in New York. All through the spring Marbury and Northcote had worked hard, discovered clues, followed them up, only to reach what seemed to be an impasse. Even Northcote had to admit that there was less zest in the life-saving business than he had expected.

Not that things had gone so badly at first.

They had left the trout brook in a sanguine mood, convinced that the clue found in the old book, *Letters from Scotland*, would soon bring them face to face with the murderer of the Robinsons, Mr Starkweather and Mrs Beaumont. During supper – the trout were cooked to perfection – discussion of future plans continued.

Mr Marbury was in favour of spending another day in Durham as he felt that a second talk with Doctor Peters might disclose some detail that would throw light on the clergyman's death. Also he advocated stopping at New Haven on their way back to New York in order to investigate the motor accident in which Lucy Robinson had been killed.

But Jim Northcote would not agree to either suggestion. He insisted that the Robinsons' misadventures, whether murder or accident, were over, and that since the discovery of a hitherto unknown branch of the Bell family, their concern should be with the future rather than with the past. If their suspicions were correct, the finding of any cousins of Mrs Beaumont's before they were found by the 'mysterious stranger' was of vital importance.

In the end Marbury was convinced, and added that, if genealogical research was in order, as appeared to be the case, the sooner they got back to New York the better.

And so it was decided. Mr Marbury explained to their landlady, Mrs Parsley, that he was conscious of a slight twinge in his back that might be prophetic of an attack of lumbago. Fishing, under the circumstances, being rather risky, he and his friend were taking the evening train to New York, hoping to return when the water in the trout streams had become less chilly than it was at present.

The train was late. It was eleven o'clock when at length the two travellers stood in the dimly lit sleeping car, swaying to the motion of the train as it ran angrily around sudden curves and negotiated the various bumps and hollows of the Boston and Maine Railroad.

"I'll take the upper berth," Northcote said – the car was full except for one section. "I rather like an upper."

"I doubt that," Marbury said. "But you can have it. Like King David in the psalm, 'I will not climb up into my bed,' if I can avoid doing so. Good night!" And he buttoned himself into his green baize bower, hoping against hope for a good night's rest, or at least an occasional refreshing doze.

His hopes were not realized. For most of the night he lay broad awake, flat on his back, weighed down by the grey blanket soggy as a buckwheat cake, so heavy that it made his toes ache, while the train rocked on through the darkness. Over and over he retraced every step of his and Northcote's investigations, and racked his brains for some scrap of genealogical information that would enable him to trace the descendants of Charles Bell. Nothing came to him. Not until morning, mountain and forest left far behind, as the track levelled and a warmer air allowed blankets to be dispensed with, could Marbury relax. Then he fell sound asleep.

But sleep had brought no useful hint. When, weary and unshorn, he met Jim Northcote – also unshorn, but otherwise annoyingly clear eyed and brisk – he was obliged to admit that he hadn't the remotest idea how their search was to be carried on.

However, a hearty breakfast at Springfield was reviving. After a large cup of coffee Marbury felt more confidence in himself as investigator and genealogist.

"I've thought of something," he said, as they went back to the sleeping car, and settled down for the remainder of the run to New York. "Charles Bell must have come to America, if he came here at all, about 1830. Not many vessels crossed the Atlantic in those days, and the newspapers always mentioned incoming boats and usually gave a list of the passengers, where they came from and where they were bound."

"And if we found the name of Charles Bell it would give us something to start with."

"Just so. Suppose you come home with me, Jim; have a bath and a shave," Marbury smoothed his chin with distaste. "And after lunch I'll see what I can find in old files at the Public Library. I haven't your morbid dislike of those marble halls." He smiled. "Not being subject to attacks of agoraphobia."

Northcote laughed. "I'll leave the shipping lists to you then. I wish you could contrive some little job for me too. Here's the tunnel. We are almost in, thank the Lord!"

Lunch was over. As they rose from the table, Marbury said: "I have thought of something you can do, Jim, while I am at the library. Philip Hone's diary may mention Charles Bell. My copy has a good index. I'll get it for you. You can sit in the garden and read Hone until I get back."

Northcote went out into the garden and made himself comfortable in a shady corner. In a few minutes Marbury appeared carrying two large volumes.

"Philip Hone," he said, "was at one time Mayor of New York. He kept a careful diary and usually noted the names of newcomers to this country; if they were in any way distinguished he called on them. I have glanced through the index and the name

Bell appears several times. Here you are! I don't need to ask you to make notes of anything useful. Anyway, you will find Mr Hone very interesting."

Looks dullish to me, Northcote thought. But he set himself to his task without protest.

Marbury took a taxi to the Public Library, went in by the Forty-second Street entrance, turned briskly to the right through a door marked "Newspapers," made out a slip and, ten minutes later, was turning the dusty yellowing pages of early issues of the *New York Evening Post*, enormous in size and bound in leather, that lay before him on a slanting topped table.

The shipping lists were, of course, what he wanted but Mr Marbury was a confirmed "browser." Again and again his eye was caught. He would pause and read "Death of the Duke de Reichstadt... Cholera diminishing in Paris... At Peale's Museum the Great Anaconda will be fed with a live rabbit... Steam Car Pontchartrain in New Orleans. This beautiful machine passed peacefully up and down the road in front of the Washington Hotel under as complete control as a Hackney Coach... Advertisements... Elegant Grecian lamps unequalled in splendour and brilliance... Black silk for Clergymen's gowns... Buhl chandeliers... Madeira, citron and boneset lozenges... Coarse linen shirts suitable for the Navy... Pickwick Papers for sale at Putnam's store."

I mustn't waste time like this, Marbury told himself at length, and concentrated on the marine news.

There was plenty of it. Numerous vessels arrived and departed, such as "Brig Flora from Phila for the Capes," or "Brig Celestia from Charleston." But not many came from British ports. Mr Marbury would read: "The Pacific, from Liverpool, Capt. Porter. Passengers: Mr and Mrs..," murmur "No Bell," and hurry on to another page. He perused list after list of passengers, now and then pausing at a name: "Mr Washington Irving," or "Mr and Miss Kemble, the well known tragedians," remembering that his grandfather had seen Fanny Kemble as Juliet; then he would turn patiently to another shipping list. At last his pertinacity was rewarded. "The Victory," he read, "Capt. Preston, from Liverpool. Passengers: Mr Schuyler Van Rensselaer of New York, Mr Charles Bell of Edinburgh."

Mr Marbury copied the entry with satisfaction, and went on his way. Not home, however; he had thought of something else. He took the elevator to the third floor, walked through the catalogue room, through the left hand reading room to the door marked History. Here, having easily accomplished the preliminaries Northcote had found difficult, he was given several very small volumes, in size and appearance much resembling prayer books. They were early issues of the New York City Directory. In the year 1830 the name of Bell did not appear. In 1832 Charles Bell, real estate, was listed at 122 Park Place; but in the next and succeeding years his name was omitted. Mr Marbury returned the books to the desk, and went home.

He found Jim Northcote still in the garden, absorbed in Hone's diary.

"Very good reading," he remarked, as Marbury sat down. "Listen to this: 'Busy moving my sherry and madeira to new house, fifteen cartloads of baskets, 2183 quarts and 254 gallons. Abolition mob broke window in Wall Street. I fear this tumult will not cease till our country is plunged in civil war. Cholera, inhabitants fleeing the city.'"

"Very interesting," Marbury broke in, "but not much to the point. I picked up several bits of information at the library. Charles Bell did come to this country. I found the date of his arrival in 1830, and his address in a New York Directory of 1832. Does Hone speak of Mr Bell?"

"He does, several times. And, remembering your dislike of dog ears, I have not turned down the corners. Wasn't that thoughtful of me?" Northcote opened the book at a page indicated by a slip of paper and read aloud:

"'July 14, 1830. Returned call of Mr Charles Bell of Edinburgh, having been out when he presented a letter of introduction from my good friend Judge McPherson. Was favorably impressed. The young Scot is gentlemanly in manner and extremely handsome.' Here's another entry a few months later: 'Dined with Mr Bell. An agreeable evening but somewhat too convivial. Mr B. would do well to avoid too great addiction to the pleasures of Bacchus.' Still later we have this: 'Bell has decided to seek his fortune elsewhere. I fear he will become a rolling stone.' And then: 'Jenkins told me today that our friend Bell is about to assume the flowery chain of matrimony. A daughter of Jacob Ravenel is to be the bride.'"

Northcote closed the book. "That's the last time the name Bell appears," he said. "None of these entries add much to what we already know, I'm afraid, except the last."

"The last is extremely valuable. Ravenel is a well known Carolina name, and if that marriage took place in Charleston it will appear in the church records. I have all the publications of the Genealogical Societies. Come up to my library and we'll see what we can find."

"Here it is!" Marbury exclaimed, after a few minutes' study. "In the records of St. Michael's Parish: 'June 4. 1838. Charles Bell Esquire of Edinburgh and New York to Miss Laura Ravenel, daughter of Jacob Ravenel Esquire of Strawberry Hill, by the Reverend Theophilus Tippleton.' We're getting on, Northcote! There are sure to be later entries. We'll divide the volumes next in order and look up every Bell in the index... Here's one right off, a baptism: 'March 14, 1841, Laura Ravenel, daughter of Charles Bell Esquire.' Good! It's my turn to find something. More children, or perhaps the death of Charles Bell."

They both turned page after page of the South Carolina Genealogical Society's many publications with the greatest care, following up every promising allusion, but without success. There was nothing more. After the baptism of little Laura Ravenel, Charleston refused to mention the Bell family in any way.

"Bell must have left Charleston," Marbury sighed, as he

replaced the books on their shelves, "not long after the date of the child's baptism. If he had stayed on, other births and deaths would have been recorded. The question is: Where did he go?"

"That's a poser! Where would a 'rolling stone' be likely to take his family in those days?"

"Heaven knows. Though we can cut out Scotland; if he had gone home his people would not have lost sight of him. But he may have rolled a long way before he landed in the grave. I doubt if he would have gone farther west than Chicago, however."

"Or north of Montreal, or south of Florida! That's a fairly large field to cover."

"It is indeed."

"And very tantalizing to stall like this with our goal almost in sight when we've gone on so swimmingly until now."

"Too swimmingly." Mr Marbury frowned. "What is to prevent the 'mysterious stranger', the murderer, in other words from beginning just where I began? The Public Library is open to everyone."

"He'd be likely to go there, too. You remember he visited the genealogical room under the name of Williams."

"And he seems to be pretty intelligent. He may have thought out some line of research that has not yet occurred to either you or me."

"He's clever, all right. But I'm not going to admit that Williams, or whatever he calls himself, is cleverer than we are. For one thing, neither you nor I would be stupid enough to commit murder. No one but a fool would commit murder, premeditated murder. Anyone might kill a man in anger, I suppose."

"Or in a fit of insanity."

"This stranger isn't insane. He can't be. You forget that in each of his three ruses – Starkweather's Wilson, Robinson's Parker, Public Library Williams – he struck those who met him as being commonplace in appearance, dress and speech. The cleverest crazy man that ever lived couldn't have achieved such complete absence of singularity."

"That's true."

"I'm sure of it. On the other hand, I do feel there is something queer about the man. He is sane but he has a twist, he's urged on by some complex."

"An inferiority complex?"

"Perhaps. Of course that idea has been worked to death. Every boastful boy and peevish girl is credited with an inferiority complex. All the same I have known men whose lives have been ruined by lack of confidence in themselves. This stranger now, I believe he is a man with a grievance. It may be that his very inconspicuousness has been a curse to him. I can imagine that it would be pretty awful to make so little impression on new acquaintances that you were forgotten the minute you turned your back."

"I daresay. If your theory is right, does it throw any light on the stranger's motive for committing murder? We haven't discussed the motive of late."

"Motive? I still feel that money must be back of it all."

"But we decided that Clare had not been killed by an heir."

"I've been thinking that over. Suppose she was killed by an heir. Not someone who expected to inherit her money, but money that would have come to her if she had lived?"

"Jim," Marbury said solemnly, "that is a most valuable suggestion."

"It gives us another motive, anyway. Why should a man set out to kill off all the descendants of a certain family unless they were heirs, heirs to an inheritance which he hoped to get for himself?"

"But where would the stranger come into the pedigree? Do you think he is descended from Charles Bell? Surely you don't expect to discover still another son of Robert Bell of Irongray! That would be rather far fetched."

"I don't know what I expect. Anyway, we haven't heard of any large estate going begging for heirs."

"Another thing, Jim. Do you realize that if our first theory that Mrs Beaumont was murdered by one of the persons who was in her bedroom on the morning of her death is correct, the stranger must be one of them?"

"You're right!" Northcote looked startled. "We may have to abandon that theory. Jane Grant and Miss Hemmingway, the two doctors, the two lawyers and the clergyman; I can't imagine any one of them committing murder, can you?" Marbury shook his head.

"After all," Northcote went on, "someone might have sneaked into her room and put the suicide letter on the dressing table while Jane was downstairs."

"Or someone may have come in later during the confusion, unobserved by the others. There was that boy from Thorley's, you know, that only Alice Hemmingway seems to have noticed. Perhaps he put the suicide letter on the dressing table; the murderer bribed him to put it there."

"If he did, I'm a poor judge of character. I dropped in at Thorley's some time ago – I forgot to tell you – and had a word with that boy. He's as innocent as you or I."

Marbury sighed. "Have you any suggestion as to our next step, Jim?"

"Not the foggiest. But don't look so woebegone! We have found out lots of important things today."

"Do you think so?" Marbury said dryly. "It seems to me that we have succeeded in accumulating some ladders and ropes, but are still waiting for a signal."

"You're right. There's not a burning house or a ship in distress anywhere in sight," Northcote agreed. "It's about time we had a bit of luck. Do you realize, Marbury, that so far we haven't had any luck."

"It was sheer luck finding that book, Letters from Scotland in Mrs Parsley's parlor."

"I suppose it was. Except for that, however, all our discoveries, genealogical or otherwise, have been due to our intelligence and perseverance. A noble thought, isn't it! To my mind, it's about time that luck stepped in and gave us a shove."

"It is." Marbury turned to a side table, where a decanter and glasses stood on a silver tray. "This is 1860," he said. "Not as good as Philip Hone's, perhaps; but it's good." He poured out two glasses of sherry. "Here's to luck!"

Northcote echoed him, and added: "God knows we need it!"

11

*"I wish all maids be warned by me
Never to trust to courtesie."*

SCOTTISH BALLAD

"Good morning, Miss Sands. I trust Miss Laura is none the worse for her disagreeable experience last evening?" Mr Price asked anxiously. "A most unfortunate occurrence. Such gross carelessness is hard to excuse. And as it was my party I feel responsible. I really hardly slept a wink last night for thinking about it."

"It wasn't your fault in any way whatever, Mr Price," Miss Sands smiled. "Just an accident that could not have been foreseen. Laura is quite all right again today. She slept beautifully and ate an excellent breakfast."

"I can't tell you how thankful I am. You are sure she was not hurt in any way? No burns, or anything of the sort?"

"No, indeed. There's a little hole burned in her dress. but she herself wasn't even scorched. It's a mercy she wasn't. Judge Evans says that a burn from fireworks often develops lockjaw."

"You don't say so! What a horrible idea! Ah, here is Miss Laura now, looking like a rose."

Laura's greeting was a trifle cool but he held her hand in his, murmuring regret and thankfulness until she drew it away with an impatient protest.

"It wasn't your fault, Mr Price. No one blames you. But I must say it was all pretty disgusting! There's a hole in my dress. A spark must have fallen on it. That shows how close..." She shuddered. "I keep hearing that hot rush like a comet or the headlight of an engine... Oh, don't let's talk about it! I want to forget last night just as soon as I can!" She flung herself into a chaise longue and lay there, staring out at the lake.

Mr Price nodded sympathetically and turned to Miss Sands. "I have just received a letter from Mr Carboy, my friend who is interested in antiques."

Laura sat up. "Does he want the sideboard?" she exclaimed.

"He writes that he would like very much to see it with a view to purchase, but unfortunately he is starting on a business trip and doesn't know just when he will return. In about a month probably. I think you'll see him then for he seemed very keen. I told him it was a choice specimen."

"How kind you are, Mr Price!" Miss Sands said gratefully, and Laura's, "Terribly kind!" was ecstatic.

"Glad I could be of service," Mr Price said modestly.

"Goodness!" Laura went on. "When I think of what it means to me to get rid of that old sideboard!"

Mr Price gave her an inquiring glance.

"If we can sell it," Laura explained, "Aunt Henrietta says she will give me the money and let me go to New York to find a job."

"Dear me," Mr Price shook his head sadly. "Aren't you rather young for that, Miss Laura?"

"I'll be eighteen in the autumn," she protested. "And eighteen isn't young. It's just the right age to begin."

"Perhaps. What sort of job had you in mind?"

"I don't quite know. I might make fashion designs. I can draw a little. Or, or I might get a secretarial position – with a diplomat, perhaps, It would be fun to go abroad."

Mr Price smiled kindly. "If I hear of anything that might suit you I shall let you know. As a matter of fact, my sister... But I had better not speak of that until I am sure... Goodbye, for the present. I am going to Boston, but I shall be back in a few days. Take care of yourself, Miss Laura, keep away from fireworks! Goodbye, Miss

Sands." He shook hands, and walked briskly away.

"Do you think he was serious about finding me a job?" Laura asked. "Or just talking?"

"He spoke as if he had something definite in his mind. But I wouldn't let myself count on it, my dear."

"Of course not. And there is still the sideboard. If only Mr Carboy doesn't forget all about it! Or, worse yet, Mr Price forgets us and never comes back! He said he would see us again in a few days, a few days might mean very soon, or not until next week. I shall die, just curl up and die if I have to wait as long as that!"

It was as long as that. Seven days went by, and still Mr Price delayed his return. Laura moped, declared that she was tired of swimming, sailing and picnics, tired of Peter and of life in general. Every morning she deposited herself in the chaise longue on the piazza, a book open on her lap, and lay there, watching the road. Then, to Miss Sands' intense relief, came reaction. At breakfast, Laura announced that she was tired of thinking of Mr Price. Old Pricie wasn't the only person in the world who could get her a job. If a person forgot you, the best thing was to forget him as soon as possible. She helped herself to another spoonful of marmalade and a third slice of toast. "I shan't waste another moment on old Pricie," she said firmly. "He isn't coming. I shall never see that Buick again, and that's that."

But Laura was wrong. One morning in the early autumn Mr Price appeared.

He was apologetic. He had been so overwhelmed with work that he hadn't even had time to write to inquire about Miss Laura's health. No need to ask, however, she looked blooming.

"This will interest you, I think, Miss Laura," he went on, and handed her a letter. "You might read it aloud. It's from Mrs Wigham, Miss Sands, that old friend of yours in Cleveland. She is a friend of my sister Gertrude."

"You don't say so! Read it, Laura."

Laura, her voice not quite steady, read:

" 'Dear Gertrude,

" 'I was so glad to get your letter. From what you say, little Laura Sands seems to be just the girl I've been looking for. You should see the creatures I have interviewed! Plucked and lipsticked out of all resemblance to humanity. That's not the sort I want to leave my child with even for a day. Her being Henrietta Sands' niece is in itself a recommendation. Dear Henrietta, I remember her perfectly. If I had time I would run up to wherever it is they live and renew our friendship, but that is impossible as we sail next week. Stupidly enough I have mislaid the address you gave me. Will you send her this scrawl? I know she'll remember me. I want a young girl to look after my child – Doris is twelve and a nice child though I say it as shouldn't – in London while I make some country visits. We shall be back here in about six weeks. I don't want a real governess, just someone who will take Doris to the Tower and all that. I'll arrange details, salary, etc., when I see her. Tell Laura to come to New York next Wednesday and we can talk it over. If for any reason we don't suit each other she won't mind having a day or two in New York. I'll expect her to spend the night, though my apartment is in confusion as we have just come in from the country, and of course I shall pay all her travelling expenses. I'll expect her at five o'clock sharp. Wish I had time for more, but I'm frightfully rushed.

" 'Yours,

" 'Evelyn Wigham.' "

Laura looked up with shining eyes. "Oh, Aunt Henrietta!" she cried. "Did you ever hear of anything so perfectly lovely! It's too good to be true!"

Miss Sands beamed. "It does seem quite providential," she said. "I remember Evelyn so well. She was one of the very nicest girls in Cleveland. Yes, Laura, I approve of this plan and we owe a great deal to Mr Price."

"Oh, we do, we do!" Laura cried. "How can I ever thank you,

Mr Price! Imagine getting a job that means going abroad and seeing London! Oh, it's too good to be true!"

"I thought you would be pleased," Mr Price said complacently. "The only objection is the shortness of time. Mrs Wigham wants to see you on Wednesday. That's day after tomorrow. Could you get ready by then?"

"Of course I can!"

"The letter doesn't say whether or not you're to bring a trunk, Laura," Miss Sands remarked. "I wonder whether..."

"If I may make a suggestion," Mr Price put in, "why not take a small bag with what you will need for the night, and check your other luggage to New York to be delivered when everything is settled."

"A good idea. I have an awfully nice little weekend bag... Wednesday! Goodness, I ought to begin packing this minute! What train had I better take?"

"Let me see. Mrs Wigham's appointment is for five o'clock. I should think the one ten from here would be the best – that is, if you don't mind the day coach. There is no parlour car on the one ten."

"That doesn't matter one bit!"

"I wonder if I ought to go with you, Laura," Miss Sands broke in. "You are so unaccustomed to travelling."

"Good gracious, Aunt Henrietta!" Laura began, but again Mr Price interposed.

"It so happens that I am going to New York," he said, "and I shall be obliged to take the train as my car needs overhauling. So if you approve, Miss Sands, I will see that Miss Laura gets safely to her destination."

And so it was all most satisfactorily arranged.

Two days went by. Slowly because it seemed as if Wednesday would never come. Like lightning because there was so much to do: mending, packing, bidding goodbye to everybody. At last it was Wednesday. Laura and Aunt Henrietta and Mr Price stood on the station platform waiting for the train. The train whistled up the track.

"Goodbye, Aunt Henrietta! Take care of yourself, darling. Your voice sounds a little hoarse. I hope you haven't taken cold. Goodbye, goodbye!"

In the train now, leaning out of the window, waving goodbye. Station platform, Aunt Henrietta's plump figure, her purple hat, dwindling fast. Gone.

"Allow me." Mr Price deposited Laura's coat in the rack overhead and her bag at her feet. They settled themselves comfortably side by side, Laura next to the window, and talked of nothing in particular. A boy selling magazines came by. Mr Price asked Laura if she wanted something to read. She thanked him and said she had a book in her bag. A boy came by with a tray of sweets. "Chawclets! Chawclets!" he cried. Mr Price stopped him and bought a box of chocolate peppermints and presented them to Laura with a smile.

"Maillard's Thin Mints, my favorite kind," she smiled back, and tore off the cellophane wrapper. "Will you have one?"

"Thank you, I never eat candy. I'll leave you now, Miss Laura, for a little while. I'm off to the smoking car. Are you sure you have everything you want? I'll be back before long."

But it was more than an hour before Mr Price returned. Laura didn't mind. Mr Price was never exciting, and today he was duller than ever. When she spoke he answered as if his mind were somewhere else and then just sat in silence, biting his nails. The longer he stayed away the better. It was pleasant to sit looking out of the window, watching the September fields and woods slip past, and to remember that before long, if all went well, she would be seeing a more exciting landscape. England. She was going abroad!

She was so absorbed in these agreeable anticipations that the train had been running slowly for some time without her noticing it. Suddenly it jerked to a stop, and at the same moment Mr Price came down the aisle.

He looked annoyed. "A hotbox," he said. "They are working on it, but no one knows how long it will take to get going again. We may not reach New York until after dark."

"Oh, dear! What will Mrs Wigham think if I don't turn up at five? Is there any way of letting her know?"

"We are near a station. I'll get the brakeman to send a telegram. This delay is very annoying. No use grumbling though. I'll go and send that telegram."

In a few minutes he returned. The telegram had been dispatched, and there was nothing to do now but wait. He sat down beside her. Another hour went by. Then, at length, the engine began to move. Heavily at first, as if unsure of itself, then more rapidly. They were off.

Dusk was falling now. Laura sat looking out of the window, watching the yellow glow fade from the sky. The lamps in the car were turned on, but she did not draw down the window shade. Now and then, the train ran into the darkness of a tunnel or a cutting, flashed out again into twilight. It's funny, she thought, while we're in a tunnel the window glass turns to a mirror; I can see my face reflected against the black walls outside. I can see some of the people in the car behind me just as clearly as if I turned around. The fat woman across the aisle, and her umbrella swaying from a hook. Now it's gone. Another tunnel. Now I can see Mr Price reading the newspaper. I can see his hand. Out into twilight again. Laura sat very still. What had she seen? In that moment of darkness, she had seen the reflection of Mr Price's hand. His hand had moved. He had kept on reading the paper, his expression did not change. But his hand had moved. And there was something in his hand: a long narrow brown and buff box – Maillard's Thin Mints – exactly like the other box – her box, that lay on the seat. It couldn't be! Some queer effect of light had deceived her. She *couldn't* have seen Mr Price changing the boxes? Substituting another box for hers? Impossible. Absolutely impossible.

Laura shivered, looking out into the twilight. What should she do? Ignore it? Or turn with a laugh, and say... What could she say? "Why have you stolen my chocolates, Mr Price? Are these chocolates better? Or are they..." She didn't know Mr Price very well. Perhaps he liked practical jokes.

She turned. "I would like a magazine, after all, Mr Price," she said. "Could you ask the boy for an *Atlantic*?" Mr Price rose at once. As he walked away, Laura opened the brown and buff box, took out a chocolate, dropped it under the seat, and began munching. When Mr Price returned she appeared to be just finishing a peppermint.

"Too bad you don't like peppermints," she said. "Thank you so much for the *Atlantic*."

She opened the magazine and turned over the pages, but she could not read. Her mind was confused. It's like a bad dream, she thought, a nightmare that keeps coming back – flash of light – streak of dark – picture against the darkness – moving hand – chocolate box. Perhaps it really had been a dream? She had fallen asleep for a second and dreamed she had seen that moving hand... Anyway, she was tired of thinking and worrying. She leaned back in the seat, and closed her eyes.

"We are almost in, Miss Laura." Mr Price was bending over her, speaking softly. "Let me reach down your coat for you."

She sat up, smoothed her hair, powdered her nose, adjusted her hat, picked up the chocolate box. Mr Price glanced at the box as she put it into her bag. Was his glance a little sly? Imagination, of course. A hangover from the nightmare...

They were out on the platform now, a red cap demanding their bags. Mr Price waved the man away. They walked on up the sloping footway, emerged into the vast loftiness of the Grand Central Station...

I am in New York, Laura thought. Actually here in New York! She looked up. A beautiful starry roof, funny little locomotive up on the balcony...

"We'll go to the waiting room," Mr Price said, "so that you can sit down while I do a little telephoning. This delay has upset my plans and I have to call up a business acquaintance."

He led her to a bench. Laura sat down, he placed her bag at her feet, her coat beside her.

"I'll be back in less than ten minutes." He walked away.

Those chocolates, Laura thought. They're perfectly all right, of course. But, somehow or other, I want to get rid of them. Drop them in the rubbish can over there? Somebody might find them... *Women* in large letters over a door. She picked up her bag and coat... In five minutes she was back again, and sat down with a satisfied smile. The chocolates had been disposed of.

Ten minutes went by. Fifteen. And still Mr Price did not return. How long should she wait for him? What was she to do if he never came back? She sat staring anxiously at the door where she had seen Mr Price disappear, wishing for his return with more intensity than would have seemed possible an hour ago. It was all very well to laugh at 'Pricie's' dullness. All very well to play a silly game with herself – make believe those chocolates were poisonous, think out a clever way of getting rid of them. That game seemed ridiculous enough now. Everything depended on Mr Price. If he did not come back, what, oh what, was she going to do?

It was nine o'clock now, by the big clock on the wall whose hand moved, not steadily, but in jerks. Nine o'clock. Dark outside, of course. And she was alone in New York... She stood up. Sat down again in sudden relief – there was Mr Price at last, at the news-stand buying a paper. He turned. Why, it wasn't Mr Price after all! This man had a moustache. She stared at him. The man raised the paper higher. It seemed to Laura that he was staring at her from behind it. She looked away, looked back. Yes, the man was watching her, peeping out from behind the newspaper. Suppose he came over and spoke to her, tried to pick her up? Nonsense, imagination again. Wake up, Laura. Think what you're going to do. Better go straight to Mrs Wigham's house. How far away was her house? This was Forty second Street. Mrs Wigham lived farther uptown. Better take a taxi...

Laura picked up her bag – and hesitated. The seat seemed an island of refuge, she could not bear to leave it. Suppose Mr Price came back and found her gone, how worried he would be...

She was still hesitating, when two people approached, obviously a mother and daughter. The girl sat down beside Laura and opened a magazine. The older woman walked away to the newsstand; Laura's eyes followed her. That man with the moustache was still there! Still reading a newspaper, still peering out from behind it!

She gave a sigh of exasperation, and glanced at the girl beside her. A nice girl. Lovely clothes, smart blue hat, and simply heavenly blue shoes...

Ten minutes past nine. Laura sighed again. The girl in blue looked up. Their eyes met.

"May I ask you something?" Laura ventured. The girl smiled encouragingly. She went on. "I have never been in New York before and the person I came with went off to telephone and hasn't come back. What do you think I ought to do? How long ought I to wait for him?"

"How long has he been gone?"

"Almost three quarters of an hour. And it's getting awfully late. Do you think it would be all right for me to take a taxi and go straight to Mrs Wigham's house? Or ought I to wait a little longer? You see when he comes back and finds I've gone, Mr Price will be fearfully worried."

"Mr Price?"

"He is the person who got me this job. An awfully nice job to go abroad with Mrs Wigham and take care of her little girl."

"I see. Why, I don't know what you ought to do. Here comes my mother. We'll ask her." She and Laura stood up. "Mother, this is Miss, Miss?"

"Laura Sands."

"Miss Sands wants to know what she had better do. She is a

stranger in New York and the person she came to town with left her here in the station nearly an hour ago and hasn't come back."

"Dear me, that is a predicament, Miss Sands, I'm Mrs Benson, and this is my daughter Beatrice." She's nice, Laura thought. They are both awfully nice. "Where are you stopping in New York?" Mrs Benson went on.

"With Mrs Wigham, on Park Avenue. I ought to have been there at five, but the train was late. I don't like to go to Mrs Wigham's hours after she expected me to come. But if I don't turn up, she will think I'm unreliable and may decide not to take me abroad."

"What is Mrs Wigham's number?"

"564 Park Avenue."

Mother and daughter exchanged glances.

"That is the number of the Colony Club," Mrs Benson said. "Mrs Wigham must be staying there."

"It can't be a club," Laura put in. "Mrs Wigham said in her letter that her apartment was all in confusion because they were only staying there until they sailed."

"Then it must be the wrong number. We'll look up Mrs Wigham in the telephone book and..." Mrs Benson glanced at the clock. "Almost time for Tom's train," she went on. "Come along, my dear I've got to meet my son, and when that's done we'll straighten out your affairs. Come along."

Laura obeyed, with a grateful heart. How kind Mrs Benson was. And she looked so competent too. As if she could handle fifty situations as complicated as this without the slightest difficulty.

All three walked rapidly out of the waiting room. Laura never so much as glanced at the man with the moustache. If she had done so, she would have seen him beckoning to a porter, but she would have thought nothing of it. The man with the moustache had ceased to alarm her. She had, in fact, forgotten him. The boy Tom was met, embraced by his mother and sister, introduced to Laura. A red cap took the bags and led the way to the taxi rank.

As they walked along, Laura said: "Mrs Benson, you spoke of

looking up Mrs Wigham's number in the telephone book."

"Of course. Wait a minute, porter." They all stopped. "Let me think." Mrs Benson thought: the Traveller's Aid? The girl would be safe with them, but they might send her to some dreary boarding house. "You'd better come home with me, Miss Sands," she said firmly. "We have plenty of room, and you look tired to death. In the morning we'll straighten everything out. Come along."

Laura came.

A taxi drove up. They all got in. The red cap put in their bags. Laura failed to notice another porter, though he stood very close to their taxi as Mrs Benson gave the address of her house.

Laura's confidence in Mrs Benson's ability had not been misplaced. Mrs Benson was a wonderful straightener out of difficulties. But even she, after prolonged examination of various Wighams in various telephone books, both Manhattan and suburban, Social Registers and club lists, was obliged to admit defeat.

"There aren't any Richard Wighams," she sighed. "They simply don't exist. Here's an R. Wigham, but he's an undertaker in Cherry Street. We shall have to give up the Wighams and concentrate on Mr S. Price." She fluttered the pages of the telephone book. "Two columns of Prices and any number of S's. The only thing to do is to try them all."

Mrs Benson moved to the telephone. Laura sat watching her anxiously. Breakfast was over, the Benson family were assembled in the library while she dialed, inquired, dialed again.

"It's no use," she said at length. "I got several S. Prices but not one of them arrived in New York last evening. I am afraid your Mr Price hasn't a telephone, Laura. What business is he in?"

"I don't know," Laura said. "He seems to travel a good deal."

"A travelling salesman, perhaps? A drummer would be impossible to find. Did he look like a drummer, Laura?"

"I don't know what a drummer looks like."

"No more do I. For that matter, you can't guess people's occupations from their looks nowadays. When I was young, you could tell actors at the first glance, and publishers invariably wore beards, and debutantes and chorus girls were as unlike as rosebuds and poinsettias..." Mrs Benson rattled on, talking while she decided what to do next. A thoroughly nice child, she thought, and so pretty. It seems a shame to send her back to her aunt. "I've tried everything that I can think of," she ended reluctantly. "I'm afraid, Laura, that you will have to go back to your aunt."

"I suppose so," Laura sighed. "You've been terribly kind, Mrs Benson. I don't know how to thank you enough."

"It has been a pleasure, my dear. Now we'll long-distance your aunt and you can tell her what has happened." They sat waiting. The call came through. Laura took up the receiver.

"Is that you, Emma?" she asked. "Oh, I'm so sorry. Well, tell Aunt Henrietta that I am not going abroad with Mrs Wigham after all. I'll be home some time today. I don't know what train. Give Aunt Henrietta my best love."

Laura replaced the receiver. "Aunt Henrietta has a bad cold," she explained. "She is in bed. I do hope it won't turn to bronchitis. What train had I better take, Mrs Benson?"

Mrs Benson was already studying a time table. "You can't catch the eleven three," she said, "and the next is an express and doesn't stop at Derby Center. You will have to take the five o'clock train, Laura. That will get you home before it's really dark, and you will have time for lunch here. That fits in very nicely. Beatrice, you and Laura might take the dogs for a walk after lunch."

"It is terribly disappointing," Laura said. She and Beatrice and two Scotties were walking down Park Avenue. "You see, I have never been abroad, and Derby Centre is such a tiny place and this plan was so marvellous."

"It's a perfect shame. But I'm sure that Mother will work it out somehow or other. She's tremendosly good at getting jobs... I suppose we ought to be going back to the house. You mustn't miss your train."

They turned, and had nearly reached the Bensons' house, when

Laura stopped.

"There's Mr Price!" she cried.

In a moment he was beside her. "Where have you been, Miss Laura?" he demanded. "What became of you last night? You gave me an awful fright, I can tell you!"

"I'm sorry, Mr Price," Laura said. "But I waited nearly an hour for you. And then Mrs Benson came. Beatrice, this is Mr Price. Mr Price, Miss Benson."

Mr Price bowed. Beatrice nodded. A very ordinary looking man, she thought; not worth making such a fuss about.

"I admit that I kept you waiting for some time," Mr Price said. "But first I got a wrong number, and then the man I wanted had to be sent for. I would have given the whole thing up, but it was a very important business transaction. I hope you will forgive me, Miss Laura."

"That's all right, Mr Price. I quite understand."

"I suppose you got in touch with Mrs Wigham?"

"I tried to. Mrs Benson did her best. But the number you gave me wasn't right and... "

"964 Park Avenue?"

"You said 564, Mr Price!"

"My dear Miss Laura." Mr Price spoke impatiently. "You are mistaken. I couldn't have said 564! But don't let's argue about it now. Mrs Wigham is expecting you."

"I'll get my bag. It's packed, I meant to go home this afternoon."

Laura and Beatrice hurried into the house. Came out again. A taxi stood at the curb. "Say goodbye to your mother, Beatrice."

The two girls kissed. "And tell her what's happened and thank her a thousand times."

"Goodbye, Laura. Call me up when you get to Mrs Wigham's, and tell me all about everything."

Mr Price opened the door of the taxi. Laura stepped in. He followed her.

12

*"Attempt the end, and never stand to doubt;
Nothing's so hard but search will find it out."*

HERRICK

When Marbury had given the toast, "Here's to luck!" and Northcote had echoed it, neither was, in fact, as pessimistic as they seemed. So many small clues had been accumulated that both felt sure the "rolling stone," Charles Bell, would be traced in time. In time, that is, to rescue his descendants if there were any descendants and they turned out to be in danger. But the weeks went by and still the elusive Charles remained in obscurity.

One hot morning Jim Northcote appeared in Marbury's garden and flung himself disconsolately on a bench. "Any news?" he asked.

Marbury looked up from the begonia he was transplanting. "Not a thing," he said. "I've searched every record I can find, without the smallest success. When the Bells left Charleston they seem to have vanished into thin air."

"There is still that Mr Bell in Dumfries to hear from. You wrote to him some time ago, didn't you?"

"Two months ago, at least. He must be away, or I should have heard by now. I'll write again."

"And then what?"

"Reconcile ourselves to failure, I suppose."

"I'm afraid we were not born to be sleuths," Northcote sighed. "Yet I don't see what more we could have done. It's all very well to say we must leave no stone unturned. We have turned over enough stones to pave Fifth Avenue and what have we found?

Nothing. Not so much as an angleworm let alone a gold moidore, or whatever it is you are supposed to find under stones."

Mr Marbury nodded sadly, gave a final pat to the begonia, rose from his knees and joined Northcote on the garden bench.

Neither spoke for a few minutes; then Northcote stirred impatiently. "This affair is getting on my nerves," he grumbled. "I keep wondering about that stranger, where he is, what he's doing. I'm sick of it. What do you say we take a rest? Leave off watching the pot for awhile? If we turn our attention to something else, the pot may begin to boil unexpectedly."

"And a change of air might brighten our wits."

"They need brightening all right! I believe I'll go to Bar Harbour tomorrow or the next day. Edith Lansing is expecting me to paint her father, you know, and I really ought not to keep putting her off. Why don't you try a whiff of country air too?"

"I believe I will," Marbury said. "I never leave my garden for long at a time, but a few weeks in the Adirondacks would do me good. As you say, we may have been watching the pot too closely."

September came, and found Marbury and Northcote together again in the garden, on the same bench and in much the same mood.

"Bar Harbour gave you a splendid sunburn, Jim," Marbury remarked. "How did Mr Bainbridge's portrait get on?"

"Oh, he was easy – a strong old face. But then I tried Daphne, Edith's youngest, and children are the very devil to paint! That soft pink round eyed empty innocence is hard to capture... Nothing turned up re Bell, I suppose?"

"Not a thing."

"Something is sure to break before long. In the meantime, I believe I'll paint you, Marbury, here in the garden. Your long thin respectability against this riot of bloom, book in hand, pince-nez on nose. I'll call it, 'Bookworm and Blossom,' or 'Philosophy and Flowers.' What do you say?"

"All right," Marbury smiled. "If you allow me to read I'll sit for you as long as you like. That is, if you promise not to spill turpentine on my lawn."

So, next morning, any neighbour who happened to look down into Mr Marbury's back yard would have seen a vast supply of painting paraphernalia brought out from the house, then an elderly gentleman enthroning himself in any easy position at one side of the grass plot, set off by an herbaceous border dazzling in colour; while, on the opposite side, a young man in a white smock took up his position before an easel and at once became so absorbed that his eyes went flashing back and forth from subject to canvas without pause for some two hours, while the sun shone, chrysanthemums gave out their bitter-sweet fragrance and an occasional cat came tiptoeing along the fence tops.

At twelve o'clock, Northcote flung his mahlstick on the grass and a paint rag at the cat, with an emphatic,

> " 'Take away my star and garter!
> Hide them from my aching sight!'

"The light has changed entirely," he explained. "But I've made a swell beginning. Come and look, Marbury." Mr Marbury approached, agreed that it was an excellent likeness on the whole.

"Is my nose really as long as that, Jim?" he asked dubiously.

"Longer, my dear boy. Inches longer! I am flattering you because I love you. It's lucky for you that I'm less modern than I used to be. Three years ago your nose and eyeglasses would have filled the whole canvas, except for one wee little chrysanthemum down in the corner."

"Then I'm glad we waited until now," Marbury said dryly. "Can you stay to lunch, Jim?"

"Not today. I have to go to Oyster Bay this afternoon to see a possible client. I'll be back tomorrow. What about another sitting on Thursday, if the weather holds?"

"That would be all right for me. While you are away I'll get on with my transplanting. Perhaps some new link in our investigation will occur to me while I am at work."

But a morning's gardening brought Marbury no inspiration. In the afternoon he went out for a stroll. Down Fifth Avenue, through Fifty-ninth Street, pausing now and then to glance at the books in the stalls of the second hand dealers along that thoroughfare. At one door, he hesitated for a moment, then went in.

"Anything new in the way of Scottish genealogy or memoirs, Mr Baker?" he asked, as a clerk came forward. "Sorry, Mr Marbury. Nothing we haven't already shown you."

Mr Marbury went on his way. Outside the Anderson Galleries in Madison Avenue he paused again in front of the notice board, and read:

"Valuable art property from the estate of the late Judge Prior, sold by the New York Trust Co. Executors. Library and important autograph letters from the collection of George Randolph Esq., of New York. Queen Anne and Georgian silver from the estate of Miss Laura Ravenel Bostwick of Cleveland, and other choice house hold equipment. To be sold at public auction, September 24 and 25."

"Laura Ravenel!" Mr Marbury gave a little crow of delight. "That was the name of Charles Bell's wife!" He hurried into the building and upstairs to the desk on the second floor, demanding information regarding Miss Laura Ravenel Bostwick of Cleveland.

The man at the desk, who knew Mr Marbury as a frequenter of auctions, was obliging. It seemed that Miss Bostwick had died some years ago, and the contents of her house had been placed in storage. Recently the executors had decided to sell some of the silver for the benefit of the heirs. "You'd better come to the sale, Mr Marbury," he added. "There are some good pieces, and they won't bring much. Too early in the season."

"September is a poor time for an auction."

"It certainly is. But we are full up later on. And it isn't as if any of this stuff came from famous collections."

"I see. Could you find me the names and addresses of these executors and heirs of Miss Bostwick?"

The man turned to a book on the desk. "Here you are," he said. "The silver was ordered sold by Miss Henrietta Sands, of Derby Centre, Massachusetts, executor for her niece, Miss Laura Sands, heir. Apparently Miss Laura Sands is a minor."

"Thank you very much. Have you any description of the silver? Coats of arms, or crests? Or do you know where it came from originally?"

"It isn't on exhibition yet, of course. But I believe some of the pieces are from Charleston and others are Scottish. The latter have the Bell coat of arms, if I remember rightly."

"Thank you. That tells me just what I wanted to know."

Mr Marbury went home, walking on air. News at last! How pleased Jim Northcote would be!

Northcote was more than pleased. He was jubilant. "Luck is coming our way at last!" he cried. "What's our next step?"

"Shall I write to this lady at Derby Centre and make a few discreet inquiries as to the descendants of Charles Bell?"

"Better see her," Northcote said. "I'll go. Though I hate to stop painting now I've made such a good start on your portrait."

"I would go, but I have a business appointment tomorrow afternoon. I could go the day after."

"Delay may be fatal. For all we know, the stranger is creeping up on his victim at this very moment, knife in hand! I'll take the first train tomorrow."

Pleasant little place, Northcote thought, as he stepped out of the train at Derby Center. Lovely lake. Wooded cliffs. Reminds you of Loch Lomond...

He stopped a passing boy. "Can you tell me where Miss Sands

lives?" he asked. "Miss Henrietta Sands?"

"The other side the lake," the boy said, and pointed. "You see the bandstand over there? Well, you cross the bridge and you'll find her house back of the bandstand, up among the trees. White. You can't miss it."

I like Miss Sands' house, Northcote said to himself, as he reached the gate. I hope the lady is as nice as her house. He crossed the lawn, went up the front steps and rang the bell... Handsome pilasters, he thought, and one of the loveliest fanlights I ever saw... Fine elms too... Why don't they answer the bell? He rang again...

A maid appeared. Northcote gave her his card.

"Is Miss Sands in?" he asked.

"Yes, she is, sir. But she can't see you."

"Would you mind giving her my card? Tell her that we have mutual friends in Cleveland." Stretching a point, he thought, but it may be true. He went on persuasively. "I'm not a Fuller brush man, or trying to sell vacuum cleaners."

The maid smiled. "I can see that, sir. But Miss Sands is sick in bed. She has bronchitis."

"I'm so sorry. There is a younger Miss Sands, I believe. Does she live in Derby Centre?"

"Miss Laura? Oh, yes, she lives here. She's Miss Sands' niece. But she's in New York just now."

"You don't know her address, I suppose?"

"No, sir, I don't. But there's Judge Evans coming up the path. Perhaps he could tell you."

Northcote thanked her, and turned away to meet the elderly man the maid had indicated.

"I beg your pardon," he said, "but I should be grateful if you could help me with a little information. I came here to see Miss Sands and find she is ill in bed."

"Glad to tell you anything I can. You say Miss Sands is ill? Then I won't go in now." The two moved toward the road. "What is it you want to know?"

"I have a friend who wants to buy a piece of property in Cleveland. My name is Northcote, by the way, but there is a flaw in the title that can't be cleared until all the heirs of a certain Charles Bell have been traced. I happened to be in New England and he asked me to see Miss Sands. She is related to the Bells in some way, I believe?"

"Only collaterally. She is a connection of the Bells by marriage. But I can tell you just as well as she could. The only living descendant of Charles Bell of Edinburgh, Charleston and Cleveland, is Laura Sands; Miss Henrietta Sands' niece."

"Really? I'll tell my friend. The maid said just now that Miss Laura Sands had gone to New York."

"Yes. She expects to go abroad with a Mrs Wigham, an old friend of her aunt's."

"You haven't her address, by any chance?"

"Let me see. I wrote it down somewhere." The Judge took out his pocket book. "Here it is. 'Care of Mrs Richard Wigham, 564 Park Avenue.'"

"Thank you very much. I shall try to see her."

"A charming girl. Pretty as a peach. I hope you are not leaving Derby Centre at once, Mr Northcote?"

"Afraid I must. A pretty place, it's a temptation to stay on. But I have to get back to New York."

"I congratulate you," Marbury said, when Northcote arrived, bearing the address of Miss Laura Sands, only surviving descendant of the late Charles Bell. "You had better go and see her at once. Where do you say this Mrs Wigham lives?"

"564 Park Avenue."

Marbury stared. "Something's wrong," he said. "That is the number of the Colony Club."

"She's staying there, of course. I'll go around and ask."

No one at the Colony Club had ever heard of any Mrs Wigham. Northcote walked sadly away. He had gone two blocks down Park Avenue when he was stopped by the traffic light. At the same moment a middle aged lady came across the Avenue. They met.

"Hello, Jim," she cried. "Where have you been all summer? Are you on your way to my house? If you were, I'll turn back. It's almost tea time."

"Thanks ever so much. You're sure you don't mind? As a matter of fact, it came to me just now as I left the Colony Club in a discouraged mood that you lived very near and might take pity on a thirsty friend. How is Beatrice?"

"Fine. She'll be glad to see you. But why, may I ask," she added, as they walked on side by side, "the Colony Club send you away discouraged?"

"They couldn't give me an address I wanted. You don't happen to know a Mrs Richard Wigham, do you?"

Mrs Benson came to a sudden stop.

"Mrs Richard Wigham!" she exclaimed. "Why, that's the person Laura Sands was trying to find, and..."

"Laura Sands! Do you know her? Do you know where I can find her?"

"On the next block, standing in front of our house. Oh, she's getting into a taxi! With a strange man, Mr Price, I suppose."

"A strange man!" Northcote shouted, and without another word, he was off.

He sprinted, ran for all he was worth, and stood panting at Mrs Benson's house only to see the taxi driving away.

Luckily another taxi was close by. He hailed it, leaped in.

"Keep your eye on that taxi," he said, pointing. "The yellow Parmalee. I want to know where they're going. But don't run too close. I'd rather they didn't suspect they were being followed."

"I get you." The driver grinned.

13

"In the first place 'tis long, and when once you are in it,
It holds you as fast as the cage holds a linnet.
For, howe'er rough and dirty the road may be found,
Drive forward you must, since there's no turning round."

JOHN MARRIOT

When Mr Price opened the door of the taxi that stood in front of Mrs Benson's house, Laura stepped in with a feeling of intense relief. Not that she found Mr Price's company so agreeable in itself. He was important as the means to a most desirable end. Mrs Wigham had been found at last. The trip abroad that an hour ago had seemed a fantastic dream had become reality.

"The Brevoort," Mr Price said to the taxi driver, as he sat down beside Laura. "And drive slowly. The young lady is a stranger in New York, and would like to see Fifth Avenue."

"Are we going downtown?" Laura exclaimed, as the taxi turned a corner. "I thought Mrs Wigham lived farther up. Aren't we going there right away?"

"Didn't I tell you? Mrs Wigham has gone to the country. She went this morning and she wants you to join her there. We're driving out, but as it's some distance I decided we had better have dinner in town first."

"I thought she was staying in New York until we sailed."

"She intended to. But the children in the apartment right next to hers came down with scarlet fever yesterday, and she has a morbid fear of contagion. She's really quite silly about it! So she just snatched her little girl off to the country. She wants me to take you to her at once. She needs you to look after the child while she is in town getting ready to sail."

"Where is her country house?"

"On the Hudson, near Tuxedo. But it isn't a country house, only a weekend cottage where the Wighams go in the spring and autumn for a few days at a time. They spend their summers at Southampton. You'll like this little place; it's simple, but very pretty. And I know you will like Mrs Wigham. She is kindness itself. When I called her up last evening and explained, as best I could, why you had not turned up, she said it didn't matter in the least so long as I brought you to her today."

"What a lot of trouble I'm giving you, Mr Price! I'm terribly grateful... This is Fifth Avenue, I suppose? Oh, I do think New York is simply marvellous!"

"It's a fine town. When you return from abroad, Miss Laura, it would give me pleasure to show you some of the sights."

"How kind you are, Mr Price!" Laura gazed out of the window, sighing with pleasure. "That must be the Empire State building!"

"I'll take you up to the top some day. The view is magnificent."

"How kind you are, Mr Price. I hope you've forgiven me for not waiting longer in the station?"

"Yes, indeed. But you certainly gave me a fright. I can't tell you how scared I was when I came back and found you gone. You knew the Bensons before, I suppose. Are they old friends?"

"Oh, no. Beatrice Benson just happened to sit down beside me as I was beginning to think you were never coming back, and I asked her what I had better do. Then her mother came, and she was very kind and said I had better go home with them. So I did."

"I see. Wasn't it rather imprudent to go home with a perfect stranger?"

"Not with a person like Mrs Benson. You can always tell, you know."

"I suppose so. Did you communicate with your aunt?"

"I called her up. But I only got Emma, our waitress. She said

Aunt Henrietta was sick in bed with one of her terrible colds, so I just said to tell her I was not going abroad with Mrs Wigham after all, and I would be home this evening. I ought to let her know right away that I'm not coming."

"I'll send her a wire from the hotel."

"Thank you ever so much. Is that the Washington Arch down there?"

"Yes, that is the Arch. And this is the Brevoort Hotel where we are having dinner."

The taxi swept across the Avenue in a U turn, and drew up at the curb. Mr Price paid the driver, gave him a moderate tip, and led the way into the lobby. He scribbled a telegram for Miss Sands and handed it to the clerk to be despatched. Then he and Laura went into the restaurant.

The dinner began well. Laura enjoyed the foreign flavour of the food. The champagne, that she had supposed to be sparkling cider until Mr Price undeceived her, prickled your tongue, but it was an agreeable prickle. The restaurant itself was fascinatingly exotic. Any one of the people at the other tables might turn out to be a celebrity. It wouldn't surprise you to find that the stout woman was Gertrude Stein and the blonde one was Greta Garbo. Through the open windows you could see more people eating and drinking at little tables on the sidewalk in the shade of tall shrubs in pots. You could imagine you were in Paris! It was all terribly exciting and simply wonderful...

Then, suddenly, Laura realized that she was tired. The dinner was too elaborate. She was no longer hungry, but Mr Price kept on ordering more things. Course followed course. He filled up her wine glass, though she did not want any more champagne. There was a dizzy feeling in her head already... Dessert... Coffee... Cigars and cigarettes... Liqueurs...

Laura yawned and looked at her watch. Mr Price sat smoking contentedly... He finished his cigar. Laura felt encouraged. He lighted another!

At last he glanced out of the window, and laid down his napkin.

"I suppose we ought to be on our way," he said. "It's a fairly long drive."

Laura sprang to her feet. Mr Price paid the waiter. Goodness! Laura thought, how frightfully expensive, and such a tiresome dinner too. He gave the waiter a moderate tip, and they were bowed out and into the lobby.

And still Mr Price lingered. He paused at the desk to make sure that Miss Sands' telegram had been dispatched, chatted about the weather, bought an evening paper. Laura fidgeted... At length they were in the street. A flower woman held out a bunch of violets. Mr Price bought it and presented it to Laura.

"Delicious," she murmured, laying her cheek against the cool freshness of the flowers and tucked the violets into the belt of her coat.

Mr Price had a car waiting just around the corner. He opened the door. She stepped in.

"What a lovely car!" she exclaimed. "It's a Chrysler, isn't it? Have you sold your Buick?"

"No, but it's being overhauled at the moment. So I borrowed from a friend. I can't afford anything as handsome as this."

They crossed Fifth Avenue and began angling through a maze of narrow crooked streets.

"What funny little old houses," Laura remarked. "Greenwich Village? It doesn't look as lively and gay as I expected. What street is this?"

"Seventh Avenue. It's getting late, and we'll make better time than on Fifth."

Then why does he drive so slowly Laura wondered. But the car isn't his, perhaps he doesn't want to take any risks.

"What street is this?" she asked.

"Riverside Drive."

"It's marvellous! And that is the Hudson, I suppose... Look at all the ships!... What a splendid bridge! Are we going over it? Good!"

"This is the George Washington Bridge," Mr Price remarked, letting the car drop to a crawl.

"If you went that way up the river," he pointed, "you would come to West Point. And in the other direction is the harbour and the sea."

They left the bridge. "Are we still in New York?" Laura asked.

"No, in New Jersey. The road runs back to the country for a few miles and then we turn north into New York again."

"How far away is Mrs Wigham's house?"

"Not very far." Mr Price slowed down, stopped the car at a corner to read a sign board, turned into a side road, and drove on. "This road is pretty rough," he remarked. "But Mrs Wigham says you can't find country solitude unless you get off the main thoroughfares."

It was a rough road, and very lonely. Twilight was falling. Now and then they passed a farm house with lighted windows. Before long, these glimpses of life were left behind and the road ran on into unbroken loneliness, dark except for the car's headlights that illuminated each rut and stone with alarming distinctness.

Progress was slow enough. With every mile the road grew steeper and rougher, and the night darker. They bumped and bumped along. The car squeaked and groaned. After negotiating a peculiarly jagged ledge of rock, the engine let out an ominous growl. Mr Price jerked on the brake. Got out. Lifted the hood, and peered in.

"There's something wrong," he muttered. Found some tools. Hammered and screwed and unscrewed... Tried this and tried that. Twisted here and twisted there.

Laura was half asleep, when, at length, he murmured that he guessed it was all right and resumed his seat in the car.

They went on bumping. Through noisy darkness now. For the wind had risen and was roaring through the tree tops. Autumn leaves strewed the ground. A branch was torn away and came crashing on to the road just ahead of them.

"We are nearly there," Mr Price said encouragingly, as the car mounted a steep hill. "The house is at the foot of this slope." He looked at his watch. "Dear me, it's later than I thought. I hope they haven't given us up, and gone to bed."

He brought the car to a standstill. "This is the gate. I'm not sure where the garage is. I shall have to leave the car here in the road for the present."

Laura, straining her eyes through the darkness, could see gate posts; behind them were some trees and the dark bulk of a house.

"There isn't a single light anywhere!" she cried. "I do wish we could have arrived a little earlier!"

"Some of the servants must be up. You'd better wait here, Miss Laura. I'll go round to the back and investigate."

He returned in a moment. "Come along," he said. "There is a light in the kitchen. We'll go in that way."

Laura got out wearily and followed Mr Price through the gate, along a gravel road, around the corner of the house, and saw, with relief, a light shining from a window. Mr Price opened a door. She entered.

The room was dimly lit by a kerosene lamp on a table. Mrs Wigham's kitchen isn't very nice, Laura thought, glancing at the rusty stove and mouldy wallpaper.

"This way." Mr Price opened another door. She went in...

"It's dark..." she began. And screamed. Only once. A cloth came down over her head: muffling, blinding, choking. She was snatched up. Dropped on the floor. Turned over and over like a stick of wood. Tied hand and foot. Around and around the ropes went. Around and around.

Gasping, half smothered, she lay flat on her back, the cloth over her face. It was jerked away. She drew a long sobbing breath, caught a gleam of light, heard a door slam shut. The light went out.

She lay there in the darkness, afraid to move, almost afraid to breathe; listening. Another door closed. Then came the sound of retreating footsteps, lost at once in the roar of the wind.

He was gone!

Mr Price! Mr Price! But why? What did it all mean? No time to think. Get away. Get away before he came back!

She strained at the ropes. They held tight. Bent her head, trying to reach the knots with her teeth. No use. She struggled, panting. Rolled over. Sat up. A queer smell. Gas? Swayed. Dizzy. Dizzy. Too dizzy to sit up. Don't try, Laura, let yourself go. Sleep. Sleep. Sleep.

14

"When list! he hears a piteous moan,
Again! His heart within him dies;
He totters, pallid as a ghost,
And, looking down, espies
a lamb, that in the pool is pent
within that black and frightful rent."

WORDSWORTH

"This is dead easy," Northcote's taxi driver remarked, as his car gained speed and swung into Fifth Avenue, not far behind the taxi which was conveying Laura Sands and Mr Price downtown. "That guy is running awful slow."

"He certainly doesn't seem to be in a hurry," Northcote agreed, as he watched the car ahead. "I wish it weren't a yellow Parmalee, though; there are so many of them we may lose it in the crowd, and his plate is covered with mud. You can't read the number."

"That don't matter. See that crack in his rear window? I can spot him quite a ways off."

"Good. Look out you don't run up on them. I don't want them to know they are being trailed."

"Leave it to me," the man said soothingly. "Leave it to me. I'm an old hand at this game. I'll take care of you." Northcote relaxed. Obviously the man was accustomed to this hare and hounds business. The taxi ran on at a discreet distance, keeping about a block in the rear of the Parmalee. Sometimes drawing almost abreast, sometimes dropping back so far that Northcote felt a moment of anxiety. But always contriving to be stopped by the same traffic lights, and never losing sight of that cracked rear window.

"It would really be better for us if they were not going so slowly," Northcote remarked, as the two cars moved languidly on, one behind the other.

"It sure would. All I can do not to bump that guy. I guess he's been told to run slow so's the lady can see the sights. She keeps looking out the window. Maybe she's never been to New York before." He gave Northcote an inquisitive glance.

Northcote was silent. If I said I didn't know the girl, he reflected, he'd just grin. He thinks I'm a jealous husband or lover; there would be more sense in this ridiculous chase if we were... How do I know that man in the car ahead is our mysterious stranger? Ten to one, he is the girl's uncle. Just what had Mrs Benson said? She had said, "That must be Mr Price." Said it without much surprise, no alarm in her voice... Northcote leaned forward impulsively. "Look here," he began, and paused.

The Parmalee had been stopped by the red traffic light at Forty second Street. Better wait a moment, Northcote thought, and see which way it went. If the couple were bound for the Grand Central Station, the girl must be going home. It would be easy enough to follow her to the ticket office and make sure that she bought a ticket for Derby Centre. Then, knowing she was safe, he could abandon pursuit with a clear conscience. But the Parmalee with the cracked window did not turn off at Forty second Street. Northcote sighed with annoyance. The girl wasn't going home after all. Where the devil was she going? To the Pennsylvania Station, perhaps. Might as well wait and see if they turned off at Thirty fourth Street.

Again he was disappointed. The car ahead kept straight on down Fifth Avenue. More than once, Northcote was on the point of calling a halt. Each time, stirred by the excitement of pursuit intensified by curiosity, he leaned back in his seat without speaking. The two cars were in lower Fifth Avenue now. As the traffic thinned out, Northcote's driver prudently dropped back a little further. They crossed Fourteenth Street, went on. Suddenly the car ahead slowed, swept around in a wide curve across the avenue, and drew up at the door of the Brevoort Hotel.

Northcote's car fell in behind. He watched the girl and her escort alight. Their chauffeur was paid. They went up the steps, and disappeared. Their car drove away. Northcote's took its place.

Again Northcote hesitated. Again his driver gave him an inquisitive glance.

"Getting out here, sir?" he asked.

Northcote got out. Paid him, praised his skill, and went into the hotel.

Just inside the door he paused.

The pair he had been chasing were standing quietly at the desk in conversation with the clerk. Northcote bought a packet of cigarettes and as they went on into the restaurant he followed. They sat down at a table near the centre of the room. After a moment of consideration he selected a table at the farther side, half facing the girl but where the man could not see him, and sat down.

The man – Mr Price, of course – was busy with the menu. Very busy. Evidently he contemplated an elaborate meal. It would be well, Northcote decided, to finish at about the same time they did. So he too must dine well. He turned to the waiter standing beside him.

"I don't know what I want," he said. "But I'd like a good dinner. Do you see that lady and gentleman over there? You can duplicate their order. Bring me whatever they are having. Not the wine, though girls are apt to like sweet champagne. Let me have a half bottle of Chablis."

The waiter departed. Northcote lighted a cigarette and turned his attention to the centre table, observing, without appearing to do so, every detail of face, dress and expression of the couple he had been chasing. The man's back was turned but he could catch an occasional glimpse of the profile, an uninteresting profile, ordinary features and colouring, no eyeglasses or spectacles, no hair on the face. Dress sufficiently good, entirely lacking in distinction.

Voice, so far as you could judge at this distance, in no way peculiar. Once it was raised all the man said was, "Waiter!" But that word would have been enough to betray a foreigner, and there was no trace of accent, not even the rough terminal indicating a Mid westerner or a Canadian. Northcote decided that if commonplaceness were the mark of the mysterious stranger this man filled the bill to perfection. On the other hand, it was a good deal easier to think of him as a harmless Mr Price than as a ruthless murderer!

The waiter bent over him. So we begin with hors d'oeuvres, Northcote reflected, helping himself to caviar. And Little Neck clams to follow? Good. I foresee an excellent repast. I wish it were not so infernally early. I should be better able to cope with a banquet some two hours from now.

The clams were consumed. Northcote resumed his contemplation of the other table. A pretty girl. More than pretty. Beautiful. Lovely colouring. A charming nose, with a nice little tilt at the very tip. Something familiar about that nose. Where, he asked himself, have I seen a nose like that? Not long ago too. Lovely modeling about the cheek bones. Lovely line of chin and throat. Slim figure. Pretty hands. Yes, take her all round, this Laura girl is a winner. Who in hell does she remind me of?

Consommé appeared at both tables. Disappeared. A fussy feeder, this Mr Price, Northcote thought. He keeps changing his mind, sending for the head waiter, asking the girl whether she wouldn't prefer something else. And she just smiles – or tries to. She's bored. Bored to death. All this argument about food doesn't interest her in the least. But she's a nice girl. I like her. Good manners. Prettily dressed, not smart, of course, what you'd expect from that fine old colonial house she was brought up in. Well brought up. She's too polite to say she doesn't care a hang whether it's cutlets or vol-au-vent. She isn't hungry either. Only drank one glass of champagne, doesn't like that sweet stuff any better than I do. Why can't Price see she's tired and wants to go home? There are shadows under her eyes. Blue? Grey? Anyway, the lashes are as long as cat's whiskers. I do wish I could remember who she reminds me of.

Another course arrived. And another. Good Lord, Northcote sighed. What an endless meal! Lucky I cashed a check this morning. Price must be well off. This dinner will set him back a lot. Probably he wants to make a good impression, hopes to ingratiate himself with the girl. Not so strange, that. She is an extremely attractive young thing. Must have been born on a Sunday: "Bonny and healthy and wise and gay."

Cigars and cigarettes at last. Gosh! The fellow was as deliberate in smoking as in eating. I've had enough, Northcote thought impatiently. Enough food and more than enough sleuthing. It's time this farce came to an end. Absurd to imagine the girl is in danger – except from indigestion. The man is a harmless Mr Price bent on treating a niece or cousin from the country to a really good dinner.

Northcote beckoned to the waiter. Gave a last glance at the girl. Half rose. Sat down again.

I've got it! he muttered. I know whom she looks like. Mrs Beaumont! She's the image of Mrs Beaumont. Or rather, what Mrs Beaumont must have been at eighteen.

It was an arresting thought. When the waiter brought the bill, Northcote ordered a Benedictine and the evening paper.

For some obscure reason this likeness to Mrs Beaumont – not in itself strange, for the two were cousins – brought the present situation into a new perspective. No one had dreamed that Mrs Beaumont was in danger, and Mrs Beaumont had been murdered! *J'y suis, j'y reste*, Northcote said to himself grimly.

It was nearly eight o'clock when at length the couple at the centre table rose. Northcote got up with alacrity, and followed them out into the lobby. They lingered at the desk for some minutes. Walked very slowly out of the front door and down the steps, paused to buy a bunch of violets from a flower seller, waited while the girl pinned it to her coat. Then they went down Fifth Avenue. Northcote strolled in the same direction. Saw them turn into Eighth Street, approach a parked car, and get in.

Northcote beckoned to a taxi.

"Do you see that claret-coloured Chrysler?" he said. "I want to know where it's going. Don't get too close. I don't want them to guess I'm trailing them."

"I get you!" the man grinned.

Northcote glanced at him. "Why, you're the man that drove me here," he said laughing, as he got in. "How does that happen?"

"I sort of thought you'd want to go on after you'd had dinner, and I felt hungry myself. So I went and had a bite and came back on the off chance."

"Good for you! What's your name by the way? Oh, here it is on the license card. Burchall. Well, Burchall, I'm glad you waited for me... Hullo. This is Greenwich Village! Where is that Chrysler going to, I wonder?"

"Nineteenth Street, I guess, to the express highway. No, he ain't. He's going up Seventh. What the hell does he want to go up Seventh for? And why did he come so far down if he was going up right away? There's plenty places to eat uptown."

"I don't know why he does anything. To tell you the truth, I never laid eyes on either of those two people until this afternoon. I have no personal interest in this pursuit. I'm acting for a friend."

The driver gave an indifferent nod – obviously he thought he knew that kind of friend – and drove on for some time without speaking. Then:

"God Almighty," he said. "I never see a guy drive so slow as what that feller does. Here we are at Riverside and he's got an open road and he goes crawling along like a sick caterpillar."

"Have you plenty of gas?" Northcote asked. "Half an hour ago I got so tired of chasing these people that I came near giving the whole thing up. Then I changed my mind. I shall follow them now no matter where it lands me."

"I'm your man then. I got plenty gas. Filled up downtown... Well, here we are at the George Washington Bridge. He's crossing, by gum; some chase, this. Weather looks bad, don't it? See them black clouds. I guess they mean rain."

Northcote agreed, wishing that he had brought an overcoat. The wind came driving furiously up the river, streaking it with foam.

The car ahead stopped at the toll house, went on. Northcote's followed suit.

"It's beginning to get dark," he said. "Look out you don't lose them if they turn off the main road."

He had spoken just in time. With an exclamation, Burchall slowed down. The Chrysler had paused, evidently to make sure of the way, then turned abruptly into a side road.

"Jeez!" Burchall grunted. "The guy that dug this road would get the chair if I had the say so."

The taxi bumped on through the darkness. The road grew narrower. It was scarcely more than a cart track now. Night had fallen. But Burchall first dimmed his lights, then extinguished them, muttering: "If that feller sees a light in his mirror way out here in no man's land, he'll get suspicious."

Luckily, the road bed was of whitish clay. It made a pale path for them. They could see just enough to avoid the ditches on either side and follow on, though the wind was blowing so hard that all sound of the car ahead was lost. They would not have known it was there except for the tail light that flickered like a red glow worm, was lost for a moment among the trees, or hidden by a hill, then reappearing.

"Have you any idea where we are?" Northcote asked, after they had driven for what seemed like hours. "We have been running north, I think. We must be some where in that wild country back of Bear Mountain."

"Search me," Burchall growled. "I ain't no hayseed. If I get home without breaking every spring I got, you won't catch me outside Manhattan again. Say, this hill is the worst yet! The car ground slowly upward. At the top Burchall jammed on the brake.

"They've stopped," he said. "They're right down there at the bottom of the hill."

"Turn off your engine."

Burchall obeyed. They sat staring from their hilltop at the lights of the other car, listening to hammer strokes that rose clinking above the uproar of the wind.

"Broke down," Burchall muttered. "Serve him right... He don't know one damn thing about his engine. Sounds like he was just hammering on the tin. Yah, how I despise that guy!" The hammering continued. "What do you say we run alongside, like we'd just happened by, and ask if we can help any?"

Northcote hesitated. "I'd rather not do that unless it's absolutely necessary. I want to find out where he's going and there, he's stopped tinkering at last. Let him get well over the next hill before you start."

The next hill was achieved. Another and another...

"When I told you I had plenty gas," Burchall grumbled, "I didn't bargain for darkest Africa. Hello, where's that tail light got to? It's out!"

"So it is. Stop right here."

They had reached the brow of a long hill. The descent stretched in front, just a pale smear soon lost in darkness. Overhead the wind boomed, trees flung themselves about, dead leaves blew into the car, blew out again.

"What on earth has become of him?" Northcote muttered. "I can't see any car down there, can you?"

"Nope. But how could you, if his lights is out?"

"I don't hear anything either. But they might be shouting and this wind would drown the sound."

"What you want to do? Shall I slip down, real quiet?"

"No. You'd better stay here. I'll go down on foot and have a look."

Northcote got out and walked off down the dark road, at first feeling his way step by step; then, as his eyes became accustomed to the darkness, making better progress. At length the ground levelled and, at the same moment, he was aware of a bulky object close in front of him. It was the Chrysler. He stopped and listened. Nothing was to be heard but the rushing wind and the growl of distant thunder. Peering through the darkness he thought he saw two gate posts, and behind them what seemed to be a house.

If only I had a light, he thought, and searched his pockets. Not so much as a match. Burchall would have a torch. He turned and hurriedly retraced his steps. But he walked carelessly, found himself off the road, floundering in a clump of bushes, scrambled out again, regained the road and went panting up the hill. As he reached the taxi a tremendous clap of thunder crashed overhead and in the glare of lightning he saw Burchall's face looking out anxiously.

"Say, what you been doing?" Burchall demanded. "Thought you was lost."

"I got off the road. The Chrysler is down there in front of a house. No sign of life anywhere. Looks queer to me."

"Man and girl gone indoors?"

"That's what I want to find out. Have you got a torch?"

"Here you are. Dumb not to have give it you before. Should I come along?"

"Not yet. They would hear the car. I must see what's going on before that man suspects anything. Give me ten minutes – time it by your watch – and then slip down as quietly as you can, and turn around at the gate and..."

"Look!" Burchall broke in. "There goes the car now! See his lights going off to the left? Road must take a sharp turn there. We didn't hear him start because of the thunder. But you can see the lights. Making good time too. Old caterpillar's waked up at last. No use trying to catch him now."

"I'm going down to have a look at the house anyway. You follow me in ten minutes, and turn when you get to the bottom so that we can make a quick getaway if we need to."

Once more Northcote descended the hill, much faster now of course for the road was lighted by his torch. At the bottom he flashed the torch this way and that; made sure that the Chrysler was indeed gone; found the gate posts; walked along a weed grown driveway, and stood staring up at a dark house. Not a light anywhere. A tangle of shrubs almost hid the front door, vines clambered up the walls only to fall again in a heavy curtain over the windows. The piazza roof sagged drunkenly, its railings were broken, one step had rotted away.

An abandoned house, Northcote said to himself, as the torch light explored the forlorn facade. No one can have lived here for years. He let the light fall on the ground, traced a dim path leading around the corner of the house, followed it, found a back door.

Here he paused. Should he knock? The house was deserted. If anyone were in hiding here it could be for no good purpose. Bootleggers, perhaps; there were plenty of them still in business.

He mounted the two steps to the door, and ran his light up the sides, looking for a bell or a knocker. There was neither. He laid his hand on the doorknob, turned it. The door would not open; it held at the top. Running the light upward he saw a bolt. It was shot. The door had been fastened from the outside. That meant the house was empty.

I must make sure, he thought. But I believe I'll wait till Burchall comes. We'll go in together. What a loathsome place this is. Smells disgustingly. Smells of mould and dead leaves and toadstools. He turned to go, and paused.

Another smell – an unexpected smell. The scent of violets! He stooped, felt along the sill, stood up. A bunch of violets! The girl had been here – might still be here, locked in!

He drew the bolt, pushed open the door, and entered. His torch showed blackened walls and dirty floor, a kitchen stove, a rusty iron sink, the stump of a broom in one corner, lamp on a broken table. The mouldy smell was strong here, but there was another odour mingled with it. Gas? Some queer sort of gas. A door led into another room. It was closed and bolted. He opened it and sending the light ahead peered in. The room was empty. No, there was a bundle lying against the far wall. A bundle of rags? A woman!

In two steps he was beside her. He dropped the torch, gathered her up into his arms and staggered out, bent on reaching the open air; for he was breathing with difficulty, the gas was in his throat. On the steps he stumbled, came near dropping the girl, recovered himself, laid her on the grass. She didn't stir. Had she fainted? Or was she dead?

The torch. He had left the torch in the inner room. Holding his breath he dashed in, saw the spot of light on the floor, snatched up the torch, dashed out again; slamming both doors behind him as he came.

He flashed the light on the girl's face. A small pale face, the eyes closed. The Laura girl! Was she dead? He laid his cheek against hers. It was cold, but she was still breathing. Her hands and feet were tied... God, what a brute! Whipping a penknife out of his pocket he cut the rope. A length of heavy clothesline, wound around and around and tied in intricate knots. She still lay without moving. He flashed the light in her face again, and her eyes opened... Stared... Closed again.

He put his arm around her. "Try to sit up," he said, and raised her so that she leaned against his shoulder.

"Everything is all right," he said cheerfully. "You're safe. Safe as a church."

She drew a long gasping breath.

"Has he, has he gone?" she whispered.

"Yes, indeed. He's miles away. You'll never see him again."

"Are you – sure?"

"Absolutely. You're perfectly safe."

"Safe?"

"Yes. Perfectly safe. Do you think you could walk? Just a few steps. I have a car here."

"Who are you?"

"A friend of your aunt's. She sent me to get you."

"How did she know?"

"Never mind about that now. See if you can stand up."

Clinging to his arm Laura struggled to her feet, stood swaying for a minute. He guided her along the path. They moved very slowly. He did not dare to hurry her, though he longed to break into a run. I'm scared, he thought, scared stiff. Never was so frightened in my life. That damned skunk may be hiding somewhere. This may be a plot. Suppose a bullet came ping out of the bushes. Two bullets. One for her and one for me. God. I'll be glad to see Burchall! They rounded the corner of the house. The taxi was not there!

Northcote stood still for one horrible moment. Then a sound came through the darkness, a light showed on the hill, swept around. Burchall was here, was turning. Ten minutes? It had seemed like years. Years or minutes, over now. Safely over.

They had reached the gate. Burchall jumped out, flung open the door of the car. Together they managed to lift Laura in. Got in themselves. The car started.

Northcote bent over the girl beside him. She had drawn her feet up on the seat, her hands fell loose in her lap, her head drooped. She lay curled up there shivering, not crying, not making a sound. Northcote had never felt so sorry for anyone in his life. Looks like a kitten the boys have been chasing, he thought. Damn damn damn that skunk. I wish she would cry. It would be easier if she cried. She just lies there and shivers.

He took off his coat and wrapped it around her. As he tucked it in she opened her eyes.

"Who are you?" she said. "Where are we going?"

"Back to New York. You can trust me, my dear girl. Really and truly you can trust me. You'll be safe in your aunt's house before you know it and all this will seem like a bad dream."

"A very bad dream." She shuddered, and brushed her hair back from her forehead. "I can't remember just what happened. Mr Price came and we had dinner and then he drove and drove. And it got awfully dark..."

"Don't try to remember now. Better not think until you feel stronger. We have a long way to go. Would you be more comfortable if I sat in front? You could lie down on the seat and take a little nap."

"No, oh, no. Don't leave me!" She caught his sleeve. "There's plenty of room. I'm frightfully sleepy." She yawned, curled up again, and in a minute she was fast asleep.

The wind was dying at last, but rain had begun. It came spattering down on the taxi roof in scanty single drops. The way was, of course, far more difficult to find now that they were no longer guided by the tail light of the other car. At every crossroad – luckily there were few – they had to pause and consider. Once as they were going over a bridge Burchall jammed on his brakes.

"This ain't right," he said. "There's a plank broke out. We didn't cross no bridge with a plank gone, or I'd of noticed it."

"We must have taken the wrong road at that last corner then. We'll have to go back."

"I don't know's I can turn here," Burchall growled, peering into the darkness.

"I'll get out and have a look with the torch... Yes, you can manage it. Keep over to the right. It's rough, but there's no ditch."

The turn was successfully accomplished. As Northcote got back into the car the rain began falling in earnest.

"Minute more and you'd been soaked," Burchall remarked, as he drove on. "You must be kind of chilly without your coat. No use asking you to take mine, I suppose. Well, here we are back at that fork again. Another five miles and we'd ought to be out on the main road. Young lady all right?"

"She's fast asleep. Though how she can sleep driving over these stones is a mystery."

"Looks like she's been doped. Say, there's the big road right ahead! You can see the lights."

Another mile or two and they were on cement, bowling along to the George Washington Bridge.

As they crossed it, Burchall said "Where you going to take her? To a hospital?"

"I don't believe that is necessary," Northcote answered. "She doesn't appear to be injured in any way. Go on downtown while I think out what I'd better do."

Northcote sat frowning, turning the situation over in his mind. I can't take her to my apartment, he reflected, and a hotel would be awkward at this hour. If it were not so late I could take her to Mrs Benson's... I have it – Marbury! Why didn't I think of him at once? I'll take her to Marbury.

He gave Burchall the address, and went on "It is very considerate of you not to ask any questions, Burchall, and I appreciate it. This must all seem pretty queer to you, and I feel I owe you an explanation. Here is my card. Come and see me between ten and eleven tomorrow. And, in the meantime, for God's sake keep your mouth shut!"

He pressed several bills into Burchall's hand.

"That's all right," Burchall grunted. "Glad I was along. I ain't much of a talker, as it happens. You'll see me tomorrow. Here we are."

"Wake up, my dear!" Northcote shook Laura gently. She yawned and sat up, then slumped back again.

"We got to lift her out," Burchall said.

They picked her up, stood her on her feet on the sidewalk, held her, guided her up the steps, and rang the bell.

"Stay until we get in," Northcote said to Burchall, and rang the bell again.

There was a long wait. Then a light flashed from the transom, there came a rattle of chains, the sound of locks and bolts unfastening. The door was opened half way and a figure peered out. It was Mr Marbury, in purple silk dressing gown and slippers, his hair standing on end, an expression of intense surprise on his face.

Northcote pushed in, his arm around the girl. "It's all right, Marbury," he said. "This is Laura Sands. Where shall I put her? She's had a fearful time and ought to go to bed at once."

"Good gracious," Marbury began. "How did you find her? What..."

"Don't talk," Northcote snapped. "Where do I take her?"

Marbury turned meekly. Northcote, supporting Laura, followed him upstairs and into a bedroom. He switched on the lights, went to the bed, turned back the covering.

"Here," he said. "Poor little thing. She looks half dead."

Northcote moved to the bed. As they reached it Laura slid from his arms and lay there with closed eyes. The two men stood looking down at her uncertainly. "Shall I call up my doctor?" Marbury asked.

Northcote shook his head. "I don't think she's really ill. Just worn out. Let's wait till morning anyway. You see, Marbury, this is a mighty queer business and we want to keep it to ourselves as far as possible."

"You mean?"

"Yes, the mysterious stranger has pulled off another of his little tricks! If we want to catch him we must let him think that this girl is dead."

"He tried to murder her?"

"He did. And came near succeeding. I'll tell you all about it tomorrow and we'll plan what's best to be done. In the meantime, we'd better make this poor girl as comfortable as we can, and let her sleep. Probably she'll sleep the clock round. I believe she's sound asleep already."

She was. They took off her coat and her shoes – she had no hat – laid her between the sheets, turned out the lights and tiptoed out of the room.

"I'll leave the door open a little way," Marbury said, "so that she can see the light in the hall if she wakes during the night, and I can hear her if she calls." He looked at his watch. "It's nearly morning. I shall dress and you had better go home, Jim, and get a good sleep. You look played out."

"I suppose I'd better," Northcote hesitated. "If she should wake tell her I'll be back right after breakfast. I..."

"Don't worry," Marbury said. "I'll rouse Sarah, as soon as I can do so without alarming her, and between us you may rest assured that Miss Sands will be well taken care of."

Northcote thanked him and departed.

15

"Out of this nettle, danger, we pluck this flower, safety."
SHAKESPEARE

When Laura awoke in Mr Marbury's best spare room she did not exclaim "Where am I?" as she might well have done under the circumstances. She lay quite still, staring about her.

White walls, white silk curtains, white Venetian blinds, white lace bedspread, white furniture. Bowl of white roses. White dressing gown over the foot of the bed, little white velvet slippers on the floor. Like a fairy story, she thought. Like Goldilocks: " 'Who has been sleeping in my bed?' said the Big Bear..."

She rolled over and buried her face in the pillows. I remember now, she shivered. That horrible horrible Mr Price. Or was it someone else who – who... And how did I get here? Whose house is this?

She sat up, and looked about her a little wildly. A telephone? There was a telephone on a stand near the window. She put one foot out of bed. A knock sounded on the door, and she crouched down again under the covers.

"Come in," she said faintly, staring at the door.

But it was not the Big Bear, the Middle-Sized Bear, or the Little Bear who entered. Only a maid. A maid with a smiling face.

One glance at that stiffly starched, blue and white respectability was enough. Laura relaxed, with the exquisite relief of a child who sees her nurse coming to the rescue at a crucial moment. She could have kissed that large plain face. There were no bears – little or big – in this house! Everything was all right.

Half an hour later, refreshed by a prolonged and boiling hot bath, back in bed again, pillows heaped behind her, a breakfast tray across her knees, both the horrid past and the uncertain future could be forgotten for the moment. She was too hungry to think of anything but food.

Even the burning curiosity as to her present whereabouts and the name of her host or hostess that still remained – direct questions being obviously impossible – was soon gratified. As the nice maid lifted the dish covers and poured out the coffee, Laura exclaimed at the beauty of a pink rosebud that lay beside the plate, and the nice maid answered – most obligingly – that Mr Marbury had put it on the tray himself. It came from his own garden.

"Mr Marbury?" Laura began, recollected herself – so silly not to know whose house you were staying in – and let her question fade out in a murmur of gratitude slightly muffled by a first ecstatic bite of hot buttered toast.

"Mr Marbury said you wasn't to hurry yourself, Miss," the maid went on. "But he hopes you'll feel up to coming down for tea. It's at four thirty in the library."

Laura nodded – silenced now by overwhelming shyness at the prospect of this encounter – and with a final smile, Sarah closed the door softly and went downstairs to the library where Marbury and Northcote were anxiously awaiting her report of their protégé.

"Miss Sands is feeling fine, sir," she said, "and she'll be down for tea. A very nice, sweet spoken young lady," she added, "pretty as a picture," and departed.

"Sarah doesn't seem unduly surprised," Northcote remarked. He had just arrived, after repeated inquiries by telephone. "What did you tell the servants?"

"That the young lady was a cousin of yours passing through New York on her way home. You were taking her to the train, after spending the evening at the theatre when your taxi was run into and pretty well smashed up. She got such a fright that it didn't seem wise for her to travel. So you brought her here to rest and recover – my house being close by."

"Pretty good, except that this house isn't on the way between any theatre and any railway station."

"I realize that. A drive in the Park would have been better, if it hadn't been such a stormy night. However, the servants seemed perfectly satisfied. I warned Sarah not to mention the motor accident, as we want it forgotten as soon as possible. Now finish the account of your adventures last night. You had got as far as the deserted house..."

"Well, as I told you, the brute – I could skin him alive! – took her to this deserted house somewhere back of Bear Mountain – a mighty wild stretch of country, you know. Tied her hand and foot in a dark room, bolted the door, and turned on some sort of asphyxiating gas – I suppose he had a tank planted in the cellar. Luckily, it gave off a peculiar smell that I noticed at once, and its effect must be slow, for I felt only a slight dizziness after I got out. And although she must have breathed it for five or six minutes she didn't seem much the worse last night except for being terribly sleepy. I hoped she would be all right after a good long rest and apparently she is. But it was a close shave! A few whiffs more in that air tight hole and she would have suffocated. A pretty story, isn't it!"

"Horrible! Thank God you were in time. The taxi driver must have found the whole thing rather peculiar."

"He did, of course. But I saw him this morning – I had asked him to drop in – and if he had been thinking of me as a possible white slaver, I managed to reassure him. Told the truth, in fact, or very near it. Said I had learned accidentally that the lady was inheriting some money and might be in danger from another heir, the man we had followed. Which suspicion was correct, as he had left her locked up in that empty house – I didn't mention the poison gas; the tale is lurid enough without that – and explained we were not notifying the police for the present, because they would let the affair get into the newspapers and our best chance of catching the brute was to let him think the girl was dead. He saw the point, and swore he would not speak of it to a living soul. I think he'll keep his word. Especially as I made it plain that silence in his case would prove extremely golden."

"Good. It is indeed a lurid tale. I can't understand why Price adopted such a complicated method of disposing of her. Why didn't he shoot the girl and bury her somewhere in the woods?"

"He was playing safe. Didn't care to risk getting blood on the car or on his clothes. Also, I think the man is proud of his ingenuity. It makes him feel big to devise so many safe ways of committing murder! And, if I'm right, a sense of bigness is as important to him as the money."

"I daresay. Have you thought what our next move is to be?"

"We must find some place where Laura Sands will be safe. She is in terrible danger as long as this murderous brute is at large. She can't go back to Derby Centre, or anywhere else where she is known."

"I shall be glad to have her stay here as long as she likes. From what Sarah says, she seems to be a nice girl."

"Nice! She's..." Northcote caught Marbury's look of amusement, and moderated his enthusiasm. "She seems to be an extremely nice girl, with lots of courage and common sense."

"You have learned a good deal about the young lady in a very short time."

Northcote laughed. "You'll admit that the circumstances were something of a test. Most girls would have gone into hysterics last night, fainted and sobbed and raised the roof. But she held on to herself, and never shed a tear. As for common sense, she did exactly what I told her to all along."

"I see." Marbury suppressed a smile. "She will, I feel sure, prove to be an agreeable guest. There's one difficulty, however. The servants will think it rather odd if she stays for any length of time."

"Let me think... A sprained ankle? No. Sarah would be on to that... I have it! Miss Sands' family want to keep her away from home for a while, because a girlfriend of hers has got mixed up in a divorce case and she may be called as a witness, and they want her not to go out in the street because she might be served with a subpoena. How's that?"

"Sounds fishy to me," Marbury shook his head. "But I can't think of anything better."

"It's all settled then. She will be safe here, of course. Price doesn't know I brought her and won't be able to trace her as he has no idea that either you or I have ever heard of Miss Laura Sands, much less met her. He doesn't even know we are interested in Mrs Beaumont's death."

"That's true. But do you realize, Jim, that if we stick to our first theory that Clare Beaumont was murdered by one of the persons present in her bedroom the morning of her death, we strike a fresh snag? If this Price had been among them, wouldn't you have recognized him when you saw him in the restaurant last night?"

"I wonder," Northcote said meditatively. "Do you know, Marbury, I am beginning to think we have ignored one person who may very well turn out to be the guilty man?"

"Who is that?"

"Green."

"Green? Mrs Beaumont's butler? But surely you would know him if you saw him again?"

"I don't think so. I can't remember ever seeing the man at Mrs Beaumont's. Green was new there, and I'm pretty sure that it was William who opened the door and brought tea the last few times I went to the house."

"But a butler? A butler seems so…"

"I know. In old fashioned detective stories a respectable butler so often turned out to be a villain that the idea seems shopworn. But as a matter of fact, when it comes to crime in the home, a butler has a better opportunity than anybody else! Do you remember that Washington Square burglary some years ago? The butler succeeded in shutting up the whole family in the wine cellar and they would have died of suffocation if Mr Slocum had not displayed remarkable skill in picking locks."

"Yes, I recall that affair."

"Well then, let us consider Green. You have seen him. What did he look like?"

"There was nothing distinctive about him that I can recall." Marbury sighed. "An ordinary looking man, clean shaven, of course."

"I thought so! Isn't inconspicuousness the only characteristic of our murderer? What's more, we don't know where Green went after he left Mrs Beaumont's."

"No, we don't. I suppose we didn't think of following him up because he was not one of the persons in her room."

"You mean, he wasn't there so far as we know. He was in the house, of course, and he could easily have poisoned the saccharine."

"We must certainly find out what became of him. Jane might know. She has gone to live with a married sister, but I have her telephone number. I'll call her up."

But as Marbury turned to the telephone, Sarah came in with the mail, and he paused to examine a handful of letters.

"Hello!" he exclaimed, glancing at the envelopes, "An English stamp. Perhaps it is from that Mr Bell of Dumfries I wrote to in the spring. He didn't answer, so I wrote again not long ago." He opened the envelope. "Yes, it is from him... He has been away... Sorry he couldn't write sooner, etc, etc... Here's something important! Very important! Listen to this:

" 'You are right in surmising that Robert Bell of Irongray had a fifth son, Charles, who does not appear in the chart sent you from the Heralds' office in Edinburgh, as I myself only learned this recently. From an allusion in an old letter I came across, I gather that Charles went to America about 1830. That is all I know about him.

" 'You may be interested in another piece of news in connection with the Bells of Irongray that I received a few days ago from a friend in Australia, a solicitor. It seems that a certain Donald Bell died there recently leaving a very peculiar will. He was of humble extraction and only distantly related to the Bells of Irongray, which family, however, he held in such esteem that he left his entire fortune – some million pounds sterling – to be divided among the surviving descendants of Bell of Irongray, with the exception of a moderate annuity to an adopted son by the name of McGuire, believed to have been a foundling. If the family is extinct, McGuire inherits everything. The executors will, no doubt, proceed to trace the various Bell descendants – unluckily I am not in line – and if you can aid in the search I would suggest your communicating with Messrs. Lobden & Lobden, 94 Glengarry Place, Adelaide, Australia.'"

"Hurrah!" Northcote exclaimed. "we seem to be getting out of the woods at last. The whole business is as clear as day now. And the motive is what we suspected: money."

"Yes, money. Now if we could find Green and prove that he was actually McGuire, the Australian heir..."

"Just so. And do you notice an illuminating detail? I said that the murderer must be a man with an inferiority complex, a man with a grievance, sick of being inconspicuous, bent on showing the world what a big noise he could make if he had the chance. Now this McGuire is a foundling. Don't you see how neatly he fits into the picture? All his life he has heard his adopted father boast about the Bells of Irongray and loathes the very name. He learns the terms of this preposterous will and starts out to get the money for himself and, incidentally, exterminate the family of whom he has so long been jealous. Why, it's perfect! Simply perfect!"

"You may be right. Anyway, I'll call up Jane and ask her for the latest news of Green the butler."

A moment later, Mr Marbury hung up the receiver, and turned to Northcote with a startled:

"You were right, Jim! Jane says Green came from Australia and often talked of returning to his old home. He has left his last situation and she doesn't know where he is now."

"Looks pretty black for Green. Now the next thing we have to decide is whether this means we should call in the police. We have a definite crime to bring to their attention, not merely suspicions as in Robinson and Starkweather affairs. Laura Sands was undoubtedly kidnapped, whether or not Price intended to murder her."

"And the case against Green is pretty strong."

"It is. On the other hand, Laura Sands' safety still remains our first consideration, and our fear that if we take our information to the police the whole thing immediately gets into the newspaper still holds good. Price or Green – let's give him a hyphen and call him Price-Green. Price-Green finds out she isn't dead after all, he goes into hiding and waits for a second chance to make away with her."

"She would have to be guarded."

"Pretty unpleasant for a young girl to know there was a detective at her heels all the time! Whereas, if we could spirit her away to some safe place she could stay there, living a normal life, until Price-Green had been landed in jail."

"That's all very well. But how are we to get him into jail unless we call in the police? You and I can't watch all the ships sailing for Australia, or trace Price-Green's car through the license number."

"I realize that. We need expert advice. What would you think of hiring a good private detective? I believe Driver & Merk are reliable people."

"An excellent idea. To go back to my question, what on earth are we going to do with her?"

"God knows! We shall have to persuade her to cut loose from all her old associations – even her aunt. You see, if Price-Green goes back to that abandoned house – though I doubt if he would risk being seen in the neighbourhood – and finds she is alive, he will hurry off to Derby Centre to make inquiries."

"An alarming thought."

"It is. So our plan must include some way of keeping Miss

Henrietta Sands in the dark as to her niece's whereabouts without arousing her suspicions. And we don't know enough about the aunt to contrive that until we have had a talk with the niece. Why doesn't the girl come? It's long after tea time!"

"The clock hasn't yet struck the half hour," Marbury smiled. "Your watch must be fast..."

He broke off. The door was opening, both turned expectantly, and Northcote sprang to his feet.

But it was only Sarah with the tea tray.

Laura stood in front of the looking glass powdering her pretty little nose for the third time. Sarah waited, smiling patiently. Laura bent closer to the glass, ran a comb through her side curls, smoothed one eyebrow. What a coward I am, she thought, and resolutely followed Sarah down the stairs.

Two men rose to meet her as the library door opened and she stood hesitating on the threshold; an elderly gentleman she had never seen before, a young man whose face was vaguely familiar. They came hurrying forward; the older man took her hand gently in his.

"How are you, my dear?" he said. "Delighted to see you looking so well. This is my friend, Jim Northcote, the knight errant who came to your assistance last evening – lucky fellow!"

Marbury spoke with intentional carelessness but Laura's eyes widened in startled recognition as she and Northcote shook hands.

She managed a breathless "I'm so grateful, so grateful to you both. I can't begin to tell you how... If it hadn't been for you... I can't tell you..."

"Don't try to, my dear," Marbury said. "We shall all be the better for a cup of tea, I think. Won't you pour it out? Mr Northcote takes his plain and I like one lump and a dash of cream. Sit here on the sofa. Another cushion? Or a footstool? Sure you are quite comfortable?"

"Oh, quite, thank you."

Maddening, Laura thought, to feel so shy. But the tea things were a help. A little difficult to fill the first cup, the second was easier. Her hand stopped trembling and her voice, as she murmured, "I just love cinnamon toast," sounded less unnatural. How tactful they are, she thought. Giving me time, talking along about gardening, and how hot it was in July, and whether the peach crop is as good as usual…

Recovery was rapid. Laura's usual high spirits and talkativeness came back – she seemed to have known these two nice men all her life – and she was about to venture one of the dozen questions hovering on the tip of her tongue when Mr Marbury raised a protesting hand:

"One moment, my dear young lady," he implored. "Your curiosity is more than pardonable, under the circumstances; but, believe me, what you can tell us about last night's adventures is a good deal more important than anything we can tell you! If you can bear to do so, please give us the whole story beginning with this Mr Price. Who is he? A recent acquaintance? An intimate friend?"

Laura shuddered. "We-we thought he was a friend. He seemed so kind. But now I'm not sure."

She had grown very white, her lip quivered, and Marbury gave her hand a reassuring pat, as he asked "How long have you known him?"

"Just this summer. He is a friend of Judge Evans at Derby Centre."

"An old friend?" Northcote put in.

"I don't know. We thought he was. Anyway, it was Judge Evans who introduced him to Aunt Henrietta. Mr Price happened to be staying at the inn and he came to call and Aunt Henrietta wanted to sell an old sideboard we've had in the attic for perfectly ages… Aunt Henrietta isn't as well off as she used to be and so she showed it to Mr Price and Mr Price knew someone who might want to buy the old thing. So then he asked us all to go over to the shore and have dinner on the Fourth of July and they set off some fireworks and a rocket came straight at me out of the bushes and..."

"A rocket! You say a rocket nearly hit you?"

"Yes, an inch nearer and I'd have been killed. There was a little hole burned in my dress. It was pretty scary, I can tell you!"

"Was Price with you when it happened?"

"Oh, yes. We were sitting on the sand... No, not at that moment, he had gone to get his coat."

Marbury and Northcote exchanged glances.

Her eyes grew round in sudden and horrified understanding. "You mean he did it?" she cried, shivering. "Oh, I never never thought of that! It would be too horrible. They said it was boys – boys hiding in the bushes – an accident..."

"Perhaps it was," Northcote put in soothingly. "Go on. What happened next?"

"Well, then Mr Price went away from Derby Centre, and we thought he had forgotten about the sideboard and everything. Then a few days ago he came back and his sister had got a letter from Mrs Wigham – she's a very old friend of Aunt Henrietta's – and Mrs Wigham wanted someone to go abroad with her and take her little girl to the Tower and St. Paul's and all that, while she made visits. And of course I just jumped for joy at the idea. So it was all arranged."

"And when and where did you meet Mrs Wigham?"

"I never met her! That was so funny. There was something wrong about her address and Mrs Benson looked and looked. She looked in the telephone book and the Social Register and everything, but she couldn't find her."

"Is Mrs Benson an old friend?"

"Oh, I forgot that part. You see, Mr Price went off and left me in the Grand Central Station and he didn't come back and he didn't come back. And a man with a moustache kept looking at me. So then I spoke to a girl and she was awfully nice and her mother came and she was nice too. And they were the Bensons and I went home with them."

"I see. And when did Mr Price turn up?"

"The next afternoon – was it really only yesterday? – while Beatrice and I were walking the dogs. I meant to go back to Derby Centre on the five o'clock train. He came hurrying up and explained how he had been detained and how worried he was and that Mrs Wigham's number was 964 not 564 and that she had gone to her weekend cottage and he would take me there. So I got my bag – my weekend bag – and I don't suppose I shall ever see that again and Mr Price said we had better have dinner first, so we did... Oh, such a long dinner... and then we drove and drove and drove..." She shuddered and broke off.

"We know the rest," Northcote said. "Mr Price seems to have laid his plans very cleverly. You realize now that he was not the benefactor he appeared to be. Had you any suspicions before last night?"

"Well, there were the peppermints," she hesitated. "I did think it was rather queer about the peppermints."

"The peppermints?"

"In the train. I imagined that I saw Mr Price taking away my box of chocolate peppermints and putting another box on the seat. I decided it wasn't possible, that I must have been dreaming. Or that he liked practical jokes – though he didn't seem at all that kind of person. Anyhow, just to be on the safe side, I threw the box away."

"A wise precaution," Marbury remarked. "I think we have all the essential facts now. Have you any plans, Miss Sands?"

"Do please call me Laura – Miss Sands means Aunt Henrietta, you know. Have I any plans? Why, no. Except that I must call up Aunt Henrietta and tell her what happened and ask how her cold is and if she thinks I'd better come home right away or try to find Mrs Wigham..."

"Mrs Wigham!" Northcote laughed. "Like Mrs Harris in Dickens, 'There ain't no sich person.'"

"But Aunt Henrietta went to school with her! And she wrote

such an awfully nice letter to Mr Price's sister!"

"My dear girl, the letter and Mr Price's sister and the wrong address were all invented by Mr Price!"

"You mean there wasn't any trip abroad, and Mrs Wigham doesn't live at 964 Park Avenue, and there isn't any little girl?"

" 'Not even a puppy, Pip,' " Mr Marbury quoted. "Let us say goodbye to Mrs Wigham once for all, and take up a much more important matter, how best to protect you from danger."

"Danger?" she faltered. "You mean he-he may try again!"

"Just so," Marbury nodded reluctantly. "At least the possibility should be taken into consideration. From what you tell us, this man Price seems to have made more than one attempt on your life."

"But why? Why should he want to?"

"That is something we still have to find out. But you had a narrow escape last night. Fortunately, Jim here was following Price's car and reached the cottage in the nick of time."

"How did you know I was in danger, Mr Northcote?"

"Well, it was like this," Northcote began, drawing his chair closer to hers. "I happened to meet Mrs Benson just as..."

"One moment, Jim," Marbury protested. "There's our next move still to consider. We must find a place where she will be safe."

"You mean I can't go back to Aunt Henrietta?" she cried.

"Not for the present, I'm afraid."

"But what am I to tell her?"

"Could you say that the Wigham arrangement has fallen through, but that another equally good position is in sight?"

"Oh, is there something else?"

"We'll find something. Would that satisfy Miss Sands?"

"It wouldn't if she were well. But she is in bed with a bad cold, and Emma, our maid, gets telephone messages rather mixed up. Shall I say that I am here, Mr Marbury?"

"Well," Marbury hesitated, "I don't like asking you to keep anything from your aunt. But this is a very difficult situation. I am afraid you will just have to trust us, my dear."

"I do trust you," Laura smiled. "Anyway, there's no hurry about Aunt Henrietta. Mr Price sent her a telegram from the hotel last evening. So if I could get a job pretty soon Mrs Benson might hear of something…"

"The Bensons must be kept out of it," Northcote put in. "Price knows about the Bensons. If he discovers his nice little plot has gone wrong and you are still alive, he will go there to inquire."

Laura caught her breath in terror, the suggestion seemed to give a horrible reality to her danger and she was on the edge of tears as she gasped "But what am I to do? I can't go back to Aunt Henrietta and the Bensons mustn't know. Oh, where am I to go! What am I to do?"

"You are to stay here, my dear child," Marbury took her hand gently in his. "Here in this house, where you will be perfectly safe, until all your difficulties are over." She wiped her eyes and managed a faint smile, as he went on anxiously: "It will be rather dull, I'm afraid. You won't be able to go out. But there are plenty of books, and the garden… Could you bear to stay on here quietly for a day or two?"

"I could, indeed!" She was laughing now. "You're an angel to let me stay. I can't begin to tell you how."

"That's all settled then," he broke in. "By the way, you must have had some luggage. What became of it?"

"Oh, dear!" she sighed. "I had my weekend bag in the car with me last night – I'm afraid that's gone for good. And I've lost my wrist bag too, and my hat. But my trunk was left in the station. It's still there, I suppose."

"I'll send for it at once. Have you the baggage check?"

"Oh, yes. Aunt Henrietta pinned the check and my money inside the pocket of my coat. I'm rather apt to leave my wrist bag lying around."

"Then I shall send to the station and..."

"Is that wise?" Northcote broke in. "Price knows the trunk is in the baggage room. He may be watching, ready to follow anyone who comes for it, and..."

"Most unlikely," Marbury put in soothingly, for Laura had whitened. "But we'll leave the trunk where it is for the present, just to be on the safe side. Make a list of what you need, and Sarah will be delighted to shop for you. And now, St. George," he turned to Northcote, "you may get on with the story you are so anxious to tell, and the damsel so obviously impatient to hear. You have the floor – fire away!"

16

"Dark cottage, battered and decayed."

WALLER

It's the most thrilling story I ever heard!" Mrs Lansing cried. "You say she is young and attractive?"

"A thoroughly nice girl." Northcote said. "Plenty of sense, awfully healthy and all that." I must make Laura sound like a nursery governess, he reflected. "Ought to get on splendidly with the children."

"Of course she will. I'll be delighted to have her."

"You're awfully kind, Edith. I can't tell you how grateful I am. Marbury and I were at our wits' end when I thought of you."

"Always glad to oblige an old friend, Jim. It's settled then. Miss Sands is to go down to Oyster Bay next week with Daphne and Muriel and stay with them as long as she likes. She won't have too much responsibility, for my sister Bertha will be there too while I'm off on the yacht. I suppose I ought to see your protégé and talk things over. Could she come tomorrow?"

"Good God, Edith, didn't I tell you she was in hiding!"

"And can't go out for fear of her life! Too marvellously thrilling! I am to meet her at Mr Marbury's then?"

"At tea time tomorrow. You know him, so your taking tea there will excite no remark."

"You have thought of every detail! I feel as if I were stepping right into the middle of an Edgar Wallace. Would it be a good idea for me to wear a false nose? Or a wig?"

"Now Edith! If you can't take this thing seriously…"

"I was only teasing you! Don't worry, Jim. I'll be there at five sharp tomorrow."

Mrs Lansing kept her word. The tea party went off very nicely. Mrs Lansing approved of Laura. Laura – after a moment's awe-struck contemplation of Mrs Lansing's make-up, not of the New England type – liked and admired Mrs Lansing. It was all arranged. Laura was to meet the children and their aunt at the Long Island Station the following Thursday at three o'clock, go with them to Oyster Bay and stay there as long as it seemed best for her to remain in seclusion.

"It may be only a few days," Northcote remarked. "We are employing detectives, and they ought to get Price into jail without much difficulty."

"What sort of creature is this Price?" Mrs Lansing asked. "Beetling brow and a wild eye, I suppose? Frightfully wicked?"

"No, indeed," Laura said. "Mr Price doesn't look at all wicked."

"What does he look like then?"

"That's what everybody keeps asking me! But I can't describe him. You know how it is. There are some people that when you are away from them you can shut your eyes and see them just as clearly as if they were in front of you. Well, Mr Price is one of the ones you can't. I don't know what he looks like – he might as well have no face! I'd recognize him, of course, if I saw him again."

"Unless he were disguised," Northcote remarked.

"Disguised?"

"Whiskers, perhaps, and spectacles."

"And a false nose," Mrs Lansing put in. "I insist that somebody ought to wear a false nose! Don't frown at me, Jim, I'll be good. Laura, can you drive a car?"

"Not very well."

"It doesn't matter, Patrick will have very little to do while I'm away."

"I think," Marbury put in, "that it would be safer for Laura not to go off the place by herself, Edith. Could Patrick, or one of the other men servants, accompany her?"

"Of course! I can't seem to believe the danger is real. Don't worry, your young lady will be guarded as if she were diamonds. Goodbye, Laura. I'm sailing on Tuesday so I shan't see you again till I get back – God knows when! A month? A year? I never decide anything before hand. Anyway, have a good time. Don't let the children bore you to death. Goodbye, Mr Marbury. Goodbye, Jim. If a cruise should happen to appeal to either of you between now and Tuesday, don't bother to let me know. Just come aboard!"

"How kind she is," Laura murmured, as Edith Lansing fluttered away. "I didn't suppose there were so many kind people in the world – or such horrid ones either," she added with a shudder. "Oh, well, I'm going to forget that disgusting Mr Price as quickly as I can. What's the use of remembering loathsome things? Is there a Mr Lansing?"

"Bertram Lansing – your aunt would know the name – died some years ago. He was a banker."

"Good! Aunt Henrietta likes bankers. But she's going to like everything about this job. Would it be all right for me to call her up now?"

"One moment," Northcote put in, as she was moving to the telephone. "Before you mention Mrs Lansing ask Emma whether Mr Price has been seen in Derby Centre since you left. If he has, don't give Emma Mrs Lansing's name and warn her not to have anything to do with him."

"All right," she nodded, and took up the receiver. A moment later she and Emma were in conversation. Miss Sands was reported better but still in bed. "Has Mr Price been back, Emma?" Laura went on... "He has?" She gave Northcote a startled glance. "Well, if he comes again, don't tell him I called up. You see, Emma, I, I, well, to tell the truth Emma – you needn't mention it to Aunt Henrietta – but Mr Price isn't – isn't as nice as we thought he was... Yes. That's what I meant. He got too – too friendly in the train the other day, and…Yes… Yes… Love to Aunt Henrietta. I'll call up again tomorrow. Goodbye."

"I had to say something," she explained, blushing pink as the men nodded their amused approval. "I had to give Emma a reason she would understand. She understood, all right. Goodness, how shocked she was!"

"When did Price come?"

"Early this morning. In a car. He asked for Miss Sands and Emma said she was too ill to see him."

"Did he say anything about you?"

"No. Emma asked him how I was, and he said, 'Fine.' Then he went away."

"So far so good. You managed it awfully well," Northcote remarked. "But I must be going now. Goodbye, Laura. See you tomorrow."

He turned away, but gave Marbury a meaningful glance as he left the room, and they went downstairs together.

"Things have taken a nasty turn," Northcote said, as soon as they were out of earshot.

Mr Marbury nodded. "Price-Green is evidently on the trail."

"Has he returned to the deserted cottage and discovered that Laura is not dead?"

"He wouldn't risk being seen in that neighbourhood unless it were absolutely necessary. But I got thinking the whole thing over last night, and this visit of Price-Green's to Derby Centre convinces me I am right. He has made one fatal mistake. He realizes it now, and will try to rectify it."

"A mistake?"

"Yes. A fatal mistake. Fatal, that is, to his expectations as heir to a fortune in Australia. You remember that Mr Angus Bell of Dumfries said in his letter that Donald Bell's adopted son, Percy McGuire, would not inherit the fortune unless it turned out that all the descendants of Bell of Irongray were dead and the family extinct. Now, according to our theory, McGuire came at once to this country bent on killing off every one of these inconvenient heirs. He succeeded in tracing them – much sooner than we did, of course, for he probably knew most of the names. Then he set to work. Makes you sick to think of the beast spying out the poor things, one after the other – creeping up on them – making friends – sinking his claws into them – pulling them down – God! When I think how near he came to getting Laura..."

"But he didn't get her," Marbury put in soothingly. "Thanks to you. Go on, Jim. Where did Price-Green make a mistake? His technique seems to me to have been flawless."

"It was – up to a certain point. He was able to get rid of Mrs Beaumont, old Starkweather and the Robinsons without much difficulty – he didn't have to bother with the Prides; they were dead already. But when it came to disposing of Laura he made a bad mistake. He forgot that her death wouldn't do him any good unless he could prove it! And how is he going to prove she is dead, unless her body is found?"

"You're right! But why didn't he think of that in the first place?"

"He was taken by surprise, and didn't have time to plan the crime properly. He had expected Laura to eat the poisoned chocolate and die in the Grand Central Station after he had left her. He was probably watching from a distance – she spoke of some man with a moustache, you remember – and when nothing happened, and the Bensons turned up, all he could do was to get their address – he probably tipped a porter to follow them to their taxi. Then, next day, he hung about the Bensons' house, hoping for a chance to speak to Laura, and got it."

"That sounds plausible. But why take her to that cottage?"

"Because he was in a hurry. When Laura slipped away from him, he had to concoct a new plan on the spur of the moment. He thought of that deserted house – must have seen it driving by some time or other, drove out there with a tank of gas – you remember John Robinson was killed with gas; hid it in a cupboard; connected it – probably by a rubber tube pushed through a crack in the door, and got back to New York in time to pick up Laura at the Bensons'. But it was quick work. He had to hurry like hell."

"And you think that, in his hurry, he forgot that Laura's body would have to be found?"

"I do. Now then, why did Price-Green go to Derby Centre? Because, believing her to be dead, and knowing he had to produce her body in order to inherit, he went there to prepare Miss Sands – in some way that we can't guess at present – for her niece's death."

"But he would have to go to the cottage in the end."

"Not necessarily. He might put someone up to finding the body accidentally, though I fail to see how he could manage that without arousing suspicion. Sending someone to get it would be riskier still. No, I think you're right. He will have to go himself. Not at once, perhaps, but before long he will go to the cottage expecting to get the body and deposit it in some place where it is sure to be found. You see what this means? The cottage must be watched by our detectives. So they can catch him when he turns up."

"Can you tell them how to find it?"

"No, I can't. It will be hard enough to find it myself. But I'll get Burchall, the taxi man, and start first thing tomorrow morning – we couldn't find the road at night. I'll take a couple of shotguns along. There are pheasants in those woods and I have a shooting license, so the police won't object."

"You think it's as well to be armed in case you find McGuire – alias Price-Green – at the cottage?"

"Just so. I'll be going now. If our detective agency turns out as good as it's said to be, a month ought to be enough for them to trace our man."

"They will make inquiries in Australia, of course? McGuire, the adopted son, must be well known in Adelaide, and if he and Green the butler prove to be one and the same individual we've got the noose around his neck."

"We have. And that sort of technical information is what a

detective ought to get easily enough."

"In the meantime, Laura is perfectly safe here. Price-Green didn't learn her address from Emma, nor has he any idea that you and I are interested in the case."

"Thank heaven for that. I'm off."

It was not yet dawn when Northcote and Burchall started out next morning. The streets were almost empty of traffic; sidewalks deserted. As they ran along Riverside Drive the landscape was still steeped in shadow; the river dim blue, the farther shore dark grey, striped with the pale lines of the Palisades. But as they crossed the George Washington Bridge and moved rapidly westward, the sun rose and thrust long pointing fingers of light on the highroad ahead.

"We timed it just right," Northcote remarked. "We shall have broad day for our mountain road. The corner where the Chrysler turned off the other night must be pretty near now."

"Here it is." Burchall stopped.

"Are you sure? Let me look at my road map."

"That mountain road ain't on no map. Nothing but a cart track."

"The map shows a road angling off from this corner, running north for five miles, swinging round to the east and ending in a dotted line. I believe you're right."

"Sure, I'm right! I kept tabs on my mileage the other night and we was just about here when that feller stopped the first time."

"That settles it. Go ahead."

"Roadbed feels just like it ought to," Burchall remarked with satisfaction, after they had gone some five miles. "We had it pretty good for a ways, then came the rocks. Here they are. Good road swings east. We go north. God! Some hill, ain't it!"

"I don't see how you made it in the dark."

"Don't know as light helps any. Just shows you there's hell ahead. Here's a crossroads. Which way do we go?"

"Straight on, I think, beside the brook. I remember hearing a brook close to the road during a lull in the storm."

"O.K."

The car bumped and lurched along. It was day now, a sunshiny day, warm and still.

"This is the hilltop where we waited so long when the Chrysler broke down," Northcote remarked. "I remember that boulder. Your headlights shone on it just before you switched them off."

"That's so. Then we got two hills more, one short and one awful long, and you're at the cottage."

"Right. Stop just before you reach it, so I can look the ground over."

"O.K."

Ten minutes more, and Northcote said:

"There it is! At least I think it's the house. Stop here until we make sure."

Burchall stopped. They were almost at the foot of the hill. A house was in plain sight.

"That's it," Northcote said. "There are the gate posts, and the gravel driveway, and the house a little way back just as mouldy and dismal as I remember it. Now, I'll tell you my plan, Burchall. You take one gun and I'll take the other. You wait behind that tree down there – the big elm – with your gun cocked, while I go along the drive, and as soon as I get to the corner of the house, you pop over to the maple, the one that's turning red so that you can keep me covered. Do you understand?"

"Sure. First the elm, then the maple. But what do I do, if I see some feller hanging round like he was dangerous?"

"I don't believe you will. The house is probably empty. If anyone does show up, use your own judgment."

"What if I see a guy drawing a bead on you?"

"Get ahead of him. Wing him before he gets me."

"O.K. I'll go to my elm."

Northcote went up the driveway, the shotgun in the crook of his arm, gazing at the forbidding facade, with its broken down piazza and overhanging curtain of vines as gloomy in the sunlight as in darkness. Queer how frightened I was the other night, he thought. I suppose it was because of Laura. Now I'm alone I feel as calm as a clock and yet I'm a fine mark for Price-Green, if he is crouching behind one of those broken window panes.

He walked on, reached the corner of the house, looked back, and saw with satisfaction that Burchall was hurrying from the elm to the maple.

On the doorstep he paused and bent, looking for the bunch of violets. It was gone!

After a moment's hesitation, he pushed open the door and entered. All was exactly as he remembered it; rusty stove, peeling wallpaper, dirty floor, lamp on a rickety table. The door to the inner room where he had found Laura stood wide open. Yet he was almost sure that, because of the gas, he had slammed both doors behind him as he hurried out carrying Laura into the open air.

He looked into the room. There against the farther wall Laura had lain, a shapeless motionless bundle wound around with rope. And he seemed to remember something else lying on the floor beside her – a small dark object – a hat! Laura's hat, of course, he remembered it perfectly. It was in the corner. There was no hat anywhere to be seen now!

So Price-Green had been here. He had taken away the bunch of violets and the hat, and the tank of gas too, of course. Useless to look for that now. Price-Green had come and gone.

Northcote walked out of the house and beckoned to Burchall, who joined him with an air of disappointment.

"We're too late," Northcote said.

"Guy's been and gone?"

"I fancy so. Let's see if we can find any footprints or wheel tracks in the road."

"Won't show much. These mountain roads is all gravel and rocks."

"Here's a patch of mud, right in front of the gate. No footprints or wheel tracks, though. But the ground has queer marks on it, as if some animal had been scratching in the mud. It looks to me as if our man had left some prints here and tried to obliterate them."

"We better go on till we come to more mud. He can't of stopped to scratch mud every time he ran into a puddle."

They got into the car and went on, watching for damp ground. Within a quarter of a mile the road turned sharp to the east.

"Go slow," Northcote said. "This is where he turned off after he left the cottage that night. You remember we saw his lights going eastward?"

"Yeah. And he was running fast. You can see where he skidded and came near getting ditched as he took the turn. Ground is awful slimy too. A wonder he made it."

They both got out and examined the wheel tracks grooved deep into the moist soil along the edge of the ditch and fading out on the shaly ground ahead. Burchall gave a grunt of satisfaction. "Them's his tires," he said. "I could swear to them. His rears didn't match. Old Goodyear on the left, and a new Firestone on the right. I noticed them when I got pretty close coming over the bridge."

"That settles it then. We'll go home."

"No use turning round, I guess. This is the way he went that night and I bet he knew the quickest road out."

"Let's try it. We can't get a worse road and we may strike the main highway sooner."

They did. Within half an hour they were out on the turnpike, headed for the bridge. Another half hour and Northcote was ringing Mr Marbury's door bell.

17

"O'er bog or steep, through strait, rough, dense or rare,
With head, hands, wings, or feet, pursues his way,
And swims, or sinks, or wades or creeps, or flies."

MILTON

"So, you had your trip for nothing," Marbury sighed, as Northcote finished his story. "No use trying to catch Price-Green at the deserted cottage now."

"No, he won't go back. But my trip wasn't for nothing by a long shot! We know something we were not sure of before. Price-Green has learned that Laura is not dead, and will act accordingly."

"Mightn't he think someone had found the body and removed it – a farmer's boy, people taking shelter from a storm?"

"Anything as startling as that would have got into the newspapers by now. No. I think he realizes she has been rescued in some mysterious way – just how, must puzzle him considerably – and is still alive."

"And he will try to find her."

"Undoubtedly. His first step was to inquire at Derby Centre."

"He didn't get her address there."

"No, he didn't. She is safe for the time being. He doesn't suspect either you or me, so he can't trace her to this house."

"What about letting her go to Oyster Bay?"

"Better make one change in our program. A car would be less risky than going in the train. I'll take her there myself and…" He broke off.

Laura – a charming figure, in white, her hair shining in the sunlight – was coming toward them across the grass. As she reached their bench, Northcote remarked:

"A pretty frock, Laura. White suits you. I'd like to paint you just as you are now. White frock and green leaves. Deep gold chrysanthemums and pale gold hair. We have a few quiet days ahead of us; will you pose for me?"

"I'd love to! But aren't you painting Mr Marbury?"

"My portrait can wait," Marbury put in. "An excellent idea, Jim. Let's begin tomorrow. I hope the weather holds."

It did. The next morning passed pleasantly and peacefully. Peacefully and pleasantly, that is, for Laura and Jim Northcote. Mr Marbury's anxiety was too great for enjoyment, although Laura's chair had been placed in a corner screened by shrubs and was supposed to be safe from observation. Marbury found his young friends' high spirits, under the circumstances, most surprising. There Laura sat, gazing placidly at Northcote placidly painting. The sun shone, sparrows twittered, chrysanthemums scattered bright petals on the grass. They talked and laughed, as if Price-Green had never existed. And yet, Mr Marbury thought, Jim knows well enough that bushes are not bullet proof. For all we know, Price-Green is crouching behind a chimney on one of those roof tops at this very moment. Jim and Laura have forgotten that she is in mortal danger. They have forgotten everything but themselves. What a thing it is to be young... Well, I for one shall be mighty glad when next Thursday comes and I see Laura and Jim starting off for Oyster Bay.

But sun and air worked their usual soothing spell. Marbury began to relax; Laura and her troubles had been nearly forgotten in drowsy contentment when Sarah came hurrying out of the house, obviously in a state of agitation.

He sprang to his feet and met her, as she got out a breathless: "You're wanted, sir! In the pantry!"

"In the pantry? Oh, dear, the plumbing, I suppose," he sighed, and followed her indoors.

Lizzie, the cook, was waiting for him with gloom on her face and a saucer in her hand, regarding its contents – two small white balls – with extreme disfavour.

"Just cast your eye on these here mushrooms, sir," she said. "Sarah thinks they look sort of queer like..." Marbury bent over the saucer, adjusting his pince-nez. One glance was enough.

"Toadstools!" he exclaimed. Sarah smiled proudly.

"How on earth did they get here, Lizzie?"

"With the rest of the pound in that there till, sir."

She indicated a container overflowing with mushrooms standing on the table. "Binder's boy he brought 'em – brought 'em late too. I called him down good and plenty. He's got a girl at fifty-two, and..."

"About the mushrooms, Lizzie," Marbury broke in. "They must be disposed of. All of them – not just those two. Don't put them in the garbage can, but into the incinerator – just to be on the safe side," he added reassuringly, and hurried out of doors again to Northcote's corner of the garden.

"Bad news, Jim!" he muttered. "Go on painting, mustn't attract Laura's attention."

"What's happened?" Northcote whispered, giving him a horrified glance, still painting busily.

"God! You're as white as a sheet."

"I've had a shock. That devil has been too clever for us, Jim. He has traced Laura to this house!"

"Good God! But how?"

Marbury raised his voice: "Laura looks tired. Isn't it time she had a rest?"

Northcote took the hint. "Laura," he called, waving his mahlstick. "That's enough for today. Light's changed."

She came running across the grass. They stood for a moment before the easel, admiring and criticizing.

Then Marbury said: "Sarah has been shopping for you, Laura.

Don't you want to try on her purchases?"

She hesitated. But after a final, "You're simply marvellous, Jim, I don't see how you do it!" she turned away. They watched her stroll toward the house in a fury of impatience, and the instant she was out of earshot, Northcote exclaimed:

"You say Price-Green knows she is here? How, in God's name, can you be sure of that? What..."

"Listen, Jim, Sarah called me in just now to show me some mushrooms that were being prepared for lunch. She thought two of them looked like toadstools. She was right. They are specimens of the Deadly Amanita. Immature; full grown they do not resemble our ordinary edible mushroom, Campestris."

"You mean they're poisonous?"

"There is enough poison in one Amanita to kill sixteen persons!"

"Good God! And you think they were meant for Laura? But mightn't they have been picked by mistake?"

"That could happen only with wild mushrooms, these were cellar grown."

"How can you tell?"

"My dear Jim. How can you tell your cobalt from your indigo? These are the sort one usually buys in the city and came from our usual grocer. But I gather, from a remark of my cook's, that the grocer's boy is apt to linger in a neighbouring house. His cart may have been left unguarded in the street..."

"I get you," Northcote groaned. "But how did Price-Green trace her? How?"

"Well, Green the butler knows me, of course, and he may have seen you without your realizing it. Jane may have said something that made him suspect we were investigating Clare Beaumont's death."

"Jane would keep her mouth shut."

"William then, or one of the maids."

"Even so, how could he connect us with Laura? He didn't get

the address of this house when he went to Derby Centre, for Emma didn't know it herself."

"She might have spoken of your having been there."

"Why should she? Price wouldn't ask, and... I have it!" Northcote exclaimed. "I know what happened! When I called on Miss Sands I gave Emma my card. She put it on the hall table. While Price-Green was talking to Emma he saw it, alluded to it, found out that I'd been asking for Laura. Guessed something was up. Found out where I lived. Hung about. Followed me to this house. Rented a room in one of the boarding houses on the next block that overlook the garden – and saw Laura!"

Marbury nodded. "You've got it. I wonder where he found those Amanitas. It might be possible to trace them. Shall I speak to the grocer?"

"Better leave that to our detectives. It may be fairly easy to trace those toadstools, for Price-Green is evidently getting reckless. In all his previous attempts he not only contrived to cover his tracks, but he was careful to aim at one particular victim. Now this mushroom affair shows utter disregard of consequences. He doesn't care how many people he kills. If he had succeeded, not only Laura but the whole household – you and me and even the servants, if they like mushrooms – would have been poisoned. Think of the risk of killing half a dozen people at one blow! I tell you, Marbury, Price-Green is deteriorating intellectually. His complex is getting the upper hand. This last effort has every earmark of homicidal mania, to my mind!"

"An appalling idea. How can we protect Laura from a maniac?"

"That's something we have to work out. The Oyster Bay plan must be given up, of course."

"We might send a detective to guard her."

"Even so, I'm not sure... I tell you what we'll do: ask Edith Lansing to take Laura off on the yacht!"

"But she's sailing tomorrow! And taking Laura would mean taking the children..."

"That doesn't matter – the children like yachting – and Edith fairly revels in quick changes. 'Anything for an unquiet life,' is Edith's motto. I don't envy her captain! The Aspasia goes wandering up and down the coast like a lost child, and Edith is forever changing her mind about going ashore. But this vagueness is all to the good in Laura's case; it will be her best safeguard. Price-Green can't trace a yacht that doesn't know where it's going! The cruise will end eventually, of course; probably at Edith's Florida plantation. But that won't be for another six weeks at least and Price-Green will be in jail by then if Driver and Merk are any good as sleuths."

"Miss Henrietta Sands may object..."

"Object to her niece's taking a trip with Mrs Bertram Lansing? Nonsense! But we're wasting time. Come on, old man!" He seized Marbury by the arm and trotted him full speed across the lawn and into the house. "Now you go and tell Laura and tell her to call up her aunt and tell Sarah to buy her a lot more shorts and slacks and whatnot and I'll call up Edith and I must see Driver and Merk – they will have to go over the Aspasia with a fine tooth comb before she sails, of course, and make sure there're no infernal machines anywhere about, and provide a detective who can go along as a deck hand or a steward..."

They were at the library door now. Northcote made for the telephone, and Marbury, dazed but willing, went on upstairs to Laura's room.

The next twenty-four hours were the most strenuous of Mr Marbury's life. What with Laura's excitement, Sarah's fussing, Northcote's running in and out and Edith Lansing's incessant telephoning, there were moments when he felt turmoil and anxiety would be the death of him. But Tuesday morning dawned at last, and midday found him standing beside Northcote on a North River pier waving farewell to the Aspasia. They watched her slim white shape move out over the blue water of the harbour. She dwindled, smaller and smaller... Vanished... They turned away.

"What a relief!" Marbury sighed. "Dear little Laura! I was never so glad to bid goodbye to anyone in all my life! What horrors we have endured since yesterday! Examining every scrap of food that came into the house for fear it might be poisoned! Keeping Laura away from the windows for fear Price-Green might take a pot shot at her!"

"Pretty hectic," Northcote agreed. "But my drive with Laura to the pier was even worse. I was chattering with fright the whole time! Suspicious trucks darting out at me from side streets. Suspicious taxis following behind – sidewalks alive with upraised hands flinging bombs – Lord! I came near bursting into tears of thankfulness when I got her across the gangplank and safe on board!"

"Well, it's all over now." Marbury said comfortably. "We can stop thinking about dear little Laura for a while. She is safe."

"I hope so," Northcote sighed. "Driver and Merk went over the list of guests and interviewed every member of the crew, and the detective they are sending – man named Curry – struck me as both honest and intelligent. But I feel as if I ought to have gone with her myself. Do you suppose I could catch the Aspasia at Quarantine?" He came to a dead stop – they had reached the street where his car was waiting. "Hire a fast launch and..."

"Don't be morbid, Jim!" Marbury exclaimed. "You are needed here. Price-Green is still at large. You and I have done our best and man can do no more. You've got to leave *something* to Providence," he added, and mounted firmly into the car.

18

*"A thousand fantasies
Begin to throng into my memory,
Of calling shapes, and beckoning shadows dire.*

MILTON

Six weeks later Marbury and Northcote were again standing together on a wharf looking out on the water. But this long rickety finger of boards wandering feebly out from a green shore was very unlike the massive structure dark with smoke where they had watched Mrs Lansing's yacht move away in the distance, and this river, the St. John's, was as unlike the Hudson as any vast estuary well could be. There it lay, stretching itself languidly in the hot sunshine, supine as one of its own alligators. Miles and miles of golden glass, empty of traffic, under a pale sky empty of clouds. The air so still that you could hear the cows on the shore, nipping at the water hyacinths as they came, and the sucking slush of their hoofs in the mud, long before they rounded the point.

A bluish haze veiled land and water, broken only by an occasional sharp flick of colour as cardinal or jay winged in and out of the live oaks and magnolias that half hid the white facade of Mrs Lansing's house. The incoming tide stroked the sides of the canoes moored at the wharf so gently that the sighing swish was a lullaby. It was very hot. Marbury and Northcote gazed at the islands of water hyacinth drifting up the river, too sleepy for conversation although they had not met for three weeks.

"Let's sit down," Marbury yawned. "The Aspasia won't be here for some time. We can see her miles away." They sat down on a bench, and again relapsed into silence.

"A soothing landscape," Northcote remarked at length. "Our anxieties seem like a bad dream here, and Price-Green a bogie left behind in the North."

"But our responsibilities will descend upon us again the moment Laura steps on shore!" Marbury sighed. "I wish this yachting trip could have been indefinitely prolonged."

"You wouldn't want Laura to be kept out at sea forever like the traitor in Hale's story! As for our responsibilities, they practically came to an end when Driver and Merk succeeded in tracing Green the butler. If they are right in believing him aboard ship bound for Australia, he must have abandoned his pursuit of Laura and she is no longer in danger. However, on the off chance of some slip up, Curry is to stay on to guard Laura until we hear that Green – otherwise McGuire – is actually under arrest."

"A wise precaution," Marbury nodded. "You have found Curry satisfactory?"

"Oh, yes. He seems to have played the role of deck steward so well that no one on the yacht suspected he was a detective, and whenever Laura went ashore he always went too, ready to ward off suspicious strangers. He is to help Patrick in the garage, while he is here, and look after the canoes, so that his presence won't excite comment."

"I gather that Laura has enjoyed the trip."

"Immensely," Northcote growled. "Dancing half the night. Deck tennis and shuffleboard and bathing all day. Don't see how she found time for the children's lessons."

"Edith wrote that she was delighted with Laura and had grown very fond of her."

"Who wouldn't be? I bet Bob Grayson and Callender and that little bounder what's-his-name have grown more than *fond* by now. God! I'm glad this damn trip is over."

"The young men you speak of are leaving the yacht at Jacksonville, I believe."

"They are, thank God. Look!" Northcote sprang to his feet.

"There comes the Aspasia now! And coming fast. She'll be here in five minutes."

"In time for tea," Marbury remarked with satisfaction.

Northcote whipped out a handkerchief and began waving furiously. "They see us," he cried. "They're waving back."

A cackle of laughter rang out from the house, followed by the patter of many feet as the servants came hurrying along the wharf – every one of them, from the cook in her flat starched cap down to the youngest child balancing itself unsteadily on small toes. All laughing, all eagerly expectant.

"Welcome home, Missis! Welcome home!" they cried, waving aprons and bandanas.

"Welcome home, Miss Daphne and Miss Muriel! Welcome home!"

The yacht swept around, sidled slowly to the wharf. A dozen hands caught at the gangplank as it was pushed out. The two children came first, galloping down in an ecstasy of delight, spinning about dangerously near the edge, with Laura running full tilt in pursuit.

Jim Northcote caught her halfway. "Laura!" he cried. "Laura!"

She stopped, smiling up at him. "Hello, Jim," she said. "Isn't Florida lovely!"

"Lovely. What a fine tan you've got! Hello, Edith!"

"Hello, Jim! How are you, Mr Marbury? Well, I've brought your girl back to you safe and sound. Daphne, behave yourself. Come along, everybody. I am dying for my tea."

Another day came, as warm and still and sleepy as the last. The sun blazed down out of a cloudless sky. The tides washed idly back and forth under the wharf, islands of water hyacinth drifted away from their moorings among the cypress knees, drifted in again. But the river – or rather, the stretch of river overlooked by Mrs Lansing's house – was no longer silent and empty of life.

The yacht lay at anchor on the edge of the channel, so near that Mr Marbury, stepping out on the verandah after breakfast, could hear the voices of the crew as they swabbed down the decks. Curry stood on the wharf bending over a canoe. As it took the water, Mr Marbury started involuntarily – the sharp splash had been too like the report of a gun! Then the children's bright figures came galloping across the lawn and along the wharf. Laura followed them. Jim Northcote followed her. Another canoe was launched.

A pretty sight, Marbury thought, as the gaily painted canoes circled about on the water. Bright spray rose in a fountain as Daphne slapped the water with her paddle, laughing. They were all laughing and calling to each other, all, that is, except Curry. Curry, a thick set young man with a pleasant face sat silent on the bench at the end of the wharf, watching.

Marbury joined him.

"A peaceful scene," Marbury remarked. "So peaceful that danger seems impossible. But I observe that you never relax your vigilance and keep pretty close to Miss Sands until she goes upstairs at night."

"That's what I'm here for, Mr Marbury," Curry said. "As for danger, the most careful watching can't keep Miss Sands half as safe here as she was on the yacht."

"But I thought your firm had traced Green the butler on the way to Australia!"

"They think they have. But I'm not so sure myself. We found the family he worked for when Mrs Beaumont's establishment was broken up, and the lodging house in New York where he stayed later on. At both places we got a hint of his being a bad egg, and a fairly good description of his appearance."

"Green had no salient characteristics, as I remember him."

"None that you would have noticed, Mr Marbury. But it seems he was bald and wore a wig. That was a help to us. We took up his trail again at a steamship office where he had inquired about a passage to Australia. We got a check up of several likely vessels, and finally through wireless found a passenger, answering to Green's general description, reported by a steward to be bald headed and wearing a wig."

"That is pretty convincing. Why are you worried?"

"I am worried because I don't see why McGuire, alias Green, should go home leaving his work in this country unfinished. Laura Sands is still alive!"

"You think the man on the ship is not Green and, therefore, not McGuire? That would mean that the murderer is still in this country and expects to stay till Laura is dead!" Marbury shuddered. "He is not discouraged, is waiting for another opportunity?"

"I do."

"But this large plantation ought to be very nearly as safe as the yacht; there isn't another house for miles around."

"Those cabins aren't houses, I suppose," Curry said dryly. "But people live in them. People that go back and forth from cabin to kitchen, chattering about everything that goes on in the big house, gossiping with neighbours farther away. The neighbours gossip too. Why, Mr Marbury, I bet that not a thing happens in the big house that isn't known from Jacksonville to Palatka within twenty four hours."

"Surely you don't suspect any of the staff of being in McGuire's pay!"

"No, indeed. Patrick the chauffeur and Mrs Lansing's maid have both lived with her for years. The others are of a fine type – loyal and affectionate. But I can't keep track of them! Every time I look into the kitchen or the garage there's a girl or boy I haven't seen before. Now on the yacht, when I once got the personnel checked up I could rest easy. I can't here."

"Not even when your charge is in plain sight as she is now?"

"No. A good shot could pick her off from the shore with a rifle as if she was a bird."

"Not without being caught."

"Right. But there's a type of criminal – the kind that assassinates kings and dictators – don't seem to care a damn whether they get caught or not."

"You think McGuire may be of that type? But surely his crimes have been carefully planned with a view to escape."

"The first ones were. But I have been reading over Mr Northcote's notes, and I agree with him. There is a conspicuous progression in recklessness. As he expresses it: 'hate seems to be getting the best of greed.'"

"Have you discussed that aspect of the case with him?"

"Haven't had the chance. If you'll excuse the remark, Mr Northcote is so interested in the young lady herself that he seems to have forgotten the danger she is in."

"I happen to be less carefree," Marbury smiled, "so I have a few questions to ask. When your firm got in touch with the police in Adelaide, did they learn anything new about Mr Donald Bell and his adopted son, McGuire?"

"In the main, only what you already know – a large fortune left to be distributed among the various heirs of Bell of Irongray. If the family is extinct all goes to adopted son Percy McGuire. But we got an interesting side light on McGuire – a jack of all trades if ever there was one! Tried the stage, studied law, veered to medicine and was doing well when he happened to add forgery to his other activities! This was too much for old Donald Bell; hence that most peculiar will. Lobden and Lobden, the lawyers in charge of the estate, have been making inquiries by letter as to the whereabouts of any possible heirs without success, and finally decided to send a man to this country to try to trace them. But that was only a few weeks ago; they haven't heard from him yet. McGuire himself left Adelaide immediately after his adopted father's death and is supposed to be travelling."

"Then he must have started out to exterminate the other heirs as soon as he learned the terms of the will!"

"It looks that way."

"The Adelaide police don't know that McGuire may be wanted for murder, I suppose?"

"Oh, no. Our agent in Adelaide was warned to keep that dark.

The police think we are after Green in connection with a burglary, and don't as yet realize that we believe him to be McGuire."

"I see. Now let us go back to what you were saying with regard to the murderer's progression in recklessness. How did you arrive at your conclusions?"

"Well, to begin with, I must admit that when Mr Northcote first gave us the case, his story of a series of murders committed by one person seemed pretty fantastic. We thought he hadn't allowed enough for accident and coincidence. But when I received reports from our men sent to investigate those murders I realized there might be something in Mr Northcote's theory after all and, thinking it over, I have come to believe he is right. Not only in tracing the crimes to one man, McGuire, but in seeing a psychological change. McGuire's ego is swelling like a balloon; as Mr Northcote puts it, 'hate is getting the best of greed.' Consider the first murder, that of Mrs Beaumont. McGuire, calling himself Green, appears to have taken the position of butler in her house in order to commit a perfectly safe crime. He stole the chart, as it attracted attention to the fact that Mrs Beaumont was in line for a share of his adopted father's inheritance; poisoned the saccharine tablets, and 'planted' the suicide letter on her dressing table having probably found it thrown away in the wastepaper basket, and all without arousing the smallest suspicion. He was equally successful with the murder of Mr Robinson in Vermont – the death of the sister in New Haven may just possibly have been an accident – probably some chemical that gave off a deadly gas was slipped into the church furnace leaving no trace. We do not know how the murder of Mr Starkweather at Mountain View was brought about for the old gentleman died alone in the woods. But McGuire must have met him there and administered a poison – probably in liquor or candy or tobacco, that affected the heart. This safely accomplished, McGuire could go back to New York believing that all the Bell descendants standing between him and his inheritance were disposed of, and planning to return to Australia by the first steamer, resume the name of McGuire and claim his inheritance.

Then he got a bad jolt. Somehow – we don't know how – he discovered, as you did, Mr Marbury, this other heir, Laura Sands. It enraged him, and he went for her at once. But the method, a sky-rocket, was too melodramatic to succeed. The poisoned candy was more in his older manner, but when that also failed, he went wild and lost his head. Kidnapping a girl and leaving her tied hand and foot to perish in a lonely house was absurd, for he had to prove her death in order to inherit, and it was reckless to the point of insanity."

"The mushroom affair wasn't so bad," Marbury remarked. "I believe your firm was unable to trace those Amanitas."

"Nevertheless the attempt was very reckless, for he risked killing off your whole household as well as Miss Laura herself. But let's recapitulate and see just where we stand: McGuire has committed several murders using various aliases; Wilson when he killed Starkweather; Parker when he made away with John Robinson; Price when he came near killing Miss Laura, and Green when he poisoned Mrs Beaumont. Your theory that she must have been killed by someone who had access to her room at the time of her death is undoubtedly correct, and Green fits the bill to perfection. Now when Green lands in Australia and is arrested for theft, his career comes to an end. But until that happens we can't be sure. On the off chance that McGuire is still in this country, Miss Laura must be guarded, for he will go on planning to kill her."

"And plan recklessly!" Marbury groaned.

"You bet! There isn't going to be any 'safety first' about his next attempt, Mr Marbury. If McGuire is still hanging around making plans, I know damn well he's plotting something sensational, something queer, something that will get him a headline in the newspapers. Notoriety is all he wants now. Safety means nothing to him."

Mr. Marbury groaned again, louder than before, but his groan was drowned in a whirring sound from overhead.

Both looked up.

"See that plane?" Curry went on. "If they wanted to drop a bomb on the house all the police in New York couldn't prevent it, and... Excuse me; Miss Laura is coming ashore and I must go."

"Does she know you are a detective?"

"I told her just before we landed. She didn't seem to mind."

Mr Marbury groaned again, louder than before, but Curry descended to a lower tier of the wharf and steadied Laura's canoe as she stepped out.

"I'm going to have a driving lesson, Mr Marbury," she remarked. "Patrick is taking me out in the big car – such fun!" and she hurried away with Curry at her heels.

Dear little Laura, Mr Marbury thought, as I watched her go. Slim figure, bright hair, pink frock, silhouetted now against the dark foliage along the river bank. So young and gay and sweet. So full of life. Impossible to think of Laura as dead. And yet, at this very moment – Mr Marbury shivered, sitting there in the warm sunlight – at this very moment McGuire might be taking aim from behind the rose hedge! There would be a flash, a report and... Mr Marbury started to his feet, realizing that his talk with Curry had so increased his anxiety that he could sit still no longer. Better go into the house, find a good book and try to forget.

"Why do we have to wait, Jim?" Laura murmured. They were sitting very close together on a garden bench over-arched by a tall clump of bamboo. "Why can't we get engaged right off?"

"Aren't we engaged? Five minutes ago, you said..."

"You know what I mean. I want to tell people. Not everybody, of course. Just Edith and the children and Aunt Henrietta and Katherine and the other girls at Derby Centre. And I'd warn them it was a secret and..."

"Tell a dozen people and expect a secret not to leak out? Why, my blessed goose, it would be in the newspapers by the next morning! And you know what that would mean?"

"Mr Price would find out where I am, I suppose. Oh, dear, I'm getting frightfully tired of bothering about Mr Price. Don't you think, Jim dear, that we might take for granted he's gone away, or dead, or something?"

"We can't, duckie," Jim sighed. "Don't tempt me! Curry says that until the brute is arrested we must go on playing puss in the corner no matter how bored we get."

"But I can't stay in the corner forever," she persisted. "Suppose we don't find Mr Price for months and months? Suppose we never find him?"

"That won't happen, darling. Cheer up. Any minute now. Damn, someone is calling us."

"It's Daphne. Teatime, I suppose. We'll have to go in."

They wandered back to the house, hand in hand. Turning a corner they met Mr Marbury also moving tea ward. Laura caught his arm. "Can you keep a secret? Then bend down and I'll whisper."

She whispered. Mr Marbury laughed. "Do you call that a secret?" he said. "Why, Edith was saying just now..."

He broke off. Daphne came skipping down the garden path. She took Laura's arm and hung on it affectionately. "You look simply marvellous in pink, Laura," she exclaimed. "Don't you think she does, Mr Marbury?"

"All colours are becoming to beauty and youth," Marbury smiled. "What about the picnic? Are we going tomorrow?"

"We are, hurrah!" Daphne clutched at the branch of a camphor tree, swung herself up on a low limb, leaped down again. "We're all going. Two cars. Mr Northcote is driving one and Patrick the other, and Curry is going too to help with the baskets. I'm so glad. I just love Curry. Don't you, Laura? Don't you think Curry is perfectly sweet?"

Laura laughed. "He's very nice. Are we going to one of the beaches?"

"Yes. To San Mateo. That's the one Muriel and I like best, because of the palms and the sand dunes. If there's a fog, the palms look like tall ghosts and Muriel and I hide in the sand hollows and make believe the ghosts are coming. It's loads of fun. But it's even nicer when the sun is out, then we play we're turtles laying eggs in the sand. I do hope it will be sunny tomorrow. Don't you hope it will be sunny tomorrow, Mr Northcote, so that you can play laying eggs in the sand?"

Northcote laughed, hoped it would be sunny. They all strolled toward the house, through the garden, past the lily pond, past the sundial. Laura and Daphne talking and laughing, Mr Marbury and Jim Northcote silent, their thoughts gloomily alike.

How many hiding places this garden provided! – under those dark masses of rhododendron – at the farther side of the gazebo – behind the balustrade along the terrace. Even the white marble vase at the foot of the steps was tall enough to shelter a man with a gun.

"This picnic idea doesn't seem very safe," Marbury said to Jim in an undertone, as Laura and Daphne ran up the steps ahead of them. "Don't you think Laura had better stay at home?"

"You can't ask the poor girl to give up every bit of pleasure," Jim grumbled. "Curry is going too. He'll keep an eye on her, and so will you and I. She will be just as safe as she is here."

"Perhaps so. Nevertheless, I hope tomorrow will be a rainy day."

19

*"The creeping tide came up along the sand,
And o'er and o'er the sand,
And round and round the sand,
As far as eye could see.
The rolling mist came down and hid the land."*

KINGSLEY

Mr Marbury's wish for a rainy day was not gratified. The morning was gloriously fine. By ten o'clock the picnic baskets were being stowed away in the cars. The passengers followed after some vacillations on the children's part, for Muriel and Daphne could not decide whether they preferred to drive with Laura and Mr Northcote, or with Curry in Patrick's car. At length this was decided, in favour of Laura.

"You can go ahead, Jim," Edith said. "Patrick doesn't like to drive fast. Daphne knows the way. When you get to the shore you'll find a gap in the sand dunes where they've put down some boards, but it's pretty soft and you'd better go into second. When you are out on the beach look at your speedometer and run south for exactly a mile and a half and you'll find the place where we usually go for lunch."

"All right. Is there only one nice place?"

"Oh, no. But you can't go much further down the coast because of the quicksands. A car was swallowed up there last summer! You'll remember, won't you, Jim? A mile and a half, and then stop."

"I'll remember." Jim pressed the starter. The run about, with Laura beside him and the children in the rumble, swept around the circle and out into the driveway.

Laura and the children were in the highest spirits. The top of the car had been lowered. Muriel and Daphne could lean over from behind, prodding Laura and pointing out objects of interest along the way: the toll gate woman's new baby; Daphne's favourite gasoline station – "So funny, shaped like an alligator. Muriel's favourite is the Grape Fruit, that's funny too!" the swamp where pitcher plants bloomed first in spring. Laura looked where she was told to look, exclaimed and admired. They chattered and laughed. Their gaiety was infectious. After the first few miles Jim Northcote forgot his anxiety. He no longer slowed down at bridges searching for dangerous breaks in the boards, peered left and right when he came to crossroads, or scrutinized every thicket and clump of woods. However, such ambushes were few and far between. The road was uninteresting. But its straightness and bareness made for security and, insensibly, he relaxed, drove fast, and began to enjoy himself.

It was otherwise with Mr Marbury in the car behind. No wayside shrub was too small for him to fancy it harboured an enemy. If an airplane hovered overhead, he wondered what a falling bomb looked like, and whether you would have time to find out before it got you. Every car that passed theirs seemed bent on overtaking the runabout, dwindling now in the distance. Even the bulge in Curry's hip pocket ceased to be consoling. What's the use, Marbury thought fretfully, of a detective with a pistol, if he sits there beside Patrick, miles away from Laura. In short, never had Mr Marbury experienced such difficulty in acting the perfect guest, and he thanked his stars that Edith Lansing was so tireless a talker that an occasional "Really?" or "You don't say so?" was enough to keep the conversation going.

"Patrick is getting farther behind every minute," Daphne remarked, glancing back with satisfaction. "Mumsy won't like that. She just hates driving slowly. But she can't do anything with Patrick. He used to be our coachman years and years ago when we had horses, and Mumsy says he thinks eight miles an hour is pretty good going."

"Why does he wear those enormous goggles?" Laura asked, "and that big cap pulled down over his forehead?"

"He says the glare hurts his eyes. Muriel and I call him Froggie," Daphne giggled. "But he doesn't mind."

"Patrick is very good natured," Laura said. "He's giving me another driving lesson tomorrow. I don't back very well and…"

A shriek came from the children: "The dunes! The dunes! Stop, Mr Northcote. This is where you turn – right through that gap in the sand – it takes you right out to the beach."

The car paused, angled to the left. The children jumped up and down in an ecstasy of delight. "Look, Laura!" they cried. "There are the palm trees we told you about! Will you play hide and seek with us in the sand hills, Laura? Some of the hollows are as deep as wells and you can't see in unless you get right on the edge. Oh, how lovely and fishy the air smells!" They were through the gap now and on the beach, face to face with the sea. Jim glanced at his speedometer and turned southward.

"This is the place!" the children shrieked, jumping up and down. "Stop, Mr Northcote! Look, there's the hollow in the dunes where we always go!"

He brought the car to a standstill. Daphne and Muriel scrambled down from the rumble and made at full speed for the sand hills. Laura and Jim sat still for a moment gazing at the vast expanse spread before them. A turquoise sea heaved gently under a turquoise sky, bringing wave after wave to shore, sent them running up the sand, let them dissolve in a lacy ripple of foam and shell. The sand dunes rose and fell in hillocks of dazzling white, scattered with palm trees that gave an oriental touch to a landscape already curiously exotic in outline and colouring. North and south the beach stretched, marble smooth and almost as hard, as far as the eye could see.

"Gorgeous, isn't it?" Northcote said. "And how remote it seems. You would never guess there were rows of big hotels a little farther down the coast."

"We have it all to ourselves," Laura remarked with satisfaction. "No other picnics, anyway. Just that one Ford and a man digging clams or something. What's become of Edith's car, I wonder? Oh, here they come now!"

Lunch was over, a lunch that left the picnickers in a lethargic condition disposed for sleep. Hot sunshine was filling the dip in the sand dunes where their tablecloth had been spread, and the party scattered, some to lie flat on their faces basking in the heat, others longing for shade and a measure of coolness, shifted to the edge of the beach where they could sit comfortably propped against a sand bank facing the sea.

Among the latter was Mr Marbury. A faint damp breeze agreeably tinged with salt was drawing in from the water. His position was well chosen, head in shadow, feet in the sun. From under his hat brim he gazed sleepily at the blue sea and white beach, finding a quiet interlude after the picnic gaiety and chatter decidedly soothing. Edith and Muriel were already fast asleep. Patrick moved quietly about gathering up the remains of the meal, and then went off to his car with the baskets. Daphne, who had been helping him, sat down beside Mr Marbury but he closed his eyes and she wandered away again. A low murmur of conversation came from further along the bank where Laura and Jim Northcote sat a little withdrawn, and beyond them Curry had stationed himself, obviously wide awake and keeping watch.

Not that there was much to look at. The Lansing runabout and limousine were parked at a little distance. Further up the beach two other cars had arrived; but their occupants, harmless family groups running about on the sand, were too far away for their voices to be disturbing. Nevertheless, Mr Marbury was glad to feel Curry near and on guard. He yawned in complete relaxation, realizing that for the first time since the yacht had brought Laura up the river he was free from anxiety. Half an hour went by in quiet contentment.

Then Edith sat up, looked about her, and called to Daphne: "Do stop running around in the sun, Daphne! Try to sit still for a few minutes."

"I am sitting still," Daphne protested. "At least, I will be as soon as I tell Laura that Patrick wants her to try driving on the beach. And it isn't sunny any more. The fog is coming in."

Edith yawned and lay down again, gazing at the sea. The fog was indeed coming in. Already the horizon had vanished, muffled in a white blanket advancing as inexorably as if it were pulled to the land by invisible hands hidden behind the sand dunes. She saw the limousine move nearer and pause. Laura sprang to her feet, got into the car, and took the wheel. It turned slowly up the beach, swept around in smooth curves, halted, went on again, backed, advanced and retreated again.

"Laura will make a good driver," Northcote said to Daphne who stood beside him. "She's getting on very nicely."

"Laura is awfully good at everything. Patrick is a good teacher too. I only hope she won't catch his cold."

"Has he a cold?"

"He's getting one. When he spoke to me just now his voice was as hoarse as a crow's."

Jim, intent on Laura's manipulation of the car, scarcely heard her. Why, he asked himself idly, were Laura and Patrick changing places?

"And it wasn't only Patrick's voice that was funny," Daphne went on meditatively. "He called me Miss and Patrick never says Miss. He says Daphne, and..."

"Something funny? Good God!" Jim exclaimed, and jumped to his feet. "Curry!" he shouted, and made a dash for his car. As he leaped in and seized the wheel, Curry was beside him.

Through the fog they could see the limousine only a few yards ahead, but going fast and southward.

"He's got her!" Jim gulped, stepping on the gas. "Price... stole Patrick's goggles... Oh, my God..."

"Steady now." Curry's pistol was out and cocked. "Our car is faster. We're gaining on them."

"But the quicksand!" Jim groaned, crouched over the wheel, sweating and swearing. "The quicksand is right ahead!"

"Steady," Curry said again. "You're doing seventy. Keep to the left, so I can aim at his tires... Damn the fog!"

For a second the limousine disappeared, lost in white cloud. It emerged, nearer now. Curry fired and missed. Fired again. The car ahead shuddered. Gave a sickening leap into the air. Recovered. Went on. But haltingly, like a wounded animal. Curry's pistol cracked again. The car faltered, jerked to a stop. Jim jammed on his brakes. At the same instant a sharp report crashed out of the fog ahead of them. They saw Price's figure sag to one side, dangle over the door, and hang head down. They saw Laura spring out, lose her balance, pick herself up and come running to meet them.

One jump, and Jim had caught her in his arms. "My darling, my darling!" He held her tight. "You're all right? Are you sure? Are you sure?"

"I'm all right," she panted. "But oh, Jim, it was horrible! I recognized him. I knew it was Mr Price after the first minute. It was horrible! Worse than in the cottage!"

"Couldn't you have signalled to me?"

"I didn't dare. I saw you sitting there on the sand, but if I had called to you he would have killed me. The pistol was on his knees."

"Did you know I was following?"

"I hoped you were. I heard you shout 'Curry!' But Mr Price heard it too. And he went faster and faster. And I didn't dare look back. And I knew he meant to run right into the quicksand. And I was afraid you wouldn't come in time."

"Darling! Darling!" Jim kissed her again and again. "You're safe now. Price is dead. Shot himself. Killed himself rather than be taken. He's dead."

"I'm glad. No, I'm not. It's so awful to be dead." She shuddered, smoothed a lock of hair back from her forehead. "I feel dizzy."

"Sit down on the running board, sweetheart. You've had a frightful shock. Don't try to talk. Sit still and think about us."

Her head dropped on his shoulder. They sat watching Curry drag a body from the car. As he laid it on the sand and covered the face with a white handkerchief, voices, excited voices, came through the fog and figures emerged ghostlike. Marbury first. Then Edith and the children. Far behind, Patrick reeled along, in his shirt sleeves, minus goggles and cap, and obviously very drunk indeed.

As Marbury approached the cars, he called to Edith: "Don't come any nearer. Keep the children back." She obeyed. Marbury paused for a moment beside Laura, kissed her, gave Jim an affectionate pat, and joined Curry where he stood looking down at the corpse on the sand.

"Dead?" he asked anxiously. "Not merely wounded?"

"Dead as mutton," Curry answered.

"It's McGuire, of course?"

"Oh, yes. It's the Australian heir all right, all right. Miss Laura's troubles are over. 'Mr Price' has made a last attempt – and failed."

"But what a narrow escape she had!" Marbury shuddered. "Why didn't McGuire shoot her before he killed himself?"

"Forgot to, I guess. His ego had swelled so big it over shadowed everything else. When his tires went, he knew the game was up. Saw the gallows right ahead, felt the noose tightening round his neck, and thought only of how to escape it. Didn't, in fact, care a hoot what became of Miss Laura!"

"Good psychology," Marbury nodded. "And, whatever the motive, his suicide will save the police a lot of trouble."

"It sure will. Once we get him identified..." Curry broke off, and bent over the body. "Let's see if he has any papers. Ought to carry a motor license, anyway. He'd be afraid to drive without." He fumbled in the dead man's pockets, drew out a wallet, opened it.

"No license," he murmured, as he examined the various papers it contained, "and not much money – only about fifty dollars... Several letters, but with the names torn off... Here we are! This chart you spoke of, Mr Marbury. It has 'Bell of Irongray' at the top. That settles it for us, and for the Adelaide police, no one but Percy McGuire would have the chart."

"And Green the butler could easily have stolen it from Mrs Beaumont. Very satisfactory – except that you were wrong in believing Green had sailed for Australia!"

"Yes, we made a mistake there." Curry stooped, touched the dead man's hair and stood up, frowning.

"Good Lord!" he muttered. "It's not Green after all. This man has plenty of hair. Green is bald and wears a wig."

"But, but, it must be Green," Marbury stammered.

"I – I know Green by sight. Take off the handkerchief. Let me see his face."

"You can't!" Curry snapped. "It's blown off. The man hasn't any face."

Marbury winced, feeling sick. The handkerchief was no longer white, and a dark stream was soaking into the sand.

"Not Green," Curry growled. "Then the Beaumont murder is still a mystery!"

"But we know that it was McGuire who killed her."

"That's not enough," Curry said impatiently. "It remains a mystery until we know under what name McGuire got access to her house."

"You're right," Marbury sighed. "Mightn't there be a clue among McGuire's other papers? You spoke of a motor license..."

Curry opened the wallet again, discovered an inner flap, extracted a paper, glanced at it, and let out a long whistle of bewildered annoyance. "His license," he grunted, "and all it gives us is another alias! I hope that name means something to you, sir," he added, handing the paper to Marbury with a somewhat sardonic grin. "It means mighty little to me."

"Good heavens!" Marbury exclaimed, as he read. "It can't be! He stared down at the body. "It might be…"

He raised his voice: "Jim!" he called. "Come here! The affair has taken a new and most surprising turn," he went on, as Northcote approached. "Who do you think this man is? Someone we have never suspected; yet he was in Clare's room that morning, and could have planted the suicide letter…"

"You mean he isn't McGuire?" Northcote demanded indignantly. "But that's absurd!"

"Oh, it's McGuire all right; alias Price, Laura's kidnapper. But I knew him under still another name!"

"Green? But we said all along it was Green the butler who killed Mrs Beaumont. Isn't this man the butler?"

"No, not the butler. The lawyer! You remember, the 'suicide letter' was sent to Atwood's office and…"

"Atwood? You don't mean this man is Atwood?"

"No. No. The other fellow. Atwood's clerk. It's Wheeler!"

"Wheeler?" Northcote muttered. "No, we never suspected Wheeler. Never thought of investigating his past. Never asked Atwood where his clerk came from. Just made up our silly minds that Green was guilty and let it go at that. What fools we were! Not that it really mattered what McGuire called himself. We got him in the end. We saved Laura."

"Did we, Jim? To my mind," Mr Marbury sighed, "it was Clare Beaumont who saved Laura. Her death bought Laura's life. If we had not hunted down Clare's murderer, where would Laura be now?"

The American Queens of Crime series

- Murder in Stained Glass — Margaret Armstrong
- Murder à la Richelieu — Anita Blackmon
- There Is No Return — Anita Blackmon
- The Blue Santo Murder Mystery — Margaret Armstrong
- The Man With No Face — Margaret Armstrong

All books available through www.lostcrimeclassics.com or from Amazon.

Printed in Great Britain
by Amazon